Also by Lazarus Barnhill
From Indigo Sea Press

The Mountain Woman Romance Series

Book 1: *Lacey Took a Holiday*

Book 2: *Caddo Creek*

The Medicine People

Come Home to Me Child

The Boston

Pastor Larsen and the Rat

indigoseapress.com

East Light

This volume also contains the novella

Charlie Cherry's Ninth Step

By

Lazarus Barnhill

Deep Indigo Books
Published by Indigo Sea Press
Winston-Salem

Deep Indigo Books
Indigo Sea Press
PO Box 67201
Winston-Salem, NC 27114

First Deep Indigo Books edition published
September, 2017
Deep Indigo Books, Moon Sailor and all production design are trademarks of Indigo Sea Press, used under license.

For information regarding bulk purchases of this book, digital purchase and special discounts, please contact the publisher at indigoseapress@gmail.com

Cover design by Pan Morelli
Manufactured in the United States of America
ISBN 978-1-938101-56-4

To those who, through their wonderful examples, taught me one day at a time.

Chapter One

Magnus stopped his Toyota at the last, lonely parking area for Scotch Bonnet Beach—only to find his entry blocked by another car. The young man behind the wheel of the old, white Chevy Impala—crowded with teenage boys leaving the beach—sat unmoving, staring at Magnus. The driver had come at the entrance from an angle and was blocking the center of the driveway. After a moment of returning his gaze, Magnus lifted his upturned hands from his own steering wheel with a shrug. The boys had to pull out of the parking lot before he could pull in.

If he had been thinking about the teenage driver, perhaps it would've surprised Magnus that the boy didn't become angry or insolent. Given the opportunity in that situation, particularly surrounded by his adolescent peerage, most young men would've at least yelled something defiant. Or made an obscene gesture. But as he steered the Chevy onto the highway and made room for Magnus Thorsen's Camry to enter the parking lot, the boy's expression was more one of dread.

The instant the Chevy pulled off the lot and headed north, Magnus put the momentary encounter out of his mind and drove across the gravel, parking in the space closest to the sign that read, "Public Beach Access—No Vehicles." He made sure the front windows were open slightly, that the air conditioner and radio were turned off. He checked the backseat and the floorboards to make sure there was no trash or dust. Of course there could not have been, since he had vacuumed the car just after he had washed it, an hour before. So his Camry—like the beach cottage where he lived—was immaculate, orderly, only waiting to be discovered.

He reached inside his glove box and took out the slender, plain brown bag that held the pint of blended whiskey he bought forty-five minutes before at the ABC store and put it in the right outside pocket of his cream-colored linen sport coat. Then he reached beneath the front seat and pulled out the small, thick plastic bag containing the snub-nose .38 revolver he had purchased thirty

1

minutes before—after a seven day wait.

"I could've been through with this last Thursday," he muttered. "But here we are a week later." He gazed at the gray, blue and violet clouds building in the late afternoon eastern sky. "The light's a lot better today, though."

He laughed and shook his head as he thought of the Indian—or perhaps Pakistani—pawnbroker who had delayed him.

"Surely we can work something out," Magnus had said the previous Thursday, pulling several one hundred dollar bills out of his wallet. "Surely to goodness you have some pistol somebody sold or traded in that you haven't registered. I don't even care about the caliber—long as it isn't a .22."

"How do I know you are not law enforcement officer?" the clerk had asked angrily. "You fill out form and wait please."

"Shit," Magnus had said. For a minute he stood at the counter considering his alternative, wondering if he went sixty miles down the road to South Carolina there would also be a waiting period.

"How long?"

"Supposed to be up to month, but I get for you in week."

"Fine," he said. "Let me sign."

He was not concerned about passing the background check. He had no felony convictions and his time in the treatment center had been voluntary, and therefore secret. The only thing he disliked was knowing that firearm permits were listed in the paper. At least, he assumed, that would happen a week or two after he got the gun, too late for his sponsor Grady or any of his A.A. friends to read it and become alarmed.

Thursday afternoon, the permit issued, Magnus showed up at the pawnshop with a feeling of fated accomplishment. He pointed out the revolver he wanted.

"You need case? Cleaning kit, Mr. Torksun?"

"'Tore-son.'" He looked at the pawnbroker's nametag. "Raj, I just need ammo."

The clerk set a small, heavy box on the counter.

"No," Magnus said slowly. "I only want to buy one bullet."

"I cannot break container," the broker said, clicking his "c's" and "t's." "Fifty cartridges is smallest box I have for .38 caliber."

Magnus stared at him. "I just need one round."

"Sorry."

He pulled out his billfold. "You don't have much interest in helping me out, do you?"

The clerk was expressionless as he replied. "I have feeling you will not be repeat customer."

On this day, as he sat in the southernmost parking area of Scotch Bonnet Beach breaking the paper seal on the ammunition box with his thumbnail, the prescient, pissy attitude of the clerk didn't bother him. He lifted a single round from the plastic sleeve, opened the cylinder, dropped in the bullet, and rolled it around to the next firing position. Then he slipped the gun into the left outer pocket of his sport coat.

He straightened momentarily, both hands on the steering wheel, and went over his mental list of tasks that had to be accomplished before he completed the last item: mail the bills, clean the cottage, wash and vacuum the car, get the whiskey, buy the gun, drive to the beach, take one last stroll. That was it.

The precise order was important. As Grady once said in a meeting: "You can take whiskey into the gun store and they don't care. But if you take a gun into the whiskey story, you're going to jail!" Going to jail, Magnus thought, would put a serious kink in his plans.

He opened the door and stepped out of the car, stretching and looking about himself at the empty parking lot. Magnus had chosen this parking area because it was so secluded. Often in years past he had come to this spot alone to drink and cook out. Many evening he would stay on the beach for hours and see no one else.

He locked the door and closed it. For an instant he stood looking at the metallic, sky blue Toyota. He had really enjoyed the car. It was pretty, with just the slightest aqua sheen when the sunlight hit it right. Then he turned his back on it, put his hands in the pockets of his jacket and walked toward the ocean.

The way down to the water was wide and hard packed. This was the access to county employees used to bring their police buggies, trucks and turtle patrol vehicles onto the beach. Private citizens were not supposed to drive over the dunes and onto the beach—though they did, and this was where they did.

Just fifty yards down the access from the parking lot, Magnus saw the beautiful, comforting, familiar vista of the Atlantic Ocean spread before him. He had heard it as soon as he opened his car door, the continual shout of water rushing to the shore, even at times like this when the tide was out. And he drew closer to the sea, walking away from the mouth of the beach access. The briny air pushed the shaggy, blonde hair from his forehead and seemed to force its way into his lungs.

Magnus wondered if there were some deep, profound thoughts he should be thinking in these last minutes of his life. No great wisdom rushed in upon him. He only decided that he would proceed before he lost his nerve. And he decided to stand where he was. If he walked on down the beach, it might take much longer before his body was found. There's a difference, he decided, between wanting to be dead and wanting to be disgustingly decomposed.

He bumped his hand against the oddly shaped, heavy bulge in his left jacket pocket. The gun was ready, only waiting for him. He reached into his right pocket and pulled out the pint of blended whiskey. For some reason he didn't look at it as he broke the seal. The thin, metal cap came off easily in his fingers and he could smell the rich, hot, sweet aroma of the liquor.

"Wow," he said, "first drink in almost 100 days. I guess it works if you work it." Somehow the cynicism in his voice embarrassed and disappointed him.

"Sir?"

The soft, strange voice was not his own. He wasn't even sure he really heard it. But, thinking someone really might have spoken to him, as he looked around he screwed the cap back onto the bottle. Glancing in either direction as he dropped the pint back into his pocket, he saw no one. It had been his imagination—the most creative and cowardly part of him.

"Sir?"

So it was a voice. A young woman's voice. And it came from behind him to his right, up closer to the dunes.

"Sir, can you help me?"

Magnus squinted at the disjointed pile of refuse on the sand that had spoken to him. There was the head of a girl in her late teens or early twenties, disheveled blonde hair haloed around it. What should've been her body made no sense to his eyes. And then he realized what he was seeing.

"Oh my god!" he said to himself, keeping his voice low. He ran toward her instantly, bounding across the fifteen yards of beach and

4

stopping just above where she was lying.

One leg, the right, was bent at an impossible angle, as was her right arm—twisted and clearly shattered. The entire upper half of her torso seemed to be trying to flee from her lower half. And she was naked. Torn, discarded pieces of her clothing—covered with dirty sand—lay around her in matching disarray.

"Oh my god," he whispered.

"Can you help me?"

"Yes."

He tore off his sport coat and put it over her from her neck down. Bent as she was, petite as she was, the jacket mostly covered her. He stood looking at her, trying to know what he should do. The jacket would keep her warm, he thought, because she was surely going to go into shock. Beyond that, he not immediately decide what to do.

"I have a phone in my car, darlin'," he said, his voice urgent and gentle. "It's just around the dunes there."

"Please don't leave me."

"What's your name, darlin'?"

"Lisa."

"Lisa, my name is Magnus. I'm not going to leave you. I'm getting my phone to call for an ambulance to take you to the hospital. I'm going to stay right here with you until they get here. Okay?"

"Please don't leave me."

"I'll be right back." He had to look away from her, not because of her hideous brokenness but because he wouldn't be able to go to retrieve his phone if he kept looking into her eyes. "I'll be right back."

He was running then—his feet sinking in the deep, soft sand—reaching into his pants pocket for the keys he thought he would never use again. It only took a few second to get back to his car. And it came to him, almost like a revelation, that he had a blanket in the trunk. It was one of those cheap, braided ones he bought for a few dollars at a gas station.

The cell phone was in the glove box. He yanked it out and activated it. As he waited for the phone to come to life, he pushed the latch and heard the trunk release. Then he was standing outside on the gravel. One of the buttons on the phone was a speed dial number for emergencies. Which one?

"Oh hell."

He pushed 9-1-1 and pressed the phone to his ear. It rang once. The answer came just before the second ring.

"9-1-1. What is your emergency?"

"I need an ambulance and the police," he said rapidly. "I'm at the last parking area on the south end of Scotch Bonnet Beach."

"Slow down please, sir. What type of emergency are you reporting?"

"Listen to me! It's a girl. Something has happened to her. Her leg and her arm are very badly broken. She's all bent. I found her lying past the dunes on the last beach access."

He could hear the woman at the other end typing.

"Is she conscious, sir?"

"Yes, but I don't see how. I've never seen anyone torn up this bad."

"What is your name, sir?"

"Thorsen. Magnus Thorsen. Why are you asking? Didn't it come up on your screen when I called?"

"Mr. Thorsen, are you with her now?"

"No. I had to run back to my car to get my phone. And I got a blanket I'm going to cover her with."

"Please go back and stay with her, sir."

"I am. I am." He lifted the trunk and pulled out the braided blanket.

"And what is the girl's name?"

"Lisa. She just said 'Lisa.'"

"How old is she, sir?"

"Uh. I don't know. Eighteen or twenty, I guess." He was trotting back down the beach access.

"And how did she sustain her injuries?"

"You got me," he said. "I don't know how somebody gets broken up that bad."

". . . All right, Mr. Thorsen. Police and ambulance have been dispatched."

"How long? 'Cause they need to be in a big damn hurry."

"They're on the way, sir. They'll get there as quickly as they can. If you will, please just stay on the line—"

At the sight of the girl, his jacket covering her, Magnus ended

6

the call and slipped the phone into his pants pocket.

"I'm back, Lisa," he called as he approached her. "I called 9-1-1. The ambulance is on the way."

He could see that her eyes were focused on him. He wondered if she could still speak.

"I have a blanket here to put over you."

"Okay."

"I'll try not to hurt you." He shook out the blanket and, beginning where her left foot protruded from beneath his jacket, gently lowered it all the way up to her neck.

"Am I covered?" she asked. Her voice was remarkably calm. He guessed that she was descending into shock.

"Yes. Completely." He knelt beside her. "How bad do you hurt?"

". . . I don't really hurt. I can feel everything. And I know I'm not right. But it doesn't hurt."

"Well," he said, choosing his words carefully, "it may start to hurt some later. But they'll be able to give you some painkiller if you need it. And you can trust me on this: everything that isn't right can be fixed. Lisa. Can you tell me what happened to you?"

It was the first time she had showed any affect. Her face darkened just a bit and her lip began to quiver. Tears welled in her eyes.

"I got raped."

"Oh. Sweetie. I'm sorry. He won't get away with it. We'll see to that." He sat down cross-legged on the sand where she could easily see him without having to move her head. "Did he beat you with something? A bat or something?"

"There was more than one of them."

"Oh god," he said, despite himself. Deliberately, but trying his best not to sound anxious or demanding, he asked, "Well, how did they hurt you like this?"

"They ran over me."

"Ran over you? In a car?"

"Yes. Twice."

"Oh," he said. "I guess you're really doing pretty good then. You're going to be okay."

". . . I played dead."

"Yeah?"

7

"They were looking out the back window after the second time. I just looked at the sand without blinking and held my breath."

It was her stillness, Magnus decided, and the obviousness and severity of her broken bones that convinced them she was dead.

"Lisa, do you know them?"

She gave her head the slightest shake, the first movement he had seen from her. "No. I was working at the beach hut. I rent bikes and surfboards on the beach down at Myrtle. I went out to lock up a bike somebody brought back and they grabbed me from behind and pulled a pillowcase over my head and taped my hands behind me. That part happened real quick."

He glanced up at the remnants of her clothes. A twisted knot of duct tape lay in the sand near them.

"Do you know where you are now?"

"On a beach."

"Have you heard of Scotch Bonnet?"

"Yes. In North Carolina. South of Wilmington. In Aberdeen County, I think."

"Well that's where you are."

". . . Seems like it took forever to get here. They put me in the back floorboard. When I would move, one of them would stomp me. And they said they'd kill me if I screamed."

Magnus had the feeling that he needed to keep her talking, to keep her alert until help arrived. And the more he could draw from her about what had happened, the more he could pass along to the police if she weren't able, or if she died. Yet he was torn as well. How cruel it seemed to make her relive all that had happened.

"You know," he said, "why would they run you over like that? I mean, your face was covered. You didn't know who they were."

"I saw them," she said.

"You did?"

"Yes. After they . . . were through with me. I heard them get in the car. I just laid there for the longest time. I didn't hear anything. I was working and working on the tape they had around my wrists and finally I got it off. I stood up and pulled off the pillowcase. I was facing the back of the car. And I heard one of them shout. 'She got loose. She sees us.' I just stood there. I was trying to figure out where I was and where I should run. And then I heard the car start and it backed right over me. Then they pulled forward and ran over me again. . . . I guess they thought I had memorized their license plate. Doing that never even occurred to me until after they drove away."

Tears were filling the hollows around her eyes. Magnus took the handkerchief from his back pocket and touched the corner of it to the edges of her eyes, soaking away the tears.

"I was praying," she said.

"Were you? That's a good thing. A good thing."

"I was praying after they drove over me again that they wouldn't get stuck in the sand. 'Cause I couldn't hold my breath and lay still forever."

He laughed softly. "You're a clever girl. I'm so glad you made it through."

She tilted her head just slightly toward him. "Do you think I'm going to make it?"

"Well you have made it, darlin'. The bad guys are gone. I'm sitting here talking to you. The ambulance is on the way to take you to get all fixed up. Everything's going to be just fine."

She smiled at him. It was amazing to Magnus that someone in her situation could smile.

"You make me feel better," she said. "Not so scared."

He dabbed at her eyes again, not to wipe away tears but to caress her face—the only part of her he did not fear to touch.

"Speaking of scared. I'll bet you have some family around here you'd like me to call. You know, to meet you at the hospital."

"No," she said. "I'm not from here. I'm from Ohio. I came here to go to school."

"Over at UNCW?"

"Yes, sir."

"And you stayed here to work through the summer?"

"No," she said. "I live here year round. I'm a rising senior."

"That's good. What's your major?"

"Political Science."

"Wow. I could be talking to the next governor of North Carolina."

"No. I don't like politics. I can't decide. . . . I was thinking I'd get an MBA."

"So, you're going to make a million bucks, eh?"

"No," she said. "I want to help redevelop the coastal communities."

"Oh? . . . You mean, like, changing building code along the ocean front?"

"No." She almost laughed. "I mean economic redevelopment. Most working class families up and down the coastline are on subsistence wages. Most of the jobs are seasonal. Not many benefits. No job security."

"I see," he said, grinning wryly. "You want to unionize all these Eastern Europeans we have selling T-shirts around here."

"No." She gave the slightest shake of her head. "I think that would only create conflict. Lots of those folks are only here on work visas, anyway."

Describing her dreams seemed to distract her from the realities of the moment.

"I'm thinking more of bringing the infrastructure up to code. I mean, think about how hard it is to get around this place. It's like a gigantic flea market, not the major vacation spot of the southeast Atlantic coast."

She sounded just like an idealistic college student to him. It was heartening to Magnus to listen to her speak, but it was clear as well to him that her voice was growing weaker and her face paler.

"I think we should try to bring the whole place up to speed. Highways. Bridges. State of the art hospitals. A major university. A really, really big convention center. Synchronized traffic lights."

"Wow. Sounds like you've given this a lot of thought," he said. "All those high-level ideas are way beyond me. When I was in college, I was hopeless in social studies and sciences."

She studied him with a curious expression. "What did you study?"

"Art."

"Oh. At UNCW? That's a really good art department."

"No," he said quietly. "I went down to Charleston. They have an art school there."

"Oh, yes. Yes, I heard about it. You must really have talent."

He smiled.

"So, are you an artist?"

"Yes. That's what I do for a living."

"What kind of artist are you?"

He started to say he was a fraud, but thought better of it. There was surely no need for the girl to carry any of his baggage. "I'm a portrait artist."

10

"Really? Do you paint a lot of portraits?"

He nodded. "I do about as many as I want to do. I do lots of different media. Charcoal, pastel chalks, oil, acrylic. It just depends on how fast folks want their portraits and how much they want to pay."

"Do you work down on the beach somewhere?"

He grinned. "No. Actually I have a studio in Wilmington. If you've been down on the river walk you may have seen it. 'Magnus Thorsen Gallery.'"

"Oh. Is that you?"

"That's me. I also have some displayed in a gallery down in Myrtle. But I live in a cottage on Fraser Beach. I have a studio there too." He heard a vehicle's tires pulling across the gravel of the parking area. "You know, I'd love to show you around my studio in Wilmington when you get back on your feet."

"Yeah?"

"Oh yeah. And I know all the restaurants along the river. I'll treat you to your favorite dish for supper."

". . . I'd like that. I love beautiful art."

He had heard a door open and close, but it did not sound like an ambulance. An ambulance, it occurred to him, would've pulled onto the beach. Maybe, he thought, it was just a random visitor to Scotch Bonnet. Or, he thought warily, those who attacked the girl coming back to see if she were really dead.

"Lisa, you didn't tell me your last name."

". . . Faucet," she said, her voice soft.

"You feeling okay?"

"Well." She seemed to be thinking. "I'm a little cold."

"I've got a coat and a blanket on you, sweetie," he said. "The ambulance will be here anytime. They can warm you right up."

It was then, as he turned to glance at the beach access that he saw the county deputy. It was a young man, tall and powerfully built, in his late twenties. His stern face was the image of observant suspicion.

"Oh, look," Magnus said. "It's a policeman. I bet the paramedics are with him." He uncurled from the sitting position he had been in, putting a hand down to steady himself.

"Don't leave me, Magnus," she said.

"I'm not. You can see me the whole way. I'm just going to tell you officer about you."

11

He hurried the twenty yards to where the young man was walking toward them.

"Is the ambulance here?"

The officer's expression was wary. He glanced repeatedly at the blanket-covered form on the beach. And he clearly didn't want Magnus—who didn't want the girl to hear their conversation—too close to him.

"The ambulance is two minutes out."

Magnus cocked his head. "If they were two minutes away, wouldn't we hear the siren?" he asked in a whisper. "They have to get here now. This girl is fading like a Long Beach sunset."

"What's wrong with her?"

"She says she was gang raped and run over twice with a car. She obviously has multiple broken bones."

The officer's gaze ran from the girl to the hard-packed sand where they were standing. He pressed a button on the radio fastened to his shirt. Stepping back from Magnus, he turned away and spoke into the microphone.

"Dispatch, this is 8. Advise MICU. Code 3. Critical."

The radio squawked back unintelligibly. The young man said something else that Magnus couldn't really hear. The officer turned back toward him.

"I didn't catch your name, sir."

"Magnus. Thorsen."

"And who is she?"

"C'mon." Magnus started toward the girl. "She says her name is Lisa Faucet. She—"

The officer had pulled out a cell phone with a built in camera. He was taking photos of the beach access and, at a distance, of the girl.

"Need to do this," he said. "The ambulance may disturb the crime scene. I needed pictures of the tracks."

Magnus looked down. Several parallel sets of tire tracks ran toward where the girl was lying beneath the blanket. It surprised him that he had not noticed them before.

"What'd you say her name was?"

"Faucet. Lisa Faucet. She's a student at UNCW. She said she was working at a bike rental place down in Myrtle."

"And how did you happen to be here?" the officer asked.

Magnus, who was trying with little success to get the deputy to come over to the girl, straightened. "Well, if you ask Lisa, I'm pretty sure she'll say it was answered prayer."

Then, distantly, Magnus heard the siren. He turned his back on the deputy and went to the girl.

"Hear that Lisa? There's your ride."

Her face had taken on a grayness. "You'll come with me, won't you?"

"Oh sure." He sat down beside her again. "They'll be here any minute. Any minute. Things are already getting better."

"Miss Faucet?" The deputy, who had been taking more photos was standing above her and looking down. "I'm Officer Miller. Are you in pain, ma'am?"

"No. . . . I've got the shivers a little. I sort of feel funny."

"Yes ma'am. The medics will be here momentarily." His voice was businesslike, unemotional. "Mr. Thorsen indicated you told him that you had been attacked by several people."

". . . I was raped. It was three or four boys." She turned her eyes, which blinked rapidly for an instant, toward Magnus. "Don't uncover me."

"We won't. The paramedics will have to, to see what's wrong with you, though."

The ambulance was drawing closer.

"I'm going to guide them," the deputy said.

Magnus leaned toward her, touching the back of his fingers against her cheek. "Hear that? They're here."

"I can hear them."

". . . Lisa, you said you're from Ohio. If you tell me who your folks are and where they live, I'll call them for you. Don't you think it would sound better coming from me than the police?"

She was quiet for a few seconds. He couldn't tell if she were thinking, or beyond talking.

"I don't think I want them to know yet," she said.

"If I were your dad, I'd want to know right away. They'll be mad if they don't know right away."

"I don't care." There was a fatigued defiance in her voice. "He's not my dad. My dad died when I was little. My mom remarried when I was ten." She seemed to lose her train of thought for a second. "He's a jerk. He's an abusive drunk. That's why my brother, sister and I all left . . . as soon as we could."

The irony of it was like a slap to him. "A drunk, huh? Well, they are pretty useless, all right. What about your mom? She'll want to know."

Her eyebrows arched. "I feel sorry for my mom. Don't get me wrong. But she wasn't there for me when I was growing up . . . with that guy in the house. . . . And I don't care if she's with me now or not." Her voice grew soft and trailed off.

The siren, which was very close, stopped suddenly. There were a few seconds of silence. Both Magnus and the girl were listening. A high-pitched beeping sound began to come from the parking lot. The ambulance was backing up. He saw the deputy appear, walking backwards and making circular motions with his hands. And then the back of the MICU came into view. It stopped on the hard packed access road—either to avoid becoming stuck in the soft sand or to avoid driving through the tracks already there.

"Magnus," the girl said, "will you stay with me?"

He struggled to find the right response. "I will, Lisa. I won't leave you. Only, we have to do this like the paramedics tell us. You really are hurt and they're in charge right now. Okay? We'll do it like they tell us."

He could hear various doors on the ambulance being opened. The medics, a young man and woman, were pulling things from the open back of the MICU. Then they were jogging across the beach toward them. Their uniforms were t-shirts with decals over the heart, black cargo pants and black boots. Magnus stood slowly and backed away from the girl as the medics came to either side of her and knelt on the sand.

"Are you Lisa?" the woman asked.

"Yes."

"I'm Shay and this is Doug. We're going to help you."

"Don't uncover me."

"I know, Lisa. We'll keep you covered up as much as we can." She was lifting the girl's head slightly and putting a padded brace around her neck. "In order to move you and to stabilize you, we have to see what's wrong. We have some warm blankets in the back of the ambulance and we're going to cover you with them."

Together they lifted the blanket and then, gingerly, the linen jacket from the girl. The medics stared intently at her. Magnus felt

14

a shiver run through him at the sight of her brokenness revealed again. Beside him he could sense the deputy straighten and turn away wordlessly.

"Officer," Shay called, "are there any more first responders in route or close by?"

The deputy, who had been facing the beach access, turned back toward her. "No. There are a couple more cruisers on the way. And the crime scene truck. But no firefighters or medics have been dispatched as far as I know."

"Well isn't this a Code Delta? Why weren't they dispatched? Okay. We're going to need both of you men to help us in about one minute."

With a latex gloved thumb, she widened Lisa's eyelids and studied her eyes for an instant.

"Okay, Doug," Shay said. "We're going to roll her slightly on her left side and backboard her. We're going to put her in the bus and work on her there. While I'm lifting her, I want you to palpate her back."

"Right," he responded.

Shay expertly put her hands beneath Lisa's right side and lifted her gently. The girl's limbs, disjointed, did not rise with her body but slid limply across the sand.

"Does this hurt?"

"No." Her voice was weaker.

"Do you feel it at all?"

"Yes."

Doug was running his hand along the underside of the girl's body. Magnus wondered what he was seeking. Then the young man slipped a long, rigid plastic board beneath her and Shay lowered her gently. Quickly they strapped her onto the backboard.

"Officer!" She looked at Magnus. "And I need your help too."

The four of them gathered around the girl. Magnus bent over, his right hand in a slot on the backboard.

"Nice and smooth on three," Shay said. "One. Two. Three."

It seemed to Magnus that the girl weighed almost nothing. The problem was walking through the soft sand in unison with the other litter bearers. A gurney was sitting on the access at the back of the ambulance and they lowered the backboard onto it gently. Then, almost magically, the paramedics pushed from the foot of the gurney and the wheels on the front collapsed, allowing them to slide it into the ambulance. They scrambled into the back with the girl and immediately raised her.

"Lower the head," Shay said. "Get two bags ready while I put her on the monitors."

"Where are we running the lines?"

She glanced at Lisa. "Left arm and left leg."

Magnus heard another vehicle pulling onto the gravel parking area. The deputy heard it too and walked toward the sound.

A feeble voice came from within the ambulance. "Magnus?"

"Yes, darlin'?"

"Don't leave me."

"I'm going to be right here, Lisa."

The medics worked in proficient haste, breaking open equipment bins and removing supplies, attaching leads to the girl and reading monitors. For the first time, Magnus began to have some confidence that the girl would live.

"I got 60-palp," Shay said. "Pulse is 140."

"One line in," Doug replied. "I'll have the other in in a second."

"Open them all the way when they're in." The woman straightened and stood watching a monitor carefully. She picked a portable radio out of her belt and keyed it. "Dispatch, this is 12."

A disembodied voice—maybe the same woman to whom Magnus had spoken—responded. "Go ahead, 12."

"Be advised. As soon as we are stable, we are transporting white female code 3. This is a level 1 trauma."

"Uh, 10-4. Trauma will be standing by."

"Line two is in," Doug said. "Running wild."

Shay was studying the monitor carefully. "Yeah, I can tell. We're up to 80 over 50. Pulse 130."

Doug had produced a couple thin hospital blankets and was spreading them over the girl. "You about ready?" he asked.

"Yes. Let's do it. Lights and sirens."

The medic made his way around Lisa and through the partition to the driver's seat of the ambulance. The engine started. Shay was securing things in the back.

"Magnus," Lisa called again. "Ride with me."

"Sir." It was Miller, the deputy. He was standing beside Magnus at the back of the ambulance.

16

"Yes."

"We need your help with the crime scene."

Magnus looked into the back of the ambulance, suddenly, inexplicably afraid to let her go without him. He swallowed. "I've got to talk to the police first," he said loudly. "Then I'll come straight to the hospital and see you."

She didn't answer.

"Okay?"

". . . Okay."

Shay pulled the door shut and the ambulance rolled forward. Magnus and the deputy stood watching. He realized as it drove off the lot onto the highway and turned on its siren, that two or three more police cars and a van with police markings had arrived. He had been so absorbed in what was happening with the girl that he hadn't realized so many officers were there.

"Sir," the deputy said, "this is Sgt. Terrell."

A short, heavy officer with a mustache but almost no hair on his head was standing beside the deputy.

"Hey." Magnus held out his hand. "I'm Magnus Thorsen."

"The artist guy?"

"That's me."

"Well, nice to meet you," the sergeant said, grasping his hand briefly. "Can you tell us what happened here?"

Magnus ran both hands through his hair. He wasn't sure what he was feeling.

"Yeah, sure," he said. "That Toyota you probably saw on the parking lot is mine. I came out here this afternoon to stroll on the beach. As I was going down toward the water—Well, here, I'll show you."

Magnus, the sergeant and the deputy turned and walked toward the ocean. He pointed toward where Lisa had been lying, her clothes and his jacket still crumpled together in a pile.

"The girl called to me when I was about here. At first I wasn't sure anyone was really talking. The second time she spoke, I saw her. I ran over to her."

"How did she look?" the sergeant asked.

"Oh. Well, she looked god-awful. She really didn't look like a person. She was naked and her clothes were lying around her on the sand. I took off my jacket and covered her."

17

"You were wearing your jacket out here in ninety degrees?"

He stared at the sergeant. Magnus knew it was his job to be suspicious, but it was distracting him and delaying the important things he wanted to say.

"You always wear a badge. I always wear a jacket," he said.

"So she told you she had been raped?"

"Well, first I ran back to my car. I left my cell phone in the glove box and I had a blanket in the trunk. After I called 9-1-1, I came back and put the blanket over her on top of my jacket—she said she was getting cold—and I asked her what had happened. She told me that she was working down at Myrtle at a bike rental place and several boys jumped her." They were walking casually toward where he had knelt so anxiously beside the girl. "They put a pillow case over her head and put her in the floorboard of a car."

"Did she know them?"

"No, but she saw them."

"She did?"

"They got back in the car and left her lying on the beach. She got loose from the duct tape they used on her and stood up. And when she did, they backed over her. And then they pulled forward over her. She pretended to be dead." He tilted his head and squinted at the sergeant. "I asked about her family."

"Yeah?"

"She's a student at UNCW. Her family is in Ohio. She says she didn't want anybody to contact them."

"Well, we have to anyway. Soon as we find out who they are."

Magnus started to reach down for his blanket and jacket.

"Don't touch that, sir!" the deputy exclaimed, alarm in his voice.

Magnus drew back his hand.

"Sorry, Mr. Thorsen," the sergeant said. "All these items are evidence now. They'll be photographed and examined and then we'll return what we can."

"What you can?"

"Well, if there is DNA on your coat or on your blanket that helps us convict her attackers, we have to hang onto it."

"Oh. I see." Magnus thought about the whiskey and the pistol in the pockets of his jacket.

The sergeant put his head down as if he were thinking. "Mr.

18

Thorsen, our lieutenant is going to want to speak to you. Would you mind waiting around?"

"Sure."

"You want to sit in one of our cruisers, where it's cool?"

A man in uniform with a video camera was walking slowly from the beach access toward them. Magnus realized he was capturing images of the tire tracks in the sand.

"All right if I sit in my car?"

"Oh. Yeah."

He nodded and walked slowly up the beach access to the parking lot. Even more vehicles were there, six or seven at least. A number of officers were milling about, most talking to one another. As he opened the door of his Camry and sat down, he wondered how many of them had a real purpose for being there and how many had just come to see what was happening.

Sitting sideways in the front seat, his feet on the gravel, he started the car and turned on the air conditioner. It was strange to him to think as he sat there that he had come to this beach this afternoon to end his life and had very likely ended up saving someone else's life. And he wondered how many of these same people would have shown up if it had been his body, rather than Lisa, that had been discovered. His plan had not changed, he assured himself. It had only been delayed. The setting and perhaps the method might have to be revised. Or perhaps not. He wondered at what expression he might see on the smooth, red-brown face of Raj if he walked back into the gun shop to buy another pistol. And another bullet.

The little sergeant—Terrell, was it?—was standing and talking to an African-American woman. Magnus noticed her because she was so striking. She was tall and lean, her willowy body accented by a gently curved neck. Her head was crowned with round billows of hair pulled upward in perfect, graceful compliment to the shape of her form, which was not concealed by the official blue jacket and skirt she wore. He recognized as well that she had an authority, a defining presence about herself.

Magnus saw the sergeant nod toward him. The two of them were walking in his direction. He turned off the motor and stood.

The black woman's face grew more interesting as it grew closer. Her features were stern, he thought, but depending upon her expression might be quite beautiful.

"Mr. Thor-sin?"

"It's 'Tore-son,'" he said. "The 'h' is silent."

He wanted her to hold out her hand. He wanted to shake it, to judge by its touch whether or not she was truly so austere. Like the other officers, though, she kept back from him.

"How do you do, Mr. Thorsen. I'm Lt. Dot Stipling."

Magnus laughed out loud. He raised his face, his eyes closed and laughed. "Ah," he said, "that's a good one."

The woman regarded him silently, her eyes widened, her mouth closed.

"Really," Magnus said, "what's your name?"

Smoothly she produced a little billfold from her jacket pocket and opened it before him. There was a badge on one side and beside it a photo ID with her name.

"I'm Lt. Dot Stipling, Chief of Detectives for Aberdeen County."

"Oh." Despite himself Magnus smiled. "Sorry, there, Lieutenant."

Apart from a hardness, an impassivity in her eyes, she was expressionless as she asked, "What's so funny?"

"Well . . . I thought someone might have told you that I'm an artist."

"No, but why would that matter?"

He sighed. "It's your name. Stipling is a form of drawing where you create an image through the use of tiny dots. Like pointillism."

She continued to stare at him.

"So, you never knew that?" he asked. "I thought you were making a joke. It's like coming up to a musician and saying, 'Hi, I'm Bea Flatt.'"

She frowned, the expression his grade school teachers used so often when he disappointed them, and said, "Mr. Thorsen, my responsibility it to determine as quickly and accurately as possible who is responsible for the attack on the young woman you found on the beach today."

"Of course."

"And the first order of business is ruling you out as a suspect."

Magnus made a little snorting sound. "Well since I probably saved her life, wouldn't that be obvious?"

"You would not be the first attacker to feel remorse and call for medical help for his victim."

"Um hmm." He did not feel threatened. She was gaming him. In part, he assumed, because of the way he had laughed at her. "Well I'm sure several officers heard her beg me to go to the hospital with her."

"That would not make her the first victim to be more concerned about her assailant than herself."

He nodded and smirked. "Look, I regret laughing at your name—obviously not as much as I should—but that gives you no right to treat me like a villain when you know I saved her life."

"Actually we are pretty sure you are not a suspect." She gestured toward his Camry. "It's because of your car. Your tires do not match the tire pattern or the track width of the vehicle that ran over the victim." She watched him closely. "So, unless you ran over her with one vehicle and brought a second back with you to report the crime, you are unlikely to be a suspect. Then there's the fact that you stayed behind."

"What?"

"If you were the perpetrator, you would never have allowed her to ride to the hospital by herself."

"Oh."

She was looking down. Magnus glanced down as well. Gravel dust was coating the toes of her blue pumps.

"Mr. Thorsen, I don't suppose you saw anybody else around here? Anybody who could be responsible for this?"

Magnus felt his mouth drop open. "Oh my god! Yes, as a matter of fact, I just might have."

The lieutenant and sergeant focused on him intently.

"When I first got here," he said. "I had to wait to pull onto the lot because a car was pulling off. It was an old, white Chevy full of boys. I was waiting for them to pull out so I could turn in, but the kid driving just sat there staring at me."

"Can you describe him, or any of the other occupants of the car?"

"Sure. White teenage boy. Seventeen. Eighteen. Light hair, cut short. Light eyes."

"What about the vehicle?" Sgt. Terrell asked.

"A cream colored Impala, '63 or '64. Pretty good shape."

"How can you be so sure about the car?" she asked.

21

He smiled. "My first car was a '63 Chevy Biscayne. There aren't too many like that still around."

"Ma'am." Deputy Miller had come walking up to the three of them.

"Yes?"

"Hospital's on the radio. They say they need Mr. Thorsen to come over immediately."

"Me?"

The lieutenant put her hand to her chin. She was deciding, Magnus knew, whether or not to let him go. "They need him now?"

"Yes, ma'am. They need his permission to treat the victim."

"Why? I'm nothing to this girl. I met her twenty minutes ago."

"Well, you've become her 'safe person,'" Lt. Stipling said, not looking at him. "I suppose we'd better get you there if they need you. Officer Miller."

"Yes, ma'am?"

"Would you please deliver Mr. Thorsen to the hospital? Code 2."

"Yes, ma'am."

"Wait a minute. What about my car?"

"Well for the next three or four hours it will be surrounded by peace officers." She handed him her business card. "If Officer Miller gets called away, phone me. We'll get you back here to retrieve your car." She looked at Sgt. Terrell. "If his vehicle description is correct, it gives us something to go on." The sergeant nodded. "In any case, Mr. Thorsen, we will be wanting to speak to you again, either tonight or in the morning."

And with that she turned away and began a private conversation with the sergeant. Magnus felt as if he had suddenly become extraneous.

The deputy began to walk toward one of the cruisers. Magnus followed him and got into the passenger's seat. The engine had been running and the car was cool. Miller fastened his belt and pulled onto Business 17 headed toward Wilmington. The cruiser picked up speed rapidly.

Magnus looked over his shoulder at Lt. Dot Stipling, standing erect, seeming to preside over the crime scene with complete, casual command.

"Is she always like that?"

The deputy glanced toward him. "Please buckle up, sir."

22

Chapter 2

At 5:45 Friday morning, Magnus finally got up. Despite the physical and emotional exhaustion he felt on Thursday evening, he had slept only fitfully. Even though he was sleeping in his own bed in his own house, he had a feeling of not belonging. He had cleaned the cottage and arranged it so intentionally for those who would enter it after his death that, familiar and personal as it was, it was no longer truly his.

He went into the kitchen and opened the package of coffee he bought on the way home the night before. He cracked an egg and smashed it in with the coffee in his old aluminum pot.

Coffee, eggs, butter, milk, orange juice, bacon, cereal. All the perishable he had thrown out Thursday morning had to be purchased again Thursday night. He had stopped at the Beach Mart Convenience Store. Arthur, the extremely talkative retired longshoreman from New Jersey, was delighted to see him.

"Magnuts! You decided to give us a chance? You gonna buy your groceries here now, huh?"

"Just this once."

"You been on vacation? Didn't see you for a couple months."

"That's right."

"Thought this was your busy season. Vacationers coming down from my part of the country. Wanting their pictures made."

"Do you not have cream, Arthur? Just this half-and-half?"

He had climbed the steps to the door of his cottage an opened the door and just stood there. It had been eerie and ironic to him—seeing the matted oil painting of his son Marty on the easel and the manila envelopes on the kitchen table, each labeled with the name of the person for whom it was appropriate. By the time he had stored his groceries and put sheets on his bed—he had stripped off the ones he had been using the day before, washed, dried and put them away—he wanted nothing but sleep. Yet sleep had come only sporadically throughout the night.

As the coffee percolated he took a shower, which involved breaking open a new bar of soap to replace the one he had thrown away and hanging new towels on the rack. Still it felt good to rinse the salt of the beach and the shock of finding Lisa and the near miss of his own dying down the drain. He put on a pair of old Levis and a sleeveless t-shirt and finished making his breakfast.

He opened the doors and windows and sat at the round table on the lower level deck. The sun was coming up—a young, shimmering, orange sphere emerging from the slate gray ocean into a broad, innocent sky. The light from the east was going to be good this morning. If he wanted to, he could go upstairs to his studio and start a couple portraits.

He heard himself sigh. Even if it had been divine intervention that hindered him from killing himself the afternoon before, Magnus had not given up on suicide. Painting might be good and usefully distracting, but he didn't want to leave anything unfinished. So the real question was, how long was he going to be needed by Lisa, and by the police? And when could he get on with dying?

They had known his name in the emergency room the afternoon before. They had been waiting for him.

"I'm Magnus Thorsen," he said anxiously to the woman at the information desk.

"The artist, right? Dr. Keith is looking for you." She had spoken into an intercom and then said to him, "If you'll just have a—"

A double door behind her burst open and a tall, impatient man rushed out.

"Are you Thor-sin?"

"'Tore-son.'"

"I need you back here now." He nodded toward the doors that were still laboriously closing, and immediately headed back through them.

Magnus followed him. "How's the girl?"

They were hurrying down a low, broad, fluorescent-lit hall littered with empty gurneys and wheelchairs.

"Stable. For now. It took some doing to get her there and she won't be for long. She has several bleeders we've got to find and fix." He glanced at Magnus. "That's where you come in. We really have to operate. Otherwise she's going to go bad on us. Sooner rather than later. And she won't let us proceed until she talks to you."

"Me?" He shook his head. "Doc, I don't know what you know

24

about this, but I'm nothing to this girl. I found her smashed up on the beach like an hour ago. That's it. Maybe I saved her by calling the ambulance, but I never saw her before."

The doctor stopped in front of some sort of nurses' station, behind which people in scrub suits were focused and moving and working.

"I don't really give a shit if you're a total stranger, Mr. Thorsen. She won't let us cut until you agree it's the best thing to do. And I'm telling you, it's the only thing to do and we have to do it now. Otherwise she's going to die."

Magnus studied the doctor. His closer look confirmed the feeling he'd had the moment the physician charged through the waiting room doors. Dr. Keith—standing before him in short sleeved scrubs that were some odd shade between forest and army green and wearing black, laced wingtip shoes—was that sort of physician who had abandoned all attempts at social graces, bedside manner and personal appearance in order to concentrate on his particular variety of medicine. As Magnus gazed at the man's awful bowl-over-his-head haircut and black, plastic rimmed glasses, he knew this was someone who was as absolutely correct about Lisa Faucet's medical condition as he was inept at human interaction.

"So where is she?"

Dr. Keith turned immediately and started down one of the emergency room hallways. "She's back here in 12."

"What exactly are you operating for, Doc?"

"Upper and lower bleeders. While we're in there, we'll reduce any simple fractures we find. I'll want an MRI after the surgery, but x-ray shows pretty clearly multiple fractures of the tibia, femur. A crushed pelvis. That's just the lower right side. She has multiple fractures of the upper right—clavicle, scapula. She has a concussion."

"Concussion? She said the car didn't hit her head."

"She didn't realize it." He shook his head. "The sand saved her. If she'd been on a hard surface instead of something she could sink into—" He stopped in front of a cubicle.

Magnus stared at the waifish figure on the elevated bed. She looked like someone who had already been through major surgery. Her skin was the color of fresh ash.

"Hi, Magnus."

25

"Hi, Lisa." He stepped into the cubicle and drew as close to the bed as he could without violating the perimeter of machines and the two silent nurses adjusting them. "Told you there were going to fix you up."

"They want to operate on me."

"Yeah. You've got to let them, darlin', so they can put the bones back in place and find where your bleeding inside."

Great teardrops formed and ran down either side of her face onto the flat, little pillow behind her head. The great irony to him was that she was surrounded by a multitude of people desperately wanting to save her life, but she was waiting on him to say it was okay—because, she believed, he was the one who cared about how she felt.

"Will you stay with me? Will you be here when I wake up?"

"You know I will."

"Okay then," she said.

"Let's go, people!" Dr. Keith barked.

Magnus felt himself duck involuntarily. He turned, but Keith was already out of the room. His voice was loud as he walked down the hall calling out orders.

"I want OR 2. Somebody find me Dr. Tracy. I need anesthesia and O positive. Let's go!"

Magnus heard a door swing open down the hallway and the doctor was gone. He gazed back down at the girl. The nurses were hurriedly disconnecting—or maybe connecting—tubes and machines.

"You're going to be good as gold," he said quietly.

Her eyes were full of understanding. Despite all that had happened to her—all that was happening in that instant and that was about to happen—she was completely aware, completely in touch with the moment.

"I'm glad you found me today."

"Me too."

". . . If I live, will you take me for mahi-mahi on the river walk?"

"Mahi-mahi? Christ, girl, there's a dozen better fish than that? We're going to try it all."

Her bed started to move, the nurses—two small, young women—leaning against it and easing it toward him. Magnus backed through the open door of the cubicle into the hall.

"Where can I—"

26

"Where you came in," one of the nurses said, without looking at him. "There's a waiting area there."

Magnus walked back down the hallway slowly, stopping in front of the nurses' station. He watched as Lisa's bed rolled from her room into the hallway, then disappeared behind another automatic double door. The door was a dull, not quite gray, not quite pale blue with a window on either side over which some opaque material had been taped.

"Why did he wait for me?" he muttered. "She could've died. Why didn't he just go ahead and operate?"

"Didn't want to get sued," a voice answered.

Magnus glanced toward the young woman who had spoken to him. She was lean and tall, wearing pink scrubs and standing above a little table covered with metal file cases. When she spoke her face was down. As he stood gazing at her, she looked up. The nurse had the exceedingly dark eyes, raven hair, long oval face and olive complexion of a Lumbee Indian.

"Sued?"

"Sure. No question he had to operate. But if she said 'no' and he exercised his authority to take her in anyway and she died, he'd get sued by her family for wrongful death. And if he waited until she passed out from internal bleeding and took her then and she died, he'd get sued for not using sound medical judgment. So," the nurse said with a shrug, "since she wasn't going to go under without you tell her she should, I guess you saved both the patient and the doctor, Mr. Thorsen."

He glanced back at the closed doors of the surgical suite. "Makes me glad not to be a doctor."

The nurse had pronounced his name correctly. He studied her.

"You know me? I mean, what I do?"

"Sure. I've been in your gallery maybe four or five times."

He took a step toward the long partition between them. "Are you working this evening?"

"Until 11 tonight."

"How about this?" he said. "You come in Saturday and I'll do a nice pastel of you. In return, you can come and tell me when the girl gets out of the operating room and how she's doing."

She was thinking it over. "Instead of me, how about drawing my daughter?"

27

"How old?"

"Six."

"Deal."

"And if I'm gone before she's out of surgery," she said, "I'll make certain someone gets you the word."

"After you're gone? That's six hours from now."

She grinned. "Mr. Thorsen, why don't you go get yourself something to eat and then come back? This is going to take a while."

There had been a hamburger stand a couple blocks from the emergency room entrance. And a drug store right across the street from it. Magnus bought a sketchpad and a very fine point pen and carried it back to the waiting room along with his double burger combo. He ate and then sat with his eyes down, sketching people who were coming and going and speaking in quiet clusters and weeping and calling people, with a hand on their cells phones and a hand on their foreheads.

They didn't realize what he was doing. It was a trick he had picked up in art school—glancing at people and putting their faces on paper, then glancing again to see if he had gotten them right.

Between striving for perfect likenesses and carefully concealing what he was doing, the surreptitious portraiture kept his mind occupied for the most part. More than four hours had passed with him drawing and occasionally checking his watch when he realized that a woman across the waiting room had figured out what he was doing. She was forty-five-year-old, dressed conservatively and lacquered with makeup and hairspray. Magnus had been drawing the craggy faced, dark-headed, despairing man silently sitting next to her—the one she addressed repeatedly, boisterously, as "Doyle." The woman's eyes had literally narrowed when she saw Magnus glance at Doyle and then resume drawing. She stood up and walked directly to him. Magnus could feel her coming and held the sketchpad to his chest.

"Excuse me," she asked, "but aren't you that artist?"

"You mean that Swedish guy?" he said. "The one with the gallery downtown? No. I get that a lot though. I think he's tall and blonde too."

"Oh." That was all she said. She retreated to her seat, leering over her shoulder at him as if expecting him to move or say something else.

Magnus knew that, if he had admitted who he was, her next question would be, "What are you drawing," followed by, "Doyle, come look at this! This looks just like you!" He closed the sketchpad and picked up a magazine. And then, miraculously, the nurse in the pink scrub suit came through the automatic doors and motioned for him.

As he got to his feet and hastened toward her, he could hear the woman talking to Doyle. "I don't care what he said, I tell you that's him."

"How is she?"

"Alive and kicking. Well, maybe not kicking."

"Will she go to the recovery room?"

"Oh Lord no. We can take better care of her back here. This back part of the ER is really an ICU." She was walking quickly and Magnus was striding to keep up with her. "They're just now bringing her in."

They stopped at the nurses' station. A little group of people clad in long surgical gowns was wheeling a bed back into the cubicle from which Lisa had come.

"It'll take 'em a second to get her situated."

Magnus turned to the nurse. "So your little girl. What's her name?"

"Cheyenne."

"Can you be there Saturday by 9?"

She pursed her lips. "Can we make it 9:30?"

"Okay."

"Just wait by the door there," she said. "They'll tell you when you can go in. Don't expect any response from her."

"Thanks. Thanks a million."

"Sure."

"Let me ask you this, though," Magnus said. "Why would a Lumbee name her child Cheyenne?"

The nurse smiled. He saw again that she had one dimple, on the right cheek.

And she had been right. Lisa had not spoken or responded to him in anyway. He stood by the head of her bed in the simulated twilight of the cubicle for fifteen minutes. Off and on he talked to her. He told her she done well. That the doctors were pleased. That he would see her tomorrow, first thing. Finally he just walked out, down the hall, through the waiting room and into the humid darkness of the Wilmington night.

He found his cell phone in his pocket and dialed a number. Magnus needed a ride back to his car and he wasn't about to ask the police, who had brought him to the hospital, to take him back to Scotch Bonnet Beach. Instead he called Grady.

"Hello."

"Grady, this is Magnus."

"I know who this is. You missed a meeting tonight."

"I need you to pick me up."

"So let me guess, white boy. You went out, didn't you? You can't drive and you expect me to take you home."

"No, Grady. I didn't drink anything. I'm at the hospital and I just need a ride back to my car. It's at Scotch Bonnet."

". . . What? What the hell happened? Are you hurt?"

"I'll tell you all about it. Can you give me a ride?"

"Shit. Gimme ten."

True to his word, Grady pulled up in his battered brown Ford Taurus exactly ten minutes later. Magnus was standing on the sidewalk by the visitors' entrance. He got in on the passenger's side, dropped his sketchbook on the floorboard and turned to his sponsor.

"Thanks."

"Buckle your ass up." Grady eased back into the street. "Scotch Bonnet?"

"That's right."

"So what happened?"

Magnus shrugged. "I finished working this afternoon. I cleaned up my house. And I still had a couple hours before time for the meeting. So I went down to my favorite place on Scotch Bonnet."

"For what?"

"To walk on the beach," he said defensively. "I hadn't been down there since I got out of treatment."

"Look, Mag-man, I don't mean to point out the obvious, but you live on the damn beach."

"Fraser Beach. It's completely built up. Scotch Bonnet is deserted. It's pristine. . . ."

"It's a great place to go drinking by yourself."

"I told you I didn't take a drink," Magnus said. "I was walking along and I heard somebody call out to me. It was a girl. A college

30

kid who was working down at Myrtle. A bunch of guys had grabbed her down there, threw her in a car, brought her up to Scotch Bonnet and gang raped her. Then they ran over her twice and left her for dead." It was only when he finished that Magnus realized how loud his voice had gotten.

Grady didn't speak for a while, as if letting Magnus calm down. They had made their way across the Cape Fear River and were almost to Hwy 17.

"So you saved her life?"

"Yeah, I guess. . . . I called the ambulance and stayed with her 'til they got there."

"Is she going to be all right?"

Magnus thought about the question. "She's probably going to live. Grady—" he glanced at him "—she was squashed like a bug. I could not have imagined someone that broken up if I hadn't see it with my own eyes. She looked like bad cubism."

"What?"

"The funny thing was, I was still out at the beach talking to the police and the hospital called. She wouldn't let 'em operate unless I was there. Unless I told her it was okay."

"Really?"

"Yeah. That's why my car's out here. One of the young cops rushed me in to Wilmington."

Grady nodded. "Well," he said slowly, "I don't mean to bust your chops, but I don't like you missing a meeting."

"One meeting. I haven't missed in almost 100 days. I've even been to meetings where you weren't there."

They wound their way over a series of overpasses and onto the highway headed south. The green reflective road sign read, "Myrtle Beach 49."

"You should've made the one tonight," Grady said. "It was on gratitude. Something you haven't showed a lot of lately."

"Son-of-a-bitch! When do I get credit for what I've done? Can we go ten minutes without you reminding me that I'm an alcoholic?"

"You only have to forget for one minute and you're out there, Mag-man. . . . You have another 'drunk' in you for sure. I don't know if you've got another 'sober' in you."

"I did something good, Grady! Drunk or sober, I saved a girl's

life. And all I've gotten—from the cops, the doctor and you—is a
raft of shit. You're just like that detective."

"Me? What detective?"

"Oh, you'd like her."

"Like who? Why?"

"Lt. Stipling. For one thing, she's blacker than you are."

"They got a black woman detective investigating this?"

"No, no, no. She's in charge of the whole thing. She's Aberdeen
County's Chief of Detectives."

"Shut up!" Grady whistled. He was thinking it over. "A black
woman is the Chief of Detectives. . . . And she gave you a bad time,
huh? And I bet you was saying ugly things about her behind her
back."

"Not really. I was thinking that she was very haughty. An ice
princess. Aloof."

". . . That's it? That's all you were thinking. She must've been
good looking."

He felt his eyebrows rise. "You have no idea. Her cheekbones
and chin were flawless. She had this long, arched neck. Hair just
sculpted on top of her head."

"Did you happen to notice anything from her shoulders down?"

Magnus had laughed. From that point on, the drive to Scotch
Bonnet had become more relaxed. Grady had stopped harping about
the importance of not drinking and Magnus had talked about the
boys in the Chevrolet and the long wait at the hospital. He had been
relieved when they pulled onto the parking lot and Grady's lights
revealed his Camry. And the sponsor had watched dutifully as his
"pigeon" got into the car and drove off the gravel toward home.

Magnus chuckled as he watched Grady's headlights pull onto
the road just behind him. "He just wants to make sure I'm not
headed to the ABC store," he said.

Memories of the previous evening replayed themselves in his
thoughts as Magnus stood rinsing his breakfast plate in the sink. He
glanced at the clock: 7:30. Still and hour and a half until the first
schedule visiting time of the ICU. The nurses had been willing to
let him stay long past the posted times the night before, but the
evening shift had knew he had saved the girl. This morning's nurses
would not. So he would have to wait to see Lisa.

He poured a second cup of coffee and went back onto the deck.

A briny breeze was coming off the ocean. Magnus sighed. Waiting to see the girl. Enjoying the morning sun. Today, this part of it at least, he was glad to be alive.

And then the doorbell rang.

"Christ." He looked at the kitchen clock again, wondering if he'd read it wrong before. "Who the hell?"

He walked through the living room to the front door and flipped open the deadbolt. When he pulled the handle he saw Lt. Dot Stipling standing before him, exceedingly close to the threshold.

"Lieutenant."

"Mr. Thorsen." She pronounced it properly.

They stood staring at each other. Magnus did not back away from the door. He had the intuition that this was one of those moments his Uncle Peder, the great business negotiator, used to warn about: "Whoever speaks first loses."

Evidently Lt. Stipling had known Uncle Peder as well, because she did not speak either. Magnus had the feeling she wasn't going to say anything, so he broke the silence.

"Can I help you with something?"

She immediately acquired that schoolmarm look again, as if she were having her patience tested by a student who should be grasping the obvious. "Do you know why I'm here this morning, Mr. Thorsen?"

He didn't flinch. "To tell me you caught the bastards who raped and ran over Lisa Faucet?"

She blinked. "Not yet. Soon. I hope. But that's not why I'm here."

"To apologize for treating me like a criminal when I saved the girl's life?"

"No one treated you like a criminal, Mr. Thorsen. We were just doing our jobs the way they have to be done. And that's not why I'm here either."

"You came to ask me how the girl did in surgery. If she's going to live and recover completely."

"She is going to survive," the detective said. "She had four hours of surgery and you were there the entire time. She faces three or four more operations. She will probably walk again, but she'll spend six to eight weeks in the hospital and will have at least a full year of physical therapy."

". . . Oh," he said. "I didn't know that. In that case, Lt. Stipling, I have no idea why you're here."

She leaned forward slightly, her chin point at his chest. "I came here to give you the opportunity to explain to me why the jacket you were wearing at the beach had a pint of whiskey in one pocket and a .38 caliber revolver loaded with one bullet in the other."

Magnus stepped back from the threshold, his hand still on the open door.

"You want to come in?"

She walked past him into the living room and stopped. He watched her as she quickly studied all of the cottage she could see. Magnus prided himself on being observant, and recognized that she was also—though her interest was differently drawn than his.

"Your son?" She nodded toward his portrait of Marty.

"Yes."

"What's his name?"

"Martin. That's my middle name. He lives with my ex in Augusta."

"Get to see him often?"

"Two or three times a year, I guess. You have kids?"

She answered without looking at him. "Yes. About a dozen. They call themselves the Aberdeen County Criminal Investigation Unit."

"What do they call you?"

This time her face jerked toward him. "Not 'Mom.'" She rested her hand on the little table by the door where he had organized his farewell notes. "I notice you have some mail here. You have people's names on the envelopes, but no addresses or postage. And they all look alike. What's in these envelopes, I wonder?"

Magnus shrugged. "Excuse me. Did you say you had a search warrant?"

"No."

He nodded. "Well, let's not talk about these, then."

"All right." She drew back her hand. "Why were you at Scotch Bonnet with a loaded weapon?"

"Well," he said slowly, "as we learned yesterday, an isolated beach like that can be a dangerous place. I have a permit for the gun. It's all legal."

"I know you have a permit. I've seen it. You got it in record

34

time, I must say." She cocked her head. "Apparently you were only expecting enough trouble to require one bullet."

"I was pretty sure I could hit what I was aiming at."

"Um hmm. And the pint of whiskey?"

"No law against drinking on the beach."

"No, that's true." Her voice had a reflective tone. "Although it probably is a pretty big deal for a person who got out of treatment a little more than two months ago and has almost 100 days of continuous sobriety."

He felt himself becoming angry and wondered if his face were growing red. "Who did you talk to in my group?"

"Whomever we might have talked to has no idea what you were about to do yesterday, Mr. Thorsen. I need to know why you were going to kill yourself." When he didn't answer immediately, she continued. "You came very close. The way I have it figured, you opened the whiskey and Miss Faucet stopped you before you could take a drink."

Somehow the reality of how close he had come to dying had not struck him until that moment. The gravity of finding the girl and the necessity of covering up his real reason for being at the beach had granted him emotional distance from the death he had intended and came within moments of achieving.

"My kitchen adjoins my lower deck. There's a great view," he said. "I'd like to sit out there."

He walked past the stairs and into the kitchen. The detective followed him silently—until she saw the vista through the doors that opened onto his deck.

"Oh."

"Beautiful, isn't it?" His voice was sedate. Resigned. "This is the best part of the day if you're an artist." He stepped over to the stove. "What do you take in your coffee?"

"Oh, I don't—"

"Come on. Do you not drink coffee? Isn't that required for law enforcement officers: firearms training, interrogation procedures, coffee bingeing." When she only stared at him, he continued. "Is there a rule against accepting a cup from people you're questioning?"

She was deciding. "Sugar. Just a teaspoon."

Leaning against the deck railing, she surveyed the beach.

35

Magnus watched as she drew a deep breath. What had Grady asked him? How did she look from the neck down? The word that came to him, as an artist, was "proportional." He might have said "voluptuous," but that implied some intent on the part of the subject. And Lt. Stipling, he reflected, was strictly business.

"Here you go."

He handed her a thick, stoneware cup. She blew over the top of the coffee and cautiously took a sip.

"This is a beautiful place. Do you have breakfast here every—" She stopped. She took another sip of the coffee. "What is this?"

"Egg coffee."

"Egg?"

"Yeah. Spherical, oval, off-white object. Slightly rough in texture. Brittle outer coating. Comes out of a chicken's ass."

"I know—" she arched her eyebrows "—what an egg is. Why do you put it in your coffee?"

He smiled. "My dad is a Swede. But Mom is Norwegian. She says that all true Nords drink egg coffee."

"Well it's unusual." She took another sip and relaxed against the railing, looking down at the beach. "It's really quite good." She looked up above her head. "You have another deck above this?"

"Yeah. That's where my studio is. The view is better."

"Better? Than this?"

"I'll show you." He could see the reluctance in her eyes. "Come on. I don't bite. . . . And I don't have any 'etchings' to show you."

Without waiting for her to respond, he walked to the stairs and started up. He could hear her light, slow steps behind him. At the top he opened the door to his studio and went in. She stopped just inside the door.

"Oh! You do have quite a view."

Magnus opened the big glass doors onto the deck and slid open the screens. He stepped out to the railing and looked down. The tide was going out. Down the beach someone was throwing tennis balls into the surf for a retriever to chase. Twenty yards away, a gull was hanging nearly motionless in the air, waiting in case Magnus had food crumbs to throw.

"Forget it. I'm not a tourist," he muttered.

It was nearly thirty-five feet from where he stood to the dunes below. Almost forty if he stood on top of the handrail. When he first

36

decided to kill himself, he thought about jumping from this upper deck to make it look like an accident. Only, if he had been pretending that he didn't mean to die, he couldn't leave notes for his son and parents and lawyer and bookkeeper. Then too, he might have survived the fall and been crippled by it. He also thought about hanging himself from this railing. The problem was that, if he didn't break his neck, hanging would be slow and awful. And no one in the family would want to live in the cottage. And its worth on the real estate market would have diminished as well.

Where was the lieutenant, he wondered. Turning from the water, he saw her walking around the room, looking at the canvases on the walls and easels.

"See anything you like?"

"They're really very beautiful."

"You think?"

She faced him. "I can't help but notice that they are all finished."

". . . Well most of them are fairly old. I didn't do any of these for customers. I did them for myself, or to try a new technique, or to demonstrate something to someone."

"Where are your 'works in progress?'"

He shrugged.

"Did you run out of clients who wanted portraits done?"

"I have a whole stack of work over there on my desk. I just haven't started them yet."

"Why haven't you?"

Magnus took a drink of his coffee. "Just waiting for my muse, I guess."

She was walking through the studio toward him. "You know what I think? I think you finished everything you were working on and didn't start anything new because you intended to take your life. Everything about this place and your actions before you stumbled onto Lisa Faucet reveals an intent to commit suicide."

She stood beside him main drawing table, her hands on her hips. It was a place, he noticed, where—with the sun streaming into the studio—the pure consistency of her complexion and the finely etched lines of her face appeared to glow with their own light. And in that instant she didn't seem to Magnus to be a police officer hounding him, but an exquisite countenance, begging to be captured on canvas.

37

"I have a friend who is a musician," Magnus said. "To him, the whole world is reducible to beat and melody. If you're a every problem looks like a nail. And if you're a police officer, everything and everyone is suspicious."

She smiled grimly. "Mr. Thorsen, you can change the subject all you want. You can have me follow you from one room of your house to another. You can try to distract me with egg coffee and beautiful artwork. But nothing changes the reality that you were going to kill yourself yesterday."

Slowly he shook his head. "That is strictly your assumption."

The phone rang.

"Now what!" he exclaimed. He looked at the little clock on the supply table. "It's just now 7:45!" The phone rang again. "How did I get so popular?"

She stared at him. "Aren't you going to answer it?"

"No."

"Might be the hospital."

There was a third ring.

"No," he said. "The hospital has my cell number. Nobody who has my home number would dare call me before 8 a.m."

"Why's that?"

There was a fourth ring.

"Because they know I'm painting."

The answering machine, with a robotic voice, spoke, "Please leave a message after the tone."

There was a protracted beeping sound and suddenly Grady's angry words were amplified through the room: "Mag-man! What's this shit in today's paper? You better pick up. I saw your name listed by a gun permit. What the hell you need a gun for? This has something to do with going down to Scotch Bonnet by yourself, don't it? You didn't tell me nothing about no goddamn gun, son. You better, by-god, be calling me back or I'm calling that hot police lady myself about this. And you better, by-god, be at the meeting tonight." There was the sound of Grady abruptly slamming down the phone.

Magnus was staring at the answering machine, refusing to look at her. He didn't know what to say, and he felt like a little boy caught in some naughty act.

"Hot police lady?"

He shook his head. "That's not what I called you."

"So he is talking about me," she said. "I take it that's you're A.A. sponsor?"

"Well he was, up until a minute ago."

". . . You have a black sponsor?"

He tilted his head and looked at her. "Yeah. Why do you ask?"

"I don't know. Just surprised me."

"Surprised him," Magnus said, "when I told him that a black woman is Chief of Detectives. . . . I told him he probably would have met you before I did, if he hadn't sobered up before he got caught."

She laughed. She had a beautiful smile. Somehow it was a relief to Magnus to see her smile.

"Mr. Thorsen," she said, her voice quite agreeable, "why don't we both put our cards on the table here?"

He grinned broadly. He pointed toward a canvas-covered director's chair that faced his main drawing table.

"Why don't you sit there?"

"What? Now you want me to sit down?"

"Just sit there. If you'll do that, I'll be glad to tell you everything I can."

Distrust, impatience on her face, Lt. Stipling pulled herself into the chair. Magnus sat behind his drawing table and picked up a worn stick of charcoal twig. He rubbed the back of his left hand in a circle several times around the heavy paper tacked to the board and quickly began to draw.

"If you don't mind me asking you a question," he said without looking up, "why are you so concerned about my health, Lieutenant?"

She watched his quick, effective motions. "Well, for starters it's my responsibility. By law we have to intervene if someone is a danger to himself or others. Imminent suicide would qualify as a danger to self. So I could lock you up and have you evaluated." When he did not respond, or even look up, she continued. "This is doubly dangerous, however, because you are a material witness in a major felony case. If you do yourself in, a group of rapists and attempted murderers might get away."

He reached for a Conte stick, his eyes flashing up at her momentarily. "Let me assure you that I have no intention of dying before you arrest the people who hurt Lisa Faucet."

She leaned forward. "That's not much consolation, Mr. Thorsen. Legal matters drag on for months and years, don't they? Suppose we find and arrest these boys. A jury hears your testimony and convicts them. Then you kill yourself. Perhaps it comes to light that you were suicidal prior to seeing them. And it comes to light that you were in treatment for alcoholism. . . . That might be grounds for an appeal. Your entire testimony would be tainted."

"Well," he said slowly, "the way I have it figured is that you won't even need my testimony."

"Why's that?"

"I'm guessing you probably got multiple sources of DNA off Lisa yesterday."

". . . I'm sure that will turn out to be the case. We're looking at a minimum of three assailants."

"I have every faith—" He changed colors of charcoal. "—that you will catch these guys. And then you'll get one or two of them to turn on the others." He looked up. "Magnus Thorsen will become nothing but a footnote to your investigation. After that, what happens to me doesn't really matter."

"So you're indicating you still intend to take your life?"

"No." He exhaled with a "pah" sound. "I didn't say that. I never said I intended to kill myself in the first place. But I will promise you that I won't do anything to impede your investigation of the crime. And I'll help you all I can."

"You know . . . I believe you are completely sincere and that you have every good intention, but it's not enough."

"Why is that?" He was rubbing a Conte stick on its side across a portion of the image on the paper.

"Well," there was some exasperation in her voice, "have you heard of making a 'federal case' out of something?"

"Yeah."

"Well this could become a federal case if we don't nail it down."

"A federal case?" There was the merest whiff of skepticism in his voice.

"Yes, actually. These boys kidnapped Miss Faucet and transported her away to rape her. That is a federal offense. And then, geniuses that they are, they took her across a state line for illegal purposes—another federal crime. Among the litany of North

Carolina felonies they committed, they're all guilty of at least two federal crimes as well.

"Now we have connected with the FBI and they have plenty to keep themselves busy with these days. They'd just as soon we handle this without them. Only, if Aberdeen County blows it, they will become involved—and they won't be too happy about it."

"Well," Magnus said, searching for a particular piece of colored charcoal, "that should shrink your pool of suspects considerably."

"Oh really? Why?"

"The morons who did this obviously don't work for Uncle Sam."

She shook her head, a smile spreading across her face. "They're kids. Inept. Inexperienced. This had to be the first time they tried anything like this because they left so much evidence."

"But still—" Magnus rubbed another color across an expanse of the page "—you haven't caught them yet. What about the car?"

She leaned back and folded her hands. "You might be amazed at how many 60's vintage Chevy sedans and coupes are still registered in the Wilmington area. Even when we select out the non-white vehicles, we have several dozen to account for."

"Why don't you make it light on yourself?" he said. "Focus only on '63 and '64 Impalas. And if I see it, I'll recognize it."

". . . You're that sure?"

"Told you I'd help you."

He picked up an aerosol can. He shook it briefly and sprayed the paper on which he had been drawing.

"Did you just put hairspray on that picture?"

He leaned back, looking at it. "First, this is not a 'picture.' It's a charcoal portrait. An original Magnus Thorsen. I sell these all day for two-fifty a pop. Second, that's not hairspray. It's workable fixative."

"Workable fixative?"

"Yeah." He motioned for her. "Want to look? The spray keeps me from smearing what I've done, but later I can go back and work on it some more if I want."

"You mean you're through? Just like that?" She slipped out of the director's chair.

"You tell me."

The lieutenant seemed almost cautious in moving to where she

41

could see the drawing. She gazed at it intently, her mouth slowly opening into a look of amazement. She raised her hand as if to feel the image, then gently lowered it. And Magnus knew he had gotten it right.

It was a soft, heavily shaded portrait of Dot Stipling's head, looking down and to her right, with an expression of wonder. There was no stress in her face, and only the slightest hint of a bemused smile on her full, parted lips. Pure, ivory light radiated across her image leaving only a hint of the left side of her cheek, while the right side of her face was adorned with a dark rainbow of complementing but distinctly stroked hues.

"The light," she said quietly. "There's something about the light."

"East light."

She turned to him. "That's what it says on the sign in front of your cottage—the name you call this place. What does it mean?"

He studied the charcoal silently, then stood beside her, hands in his pockets. "Most artists—especially portrait artists—use 'north light.' The images they are painting or drawing are theoretically illuminated with a light source coming from over the artist's left shoulder. . . . But being left-handed, I always found that cumbersome. I felt as if I were obscuring that light as I worked. So one day when I was a rebellious teenager, I broke the rule. I imagined my light source was coming from my right elbow, an 'east light.' I've used it ever since. It gives what I do a different sort of feel. That's why my studio is arranged like this. On good mornings, like this, I catch the east light. It's my inspiration, I guess."

Lt. Stipling had been watching him as he explained. He could hear the odd sound of her breathing, through her nose but heavy. He wondered if she had been doing that all along, only he hadn't heard her.

"Why do you want to kill yourself? You create such beauty," she said. "Why would you want to die when you can do this?"

Magnus looked down at her, her face inches from his. Wordlessly he pulled the paper free of the tacks that held it and began to roll the portrait, the image inside.

"Quite the contrary, Lieutenant. I've said that I'm going to do everything within my power to live. I intend to help you find the people who hurt Lisa Faucet."

42

"And after that?"

He sighed. "Well, as we say in the program of Alcoholics Anonymous, 'first things first.' 'One day at a time.' Would you like this charcoal?"

"Well—" She laughed, embarrassment in her voice. "Yes. But, I don't have two hundred and fifty—"

"It's my pleasure," he said. "I give it to you as a favor. And I ask a favor in return."

"Uh . . . what?"

"Sometime—after we catch these bad guys, maybe—I want to do another portrait of you."

"You can do that again?"

"Different pose," he said. "Different medium." When she didn't respond, he continued, "Just think it over."

He slid the rolled paper into a cardboard cylinder and handed it to her. She held it against her chest, studying him.

"I'm guessing," she said, "that you're going to the hospital? That's really why I came so early. We could've discussed all these things last night, if you had called for a ride the way I told you to."

He nodded. "First visiting hours at the ICU start in about an hour."

"Well, I'm sending someone there to speak to you and get your help."

Chapter 3

"Mr. Thorsen?"

He had been watching the clock beside the ER/ICU door, waiting for the moment when he could go in to see Lisa. The familiar voice drew his gaze toward two young men standing next to him.

"Officer Miller. How are you?"

"Fine, sir. This is Chip Logan. He's our sketch artist."

The thin, short, exceedingly youthful figure beside the deputy stared big-eyed at him. Magnus thought he looked vaguely familiar.

"Sir," Miller continued, "we know you're waiting to go in to visit the victim—"

"Lisa. Lisa Faucet."

"Yes, sir," he went on, undeterred, "but Lt. Stipling asked if you would just take a few minutes to work with Mr. Logan and come up with a likeness of the Chevy driver."

". . . You want me, right now, to describe the kid to your sketch artist?"

"Yes, sir. It will only take ten or twenty minutes."

"Visiting hours are only thirty minutes."

"Please, sir."

"Ah." Magnus lumbered to his feet.

"We have a conference room reserved over here, sir."

Magnus nodded. He followed them toward the small, windowless, gray room. He knew all about family conference rooms in hospitals. They were behind unmarked doors that always remained closed, doors you might walk past 100 times without realizing they were there until the oncologist called your family in to tell you that—despite all the chemo, radiation and surgery to which Auntie Jean had been subjected—she wasn't going to live out the week. So when they went in and closed the door and sat down at the little table, adorned only with a box of tissues, Magnus was immediately uncomfortable.

Skip Logan sat down to his right, so that Magnus could watch him draw. He had a canvas carrying bag and began to take out graphite pencils, eraser and drawing tablet. The deputy sat across the table from them, erect in his chair but with a distant expression.

"We met before, Mr. Thorsen," the young man said.

"Really? I thought I knew you from somewhere."

"Three years ago," he said. "You came out to North Aberdeen High School to judge our spring art contest."

"Oh. There you go, then. You had an entry?"

"Yes. I had three pen-and-ink drawings entered."

"Did you win?"

"Uh. No. Got a green ribbon on one of them."

"That's good," Magnus said. "Obviously you've stayed with it."

"I'm about to finish up my associates degree from the community college in New Hanover County. Then I'm going to transfer to UNCW and get a bachelor's in art and graphic design."

He was clearly more excited to talk to Magnus about art than to draw a sketch of the driver.

"I really applaud you, Skip—is it?" Magnus nodded slowly. "And what you're doing here is good as well. Just goes to show that you can make a living as an artist. Speaking of which—"

"Oh! Yeah. I'm ready. So, tell me the shape of his face."

"Long round. Just a little wider at the top than the bottom, broken by a strong definite chin. He has short, light brown hair that stands— Don't draw him flat like that. You lose perspective."

"Well," Skips voice was apologetic, "this is how they want me to draw, Mr. Thorsen. They say it reproduces better."

He looked from the elongated, #2 pencil drawn oval on the sketchpad to the artist. "Right. Well, let's do it like they want you to then. . . . He's about eighteen, I'd guess. Fair complexion. . . . I hate to say this, Skip, but that's too long. You got him looking like Joe Palooka there."

"Who?"

"An old cartoon. Never mind. You got his head a little too long."

Skip flipped a page on his sketchpad, ready to begin again. Magnus eyed him warily. This time the circle was drawn too short and fat. He could sense that he was making the artist nervous. He sighed.

"Listen, Skip. I know you know what you're doing. I have no doubt that, if we stayed at this, you'd hit it perfectly eventually. But the truth is, I have a pretty young lady waiting to see me. And I make it a practice not to be late for appointments with women. Do you mind?"

He didn't wait for the kid to respond. Instead he reached across and took the pad and pencil out of Skip's hand. He rolled the General #2 between the fingers of his left hand, flipped a page on the tablet and rubbed the edge of his hand in a circle around the blank sheet three or four times. Then he started to draw. Deputy Miller apparently displeased at what Magnus had done, leaned forward in his chair and clenched his teeth, but said nothing.

Then the image began to flow from his memory through the pencil onto the paper—the image that had awakened him more than once the night before: the wide-open, pale eyes and fair skin, short upright hair and strong chin. He drew the muscled neck and the darkness around his closed lips. And when he did, the look of dread he remembered was there.

It did not take long for his experienced hand to finish the drawing—only a couple minutes. As he watched, the sketch artist slowly leaned closer and closer. There came a point when the young man studying the drawing took on an expression of reluctant recognition. When Magnus dropped the pencil on the pad and pushed them toward him, Skip didn't pick them up. He had, Magnus thought, a similar look of dread.

"Oh my god," the kid said slowly.

"What?" Miller asked.

"This is the most perfect likeness of Randy Plank I've ever seen. It's more like him than a photograph."

"Who's Randy Plank?" Magnus asked.

The deputy turned the sketchpad toward himself. He gazed at the likeness. As always, he remained emotionless, though it seemed to Magnus that recognition flashed in his eyes, followed by something like weariness.

"He was the North Aberdeen High quarterback the last two years," Skip said. "Probably one of the best in the state. Took the Ospreys to the semis this year."

Miller produced a cell phone and engaged it. Magnus wondered why he didn't use his radio as he had the day the before. The officer pushed a button.

"He was recruited by nearly every major college in this state, I

46

heard," Skip continued. There was a sadness in his voice. "I think he signed out-of-state, though. Southeast Conference, maybe. He has mad skills in the backfield."

"Lieutenant? This is Miller. . . . We have a suspect, ma'am. No, not just a composite drawing. We have a named suspect."

Skip had grown silent. He and Magnus listened solemnly to the portion of the conversation they could hear.

"Randall Plank. . . . Yes, ma'am, that one. . . . In the conference room at the hospital. Myself, Mr. Thorsen and Skip Logan." Miller listened for a few seconds and then said, "Here he is, ma'am." He handed the cell phone to the young artist. "Lt. Stipling wants to speak to you."

Skip took the phone gingerly and held it to his ear. "Hello, Lieutenant. . . . It's a perfect likeness because Mr. Thorsen drew it. . . . No, ma'am. I'm not a sworn officer." Skip was nodding, as if Lt. Stipling could see him. "I do understand. No, I'd never do that. . . . Okay. Goodbye." He closed the phone and handed it back to the deputy. "She's afraid I'm going to tell Randy we're looking for him. She said she'd arrest me if I contacted him or if I ever told anybody else about this sketch."

Magnus felt himself smile. "Hey, don't feel bad. I saved a girl's life and for half an hour they treated me like a suspect."

Miller was standing up. "We have to go, Skip."

The young man began scooping up his drawing supplies and drumming them into the canvas carrying bag. For him, Magnus thought as he watched, this had been an experience of loss in several ways.

As he pushed to his feet, he put his hand on the kid's shoulder. "Want some advice?"

The boy stopped instantly, looking at him.

"There are three things you have to possess to become an artist, Skip. Talent. Experience. And confidence. The talent you have. No problem. Keep doing what you're doing. That's the practical experience part. And with practice and experience, the confidence will come."

His face lightened. Magnus shook his hand.

"Ready?" Miller asked.

"You know, Officer Miller," Magnus said, following them through the conference room door, "when you get upset, your

47

(continued)

forehead turns white and your chin gets dark."

The deputy glanced toward him for an instant and then walked quickly toward the hospital exist with the sketch artist beside him. Magnus looked at the ICU/ER clock. He had lost ten minutes of his visiting time.

Despite the fact that there were no exterior windows, the hallway seemed brighter to him as he quietly made his way around the empty gurneys and down the corridors to the Lisa's cubicle. He stood in the hallway outside the door and gazed in at her.

Her color was remarkably better this morning, though her expression was one of extreme weariness. Her right arm was swathed in some sort of apparatus that looked like a rug turned inside out, and inside that was a cast. She was lying mostly flat, her right leg framed with a black metallic skeleton through which metal pins, emerging from her bare skin, were screwed in place. He had seen these orthopedic gizmos the night before, but had mostly ignored them as he concentrated instead on the girl.

There was another young woman in the room with her, a plump girl with a round face, short dark hair that was cut so it looked like a roof, and eyeglasses with small, rectangular frames. Magnus could not help but envision her as pink Dutch barn with a brown thatched roof and little loft windows. And she was talking. It wasn't clear that Lisa was listening, but the girl was chatting away in an animated voice.

"Magnus!" Lisa saw him and spoke and smiled. Her face brightened instantly.

"So you remember me?"

"How could I forget my hero?" Her voice was slow, sleepy. Still it had an unmistakable flirtatious quality that Magnus had not remembered from the previous day. "This is my roommate Katie Morgan." She motioned with her left hand toward the girl.

The girl stood and reached across the end of the bed to shake Magnus' hand. She started talking immediately.

"Hi. I'm Katie. I'm Lisa's roommate. I have been for two years now since we got liberated from the dorm."

Magnus let go of her hand and stood at the end of Lisa's bed. The girl sat back down and kept talking.

"We've actually known each other since we were, like, freshmen. But we've never had a class together. I'm a music major.

Piano, you know. So you must be the artist guy who saved her life?"

He opened his mouth, but she continued.

"That was a great thing you did. She would've died. That's what that one geeky doctor said." Her eyes widened. "Not that she's going to be okay tomorrow. She has to have a couple more operations at least. I came down to stay with her to keep her company because her mom and sister are coming, but they can't be here 'til tomorrow. Lisa doesn't have anybody else, you know."

Magnus looked away from the roommate to Lisa. "How do you feel?"

"Like shit." There was resignation in her voice. "And if I let my medicine run out, it hurts like fire."

"Your medicine?"

"Her morphine," Katie answered. "She's on the pump. She can push it ever ten or fifteen minutes. As she gets better they'll set the doses farther and farther apart. They say you actually use less morphine this way."

Magnus nodded at her and turned back to Lisa. "So your medicine works for you?"

"Yeah. When it first hits, I feel like I'm floating down in a feather bed."

"Hmm," he said. "Maybe I can get the nurse to fix me some to go. So then your doctor came in to see you this morning?"

"Oh my god!" Katie was rolling her eyes. "Just a minute ago. You should've been here. What a total dorky guy—"

"Yeah," Magnus interrupted, "but he's really the one who saved her life."

"Dr. Keith," Lisa said laconically. "I don't remember what he said."

"He said," Katie began, "your signs are stable. You have to have another surgery on your pelvis in the next few days as soon as you've recovered enough because your something is squeezing on your something and, when your leg bones mend, you won't be able to walk otherwise. He wants to call in an orthopedic specialist and a—" She was thinking. "—was it gynecologist—for that surgery. Then you have to have your wrist fixed later on."

She was going to keep talking, but Magnus cut her off again. "How long in the ICU and how long in the hospital? Do you remember if he said anything about that?"

49

She didn't say anything for a second or two. Her face softened and flushed ever so slightly. The big tears he remembered from yesterday formed and began to run down her cheeks.

"In the ICU?" Katie said obliviously. "I think that depends on when her next surgery is. But overall he said six to eight weeks. I think. Isn't that right, Lisa?"

"Gosh, Katie," Magnus said, "you were here when I got here. Do they let you come before visiting hours?"

"Well I told them I was family," she said in her chatty tone, "which I'm not, of course, but right now I guess I'm the closest thing Lisa's got."

"Yes." He nodded. "It's good they'll just let you stay like this. You know, I'm going to have to go in about fifteen minutes, but I'm a little queasy. I guess it's the sight of all this medical stuff."

She giggled. "A big, macho man like you? Mom says that, underneath, all men are really sissies."

"Smart woman. I hope she doesn't tell anybody else. But let me ask you a favor, Katie, since you can stay and I can't—and if I puke they'll kick me out now."

"Puke? Yuck. What favor?"

"Is there like a soda machine around here? I'd pay for each of us to have a soda."

"Right where you came in, in the ER waiting room. Drinks are a dollar each. How could you miss it?"

He was taking out his billfold. "This whole ordeal gets me worked up and I just get beside myself. I can't think straight, I guess." He sighed. "Here are two dollars. Get yourself whatever you want. I'll have a diet whatever."

Katie hopped up and took the money. "Well I'll be right back. It was right by the door where you came in." She scurried out of the cubicle, still talking as she went down the corridor.

Magnus turned to Lisa, who was watching him with half-lidded eyes.

"That was so sly," she said in her drowsy voice.

He sat down in the chair on the left side of her bed. "Well, it bought us ten minutes."

"No it didn't. . . . She'll be back in thirty seconds."

"I don't think so. The 'exact change' light is lit up on that drink machine. She'll have to go get change."

Lisa chuckled. And grimaced.

"If she were my roommate—sorry to say this—I'd have to have a constant supply of morphine."

"Yeah," she said slowly. "Katie talks a lot. Sometimes it's worse than other, like when she's stressed out. . . . She talks more when she doesn't know what to say. . . . I guess that's weird."

She seemed to doze as Magnus watched her. Then she opened her eyes, looking at him.

"I'm glad to hear your folks are coming."

"My sister is bringing my mom. Next week my brother is coming."

Magnus decided not to ask about her stepfather. "They will be very glad to see you. To see you're doing okay." When she didn't respond, he asked, "I guess you'll be glad to see them too."

"I guess. . . . Long as they keep me on drugs." She gazed at him. "I'm glad you came this morning. They told me you were here last night when I got out of surgery."

"Yeah. Well, I did promise. And I wanted to make sure you were okay."

"Some policemen have been here too. Off and on they stand outside the room and talk to the nurses."

"Checking to make sure you're doing all right, I guess."

"Are they guarding me?"

He thought it over. "I don't know. I wouldn't think so."

". . . Why not?"

"Because even a bunch of teenage boys could never get a Chevy Impala into this little room."

She laughed, and then cried out.

"Oh," he said apologetically, "I forget. I don't mean to make you hurt."

"You make me laugh. I guess they haven't caught them yet?"

He wasn't sure how much to say, but he wanted to answer quickly so she wouldn't think he was holding out on her. "I don't think they've caught 'em yet," he said, "but I think they have some very good leads."

"Well . . . if they haven't caught them, and they're still out there, why aren't they guarding me?"

"Honestly? There hasn't been any news about you on TV or in the newspaper. If I don't miss my guess, the police are keeping this

51

under wraps until they're ready to arrest the boys."

"Why?"

"Well, darlin', as far as those boys are concerned, no news is good news. It makes them assume they got away with what they did. Since you haven't been on the TV, they think you're still at Scotch Bonnet Beach and nobody has found you."

"My body, you mean."

"Yeah." Magnus shrugged, averting his eyes. "They probably think you're still there. If I don't miss my guess, the police are probably closing in. And when they arrest them, that will be big news."

"Why do you say that?"

"Well, you'll be like a hero. Reporters will come and interview the girl who survived being run over twice. 'Tough UNCW Coed Still Going Strong.'"

Her face seemed to mellow as she stared at him. "You're the hero. You're the one who saved me. They'll interview you and give awards."

This time it was Magnus who felt the sudden surge of dread. "Oh no, Miss Lisa. I've got all the notoriety I ever want. All I did was push a button on my cell phone."

The idea that he might be thrust fully into public scrutiny—even for heroic actions—had not occurred to him. That sort of acclaim, he thought, would robe him of his intended suicide for an even longer period of time—not because he would be closely watched, but because people would always try to connect his killing himself with his saving the girl. People would find, he thought, some emotional connection between the two events. They would say that Magnus suffered post-traumatic stress because of the seeing the girl horribly injured, or they would say that Magnus couldn't handle the acclaim of being a hero. No one would ever believe the proximity of the two events was mere coincidence. He pictured himself leaving a note: "Hey everybody, I planned to do myself even before I saved the girl." No one would believe it. But then, he wondered, why would he care what rationale strangers placed on his suicide?

"You said your mom and your sister will be here tomorrow. Well if the news of this breaks while they're here, you can have them talk to the reporters for you," he said. "Just leave me out of it, if you don't mind."

She was studying his face. "You're not trying to renege on our deal and back out of my life, are you?"

"Oh, no. I wouldn't do that. You and I are going for a big fish feast on the river walk. After that we may go dancing." He smiled. "Although we may have to wait a little while for our date."

She groaned. "O god. Six weeks." She felt for the little gray device pinned to her hospital gown and pushed it with her thumb. "Mmm. . . . Six weeks without . . . makeup and real clothes. Six weeks of learning to walk again. Six weeks off work. Going broke. Looking like shit."

"Trust me, you don't look bad."

She shook her head. "Magnus, I look awful. Katie told me how bad I look."

"What a nice friend she is."

"Well at least she's honest. My hair is so greasy and yucky you can't even tell what it's supposed to look like."

"I can."

"No you can't."

"Oh yes I can." His voice was insistent. "It's my job to know how people are supposed to look. I see where beauty is in a person when most people don't. Especially if those people are music majors."

"Oh, Magnus. . . ." She closed her eyes. "I just love you. You're still rescuing me."

"You think I'm joking. I'm not." He was thinking. "I'll prove it. Tomorrow I have to do a charcoal over at my studio for a one of the ICU nurses. I owe her a favor for getting me in to see you late last night. But after that, I'm bringing my stuff and coming over here."

". . . And?"

"And showing you just how beautiful you are—with your Erector Set leg and all."

She laughed. It didn't seem to hurt her as much.

"What's an Erector Set?"

"It's an old toy. Never mind. Just try to be here about lunchtime tomorrow."

She laughed again. "I was going to go out and walk around . . . but I guess I can wait."

Then they could hear Katie coming back down the hallway,

53

talking to herself. She walked into the cubicle with a soda can in either hand.

"That was quick," Magnus said, getting up to give her back her chair.

"No it wasn't," she said, incredulity in her voice. She handed him a diet soda and sat down. "The machine in the waiting room was only taking exact change. They didn't have any money at the information desk. Can you imagine? They sent me up on the labor and delivery floor to the visitor's lounge to the machine up there. I almost never found it."

"Oh my," Magnus said. "Wouldn't have asked you to go if I'd know it would be that much trouble."

Lisa was smiling at him, and then turning toward a figure in the doorway of her cubicle.

"Hello?" she said.

Magnus turned, expecting to see a nurse or Dr. Keith. Instead it was a familiar, austere black woman in a navy business suit.

"Oh! Lieutenant." He stepped toward her. "I don't believe you've met my friend, Lisa Faucet."

"Hello, Miss Faucet."

"Hello, Lieutenant. Are you investigating my crime?"

Lt. Stipling smiled. "You mean the crime that happened to you?"

Magnus extended his upturned hand toward the other young woman. "And this is Lisa's roommate, Katie Magpie."

"Magpie? Morgan! Katie Morgan. How did you get that? It's never been Magpie."

Magnus, smiling slyly, exchanged a glance with the detective.

"So, Lieutenant," he said, "Lisa was just asking me about your investigation."

"Have you arrested them?" Lisa asked in her drowsy voice.

"Not yet, Miss Faucet. But we are making real progress, thanks to your friend, Mr. Thorsen."

"Isn't he good?"

"He's a wonderful artist. That's for sure. And he's a good witness." Lt. Stipling stepped closer to the foot of the bed. "That's why I'm here, actually. I know you three are visiting, but I was wondering if I could borrow your friend, Mr. Thorsen, for a while?"

". . . I guess."

"And do you have the time to help us, Mr. Thorsen?"

"I think I can make myself available." He leaned over the bed and grasped Lisa's left hand. "Don't forget about tomorrow."

"What's tomorrow?" Katie asked.

"Will you remind the nurses to wash her hair in the morning?" he asked the roommate. "She's getting her portrait done." He saw Lt. Stipling glance at him.

"Wow," Katie said. She turned toward Lisa. "Is it like 'before and after'?"

Magnus and Dot Stipling were out of the cubicle before Lisa answered.

The lieutenant looked at him. "I take it her roommate is a rather talkative airhead."

"You have no idea." When they were beyond the nurses' station and could not be heard by anyone, he asked, "Have you caught your football player yet?"

"Actually we have him under surveillance at this time."

"That didn't take long. When will you arrest him?"

They exited the exterior emergency room doors and stood beneath the portico. The lieutenant was looking around them, apparently to make certain they were alone.

"That depends," she replied. "Will you help us?"

"Sure. You want me to identify him?"

"Hope you don't mind riding with me." She headed toward the parking lot. "We're pretty sure you can identify him, assuming you can remember him as well as you can draw him. What we want you to do is identify the car."

"Oh. Okay."

Magnus followed her to the passenger's side of a spotless, silver blue police car. It had no decals identifying it, but a short, wire antenna protruded conspicuously from the trunk. She held the door open as he slid into the sea and then she closed it firmly.

"So chivalry is not dead," Magnus muttered as she walked around to the driver's side.

The car was as immaculately clean on the inside as it was on the outside. Apart from the police radio and some sort of small computer screen and keyboard, it was like any other car—that belonged to an obsessive neatness freak. It had a distinctive scent though. Not perfume. What was it?

55

He started talking to her again as they drove off the parking lot and pulled away from the hospital.

"After I confirm it's the car, then you're going to arrest him?"

"Probably not," she said. "With him under surveillance, our hope is to build an airtight case before he knows we're onto him. We'd only arrest him at this point if he figured out we're watching and tried to run."

Magnus rolled his head toward her. "Now see, there you lost me. You have an eyewitness who has identified him. His DNA is got to be on the girl. If this car we're going to see is the right one, I'll know it. So why are you taking the chance of not locking him up?"

Her tone remained perfectly even. "Building a case, especially in a crime this severe—with multiple assailants—is a process, Mr. Thorsen. Fortunately, this is an unusual situation in that we have a pretty clear idea of who our chief suspect is and what he did. We have a distinct advantage we usually don't in that he has no idea that we are observing and investigating him." She signaled and made a turn. "I understand that, to you, this seems open-and-shut. But a hundred things can go wrong. There are lots of loose ends we have to tie up. Things we have to figure out. A chronology we have to work out. . . . This is like picking tomatoes. You don't want them green and you don't want to wait too long. You want to catch them at that perfect moment. There's an instant when a suspect is 'ripe' for arrest. I think most folks don't know that about criminal investigations."

He was studying her profile. The longer he knew her and the closer he observed her, the more she became a visual feast for him. The expressiveness of her lips as she spoke. The shades and flecks of different browns in the irises of her eyes.

Her radio crackled softly and familiar voice spoke. "12 to 3."

She lifted the mike from its cradle with an effortless, practiced motion. "3. Go ahead."

"ETA, ma'am?"

Lt. Stipling looked at her watch. "0-9-3-0."

"10-4. We'll meet you there. 12 clear."

"Clear." She replaced the mike.

"Uh," he said, "if I can ask, where are we going?"

She slowed and turned onto another street and said, "Oleander.

Over near the tracks. There are some storage units there."

"Yeah?"

". . . Well, Randy Plank drives a Pontiac. But his grandfather, Mr. Houck, has an older model car that he keeps under lock-and-key at this place," she said. "We're wondering if it might be the car we're looking for."

"What kind of car does he have?"

She hesitated, looking at him from the corner of her eye. "If I shared that information with you—unlikely as it is that anyone would ever find out—it would be perilously close to witness tampering. You're supposed to tell us about the car. Not vice-versa."

Slowly he began to smile. "You know, for a person with such a gracefully curved neck, you sure are a straight arrow."

She lifted her hand gradually and ran it across her throat and then touched where her hair met the flesh on the back of her neck.

"How is it with you and Miss Faucet, today?"

"What?" he asked.

"I wondered how she would act once the crisis had passed," the lieutenant said. "She still seems very attached to you."

"Well, the crisis isn't over." He gazed out the passenger's window as they cruised swiftly down Oleander Street. "She has another surgery, probably early next week. That's to repair her pelvis and abdominal organs. Then later on they have to fix her wrist. It'll be six weeks at least before she gets out of the hospital."

"Is that when you're taking her for fish?" When he turned to her, she continued. "It's my business to know those sorts of things."

"Maybe then you know about me," he said, "that I keep my promises. And so now you know I don't intend to do myself in."

"For six to eight weeks, anyway. You know, Mr. Thorsen, the girl is in love with you."

"Oh please! She just said that. She said she loved me because I was still rescuing her."

The lieutenant was staring at him. "I didn't know she said she loved you."

Magnus took a deep breath. To a lesser degree he felt the same way he had that morning when Lt. Stipling overheard Grady on the answering machine.

"Look," he said, "you're going to think whatever you're going to think about me. I may be a lot of things, but I'm not a pervert. Lisa

Faucet is young enough to be my daughter—if I had one. She is at a very vulnerable place right now. She's been taken advantage of enough already. All I want to do is be good to her. I have no romantic inclinations toward her at all. After what I saw yesterday, I'm not sure I ever could. And as far as what she might be feeling, she's basically an adolescent and nobody can control what an adolescent is feeling—or should pay any more attention to it than necessary."

The lieutenant was thinking it over. "Well, if I don't miss my guess, she probably wonders on some level whether or not anyone will ever find her attractive again. For a couple reasons. And you are her safe person, like I said. So . . . you have a chance to make her feel good about herself, and to restore her faith in people. . . . The thing you have to remember is that people her age lots of times get love confused with sex."

They turned onto a parking lot. Magnus read the sign on the front of the building as they pulled up to it: "Ables Self-Storage." It was a place he had driven past hundreds of times, a business that had been located in the same spot as long as he could remember. Before this moment he had never given it a second thought.

The instant after Lt. Stipling parked, a marked police car pulled up beside them. Sgt. Terrell put his cruiser into park, opened the door and got out without shutting off the engine. Magnus opened his door and got out.

"Hello, Sergeant."

"Mr. Thorsen."

Magnus didn't bother trying to shake his hand. That only seemed to irritate peace officers, he had decided. And, anyway, the sergeant was holding a small packet, a document folded over and bound with string.

"Is that it?" the lieutenant asked.

"Yes, ma'am."

Another vehicle, the SUV with "Aberdeen County Crime Scene" on its side, pulled onto the lot.

"Mr. Thorsen," Lt. Stipling said, "you can come with me. Sergeant."

Sgt. Terrell handed her the bound document, which she slipped into her small, blue efficient-looking purse. Magnus tried to get to the front door and hold it for her, but she beat him there and nodded for him to go first.

As they entered the office of the storage facility, Magnus studied the man standing behind the counter. He was in his late forties or early fifties, his dark hair cut short. His posture was ramrod straight and his businesslike expression had only the slightest hint of pensiveness to it. Magnus guessed that the lieutenant was about to deal with someone who was as "no-nonsense" as she was.

She smiled graciously at the man, standing with his hands on his hips, and said, "Mr. Able?"

"Yes, ma'am."

His accent was pure, down east North Carolina. He was, Magnus judged, a native of this area. And likely his family had been natives before him.

"I'm Lt. Dot Stipling, sir. I'm the Aberdeen County Chief of Detectives."

"Yes, ma'am."

"This is Mr. Magnus Thorsen."

"Yes, ma'am. I recognize him."

"I know you're wondering why three Aberdeen County police vehicles have pulled up on your lot simultaneously."

"Yes, ma'am."

"Well, I can assure you it has nothing to do with you or your business here."

"Yes. Well, I have nothing to hide, ma'am."

"Certainly not, Mr. Able. The thing is, we're searching for a vehicle. In addition to renting storage spaces, you also park vehicles inside your compound, don't you?"

"Yes, ma'am. We store any vehicle, provided the owners can produce a title. So far as I know, none of the boats, cars or trucks here are stolen."

She shook her head. "We don't think the one we're interested in was stolen. We investigating the possibility it was used in a crime without the owner's knowledge."

"I see." His lips formed a tight, short line. "Yes, ma'am."

Lt. Stipling produced the document from her purse. "Mr. Able, this is a search warrant."

"That's not necessary, ma'am. We're law abiding citizens and we expect our customers to be as well. You all are welcome to search for any vehicle you want on the premises."

"Well," she said, "I'm really wanting to explain to you that the warrant allows us to search the vehicle should we find it here. So, if the owner were to come to you and ask why you let us in and let us examine his car, you'd have this to show him as a way of protecting yourself."

She handed him the warrant, which he took and held silently at his side.

"Let me open the gate for you." He pressed a button, unseen behind the counter.

"Thank you. I notice, Mr. Able, that you have a computerized entry system here. I guess that's to let you know when people come and go?"

"Yes, ma'am."

"Might we impose upon you to check something for us?"

"Certainly."

"One of your customers who keeps a vehicle here is Mr. Edward Houck."

Able stiffened, even straighter than he had been standing. "I know Mr. Houck. He is a fine gentleman and a long-time customer of mine."

"Yes, sir. I'm sure he is. And we don't suspect him of any wrong doing at all. We are wondering, though, if someone might have taken his car out yesterday?"

The man was staring at her, his face now marked with reluctance. For only a moment he hesitated and then turned to the computer screen on the desk behind the counter.

"Occasionally people can come in and go out without there being any record," Able said as he typed in a password and maneuvered the cordless mouse. "If the gate is open when you arrive or leave, there is no record. The computer only keeps track when you use your code to open the gate." He was staring at the screen. "Mr. Houck's code was used to open the gate at 11:44 a.m. Thursday and then reopen the gate at 11:53. That would be coming in and going out, I assume. It shows that his code opened the gate again at 5:52 p.m. and then reopened the exit at 5:56."

"So," Lt. Stipling said, "it seems possible that someone came in and got his car at about 11:45, then returned it just before 6 in the evening."

"Yes, ma'am." Able's voice was softer.

"Would you have an idea of where we might find that vehicle if it's in your complex here?"

"Yes, ma'am. As you go straight back through the gate, turn left on the third row. It's about halfway down on the right."

"May I ask, sir," she said, "do you have time-coded video from yesterday?"

"Yes, ma'am. It's kept off site through a video link in case someone tries to break in and steal the evidence that they were here."

"That's a very good idea," she said. "We may come back and contact your security company for that recording."

"Yes, ma'am."

Lt. Stipling seemed to be considering her words carefully. "Mr. Able, I have to ask a favor of you," she said. "These crimes we are investigating are of an extremely serious, violent nature. Again, Mr. Houck is not personally involved in any way. It's exceedingly important that no one knows why we came here today, what we were looking for, or what we might have found."

"Yes, ma'am." Able held eye contact with her. "My family and I have had our business here for eighteen years. We follow all city ordinances and abide by all pertinent state laws and codes. We have no intention of compromising the work of the police, ma'am. Even though you're from outside of our county."

Lt. Stipling nodded genuinely and then surprised the hell out of Magnus by grasping and shaking Able's hand. They turned and she held the door open for him again.

"How come you've never shook my hand?" he muttered.

She glanced at him. "You never promised not to compromise my work." She motioned toward the open gate and called out to the others on the parking lot. "Straight back to the third row, turn left."

The three police vehicles processed slowly through the compound. Many of the storage units had exterior doors. Others, Magnus decided, were climate controlled and were accessed from inside the building. The outsides of those units had few doors and it was alongside those long, low structures that people had parked covered boats, work trucks, delivery vehicles, motorcycles and antique cars. Midway down the third row, he saw a canvas-covered form that he knew immediately was an old, full-sized Chevrolet. He felt himself smile.

The police cruiser and SUV pulled passed them and parked alongside and behind the Chevy, blocking its path as if it might of its own accord start up and drive away. Magnus got out and stood before the car. Sgt. Terrell was in front of the vehicle as well, quietly giving instructions to the two uniformed officers who got out of the crime scene unit. Wearing latex gloves, they loosened the canvas cover and rolled it back, exposing the grill, hood and then windshield of the car.

"That's it," Magnus said. "I told you. A '64 Impala."

"How can you be sure this is the car?" Terrell asked.

"It's missing one, short lateral grill piece by the driver's side headlight. Apart from that, the thing is in mint condition."

"How could you remember that from yesterday?" There was skepticism in the sergeant's voice.

Without looking at him, Magnus said, "The same way I remember that you have a scar your right eyebrow doesn't fully conceal."

". . . Damn."

"You should see the likeness he drew of Plank," Lt. Stipling said. "If he says this is the car, he's sure of it." Then she called to one of the forensic men, "Can we get into it without breaking anything, Thomas?"

"Yes, Lieutenant. There's nothing electrical to damage on this old-timer. I'll have it open in a second."

The other investigator spoke up. "Ma'am, this vehicle has recently been washed. However there is sand in the tire treads and on the rims of the underside of the bumpers."

"They tried to cover their tracks," she said reflectively.

"You want us to impound this car, Lieutenant?" Terrell asked.

She thought about it. "No. Let's do as thorough a check for physical evidence as we can here. Then let's lock it back up and leave it for now. Chances are Randy will want to stay as far away from here as he can for the next few days. He's still waiting to hear that somebody found the victim's body, if I don't miss my guess."

"Do we not have enough to move on him now?" the sergeant said. "I mean, I don't remember us having an eyewitness this good. You and I know these tire treads are going to match those at the beach. We're probably going to isolate his DNA from the girl. I think our case is solid, Lieutenant."

She shook her head. "Actually it's mostly circumstantial. This kid is a quarterback. A leader. Cool under fire. . . . Suppose he wore a condom. No DNA from him. If he doesn't roll, we won't be able to find out who the others were or compel them to take DNA tests. Sure, Mr. Thorsen saw them leaving the beach, but what if Randy says they were down there drinking. Or smoking dope. Or even that they paid the girl. That they had group sex in the sand and accidentally backed over her. Then they got scared because she looked dead and they drove off." She pursed her lips. "We need this kid to do something to incriminate himself."

Magnus had been watching the officers open the four doors of the Impala and methodically examine the vehicle.

"I had a Biscayne," he said. "Guess I told you that yesterday. It was a lot like this car. Big back seat. Lost my—" He stopped and turned to Lt. Stipling. "You know what you ought to do?"

"What, Mr. Thorsen?" she asked skeptically.

"Have Lisa call him. Record the conversation. Once he realizes she's not dead, he's going to freak out and say something to incriminate himself."

Sgt. Terrell showed the same astonished look he had when Magnus described his scar. "What do you think, Lieutenant? That might work?"

Lt. Stipling was looking past the car, into the distance, considering possibilities. Slowly she said, "I have a better idea."

Chapter 4

At least Katie was gone.

Magnus leaned against the doorway of the cubicle looking in a Lisa. She seemed to him to be very weary. And—though her eyes were closed—not quite sleeping.

"You talk to her," Lt. Stipling whispered. "I'll wait out here."

Magnus made his way around her bed to the empty chair and sat down. He was debating about the best way to rouse her when she opened her eyes.

"Hey," he said quietly.

"Hi, Magnus."

Probably, he thought, she needed her rest more than anything. And his great desire was to leave her alone and let her sleep. Only he had agreed to disturb her, to ask for her help.

"I see you got rid of your roommate."

Lisa gave him a slow, sleepy smile. "It wasn't me. Somebody complained. . . . There's an old man in the next room over. He has a blood vessel in his abdomen that turned into a balloon and started to burst."

"An aneurysm?"

"I guess. . . . Anyway, he's not taking enough painkiller to endure Katie's constant talking."

Magnus chuckled.

"I didn't think I'd see you 'til tomorrow."

"Well," he said slowly, "the police asked me to come back. They asked me to ask if you would help them."

". . . Help them?"

"Lisa, they know who attacked you. Or at least, they know the one who drove the car. What they want to do is trap him into confessing. Once he does that, they think he'll have to give them the names of everyone who—was in the car with you."

The fearfulness he had heard that morning when they discussed her attackers was back—and stronger—in her voice. "What do they want me to do?"

"You don't have to face him," he assured her. He studied her expression, wondering how she would react. "They have his cell phone number. They want you to call him on his phone."

"Call him? Talk to him?" Her face seemed to grow rounder and softer, as if she were becoming a child, a frightened little girl. "I can't do that, Magnus."

He nodded. He looked down and continued softly. "I understand that. I'm not sure I could either, if I were you. I promised I would explain their plan to you though. Is that okay?"

". . . Okay."

"I guess the police are thinking this kid doesn't know you're alive. If you call him, you'll have control over him. You'll show him that you know who he is and where he is, but he won't know anything about you—where you are or what you intend to do."

She was thinking about what he'd said. "Well, wouldn't he think it was a trick? Wouldn't he think the police or someone had figured out he was the driver and were just trying to fool him into believing it was really me he was talking to? How would he ever believe it was really me?"

Magnus nodded his head. "He would if you told him something that only you could know."

Her expression was a little less fearful. A little more curious. "What would I say to him? What am I supposed to tell him?"

"They have a script. That Lt. Stipling woman wrote out what they want you to say."

"Are they going to put me in wheelchair and take me out somewhere to a pay phone?" She asked with the slightest irritation in her voice. "Do I have to go to the police station?"

He smiled. "I guess they have a set up. They bring in some equipment so you can do it right here."

She took a deep breath. "Like he won't hear all my machines beeping and clicking and know right where I am?"

"Is it okay if I bring in Lt. Stipling? She can let you read the script and tell you how it would work."

"You'll stay with me?"

"Yes, darlin'."

"I'm not promising anything."

"I know. It's okay," he said.

The lieutenant was down the hall a little way having an earnest conversation with a woman in the sort of uniform that nurses had

65

worn when Magnus was a little boy. There seemed to be a whispered dispute of significant proportions going on between them. As Magnus watched, it appeared to him from the women's expressions that some sort of mutually acceptable—if grudging—agreement had been achieved. The detective, her jaw set, walked toward him.

"Is the girl on board?" Her voice was firm.

"She's willing to hear what you have in mind," Magnus replied.

The lieutenant looked down into the leather attaché she had strapped over her left shoulder. Magnus smiled. The precise little blue purse she always carried had somehow been transformed into this somewhat larger, but compact, efficient-looking carry all. She produced a manila folder.

"Give her this. Or read it to her. Whichever. I'll be there momentarily. We're bringing in our gear."

Magnus took the folder wordlessly and walked back into Lisa's room. She was more alert this time, her expression pensive.

"Can you read this by yourself, sweetie? Or do you need me to?"

"Let me try."

She reached out with her left hand and took the folder. Inside was a single sheet that she held at a strange angle and read. She gazed at it so long Magnus thought she wasn't really able to understand it. Finally she dropped it onto her chest and leaned her head back.

"Can I have some water?"

Magnus held the little cup and bent the straw to her lips. She only took a sip. It seemed enormously unfair to him to ask her to do this. Still, he thought, it was a good plan.

"Miss Faucet?"

They both turned to the doorway of her cubicle. Lt. Stipling was standing just outside, leaning slightly across the threshold.

"I'd like to come in and bring a couple officers with me."

Lisa looked as if she were still deciding, but the lieutenant had turned away and nodded to someone in the hall. Walking around her into the room was Sgt. Terrell, carrying a bulky black case, and after him came the two forensic officers Magnus had seen at the storage facility. They too were carrying equipment in heavy, thick cases.

"Hello, Miss Faucet," Terrell said. "Saw you yesterday, but I don't think you remember me."

Lisa didn't respond to him. Neither did she respond when one of the policemen looked up at her as he was trying to find an acceptable place to set down—or maybe set up—his equipment and said, "Hey."

"Miss Faucet." Lt. Stipling was at the end of the bed. "The decision on whether or not to do this is up to you. I understand you had major surgery and that was after some major trauma. I'm not trying to be insensitive, but I do have to be blunt." She paused, holding Lisa's eyes with her own. "The people who did this to you are still out there. We believe we know who one of them is. If we are able to trap him into admitting what he did, in order to lessen his own consequences, he will most likely turn in the others. This is our one best chance to arrest and prosecute the people who did this. If we are not successful in getting this suspect to turn on the others, if we don't have the leverage you can give us, it will be very difficult for us to protect you in the future. . . . Will you help us apprehend and punish those who hurt you?"

Lisa nodded. And, like a little chain reaction, the lieutenant nodded at Terrell, who nodded at the friendlier tech officer, who in turn stepped to the side of the bed. He was holding a telephone headset.

"I'm going to put this on your ears, Miss Faucet," he said. "You'll be able to hear and talk without needing to use your hands."

As the officer was positioning the device, Lisa rolled her eyes toward Lt. Stipling. "When I call him, what will his caller ID say?"

"It will come up 'Unknown name. Unknown number.'" She was standing in the doorway, motioning for someone outside the room.

"Well, if he doesn't recognize the phone number, what if he just doesn't answer?"

The lieutenant gave her a momentary smile. "In my experience, Miss Faucet, there are no teenage boys who will refuse to answer any mysterious call on their cell phone as long as they believe it isn't their parents. 'Unknown name' will only make it more likely he will answer."

It was a nurse she had been motioning for, a petite girl who seemed to Magnus to be scarcely out of her teens. She entered the cubicle with swift, expert moments and went quietly from one machine to another, pressing buttons. Little by little the cubicle grew silent.

Sgt. Terrell handed a headset to Lt. Stipling, which she held at her side as she watched the nurse. The tech men were kneeling, turning equipment on even as the nurse was turning things off.

"Are we ready?"

"Almost, Lieutenant."

"Miss Faucet," Lt. Stipling asked, "are you familiar with the script? Are you comfortable with it?"

". . . What if he says something off the wall? Something the script doesn't cover?"

"Be aggressive. Be in charge. You're bound to have some anger about this in there somewhere. Let it out. Only two things to remember," Lt. Stipling said. "Do not let on that you're hurt and in the hospital. And under no circumstances mention the name 'Scotch Bonnet Beach.' Understand?"

She took a breath. "Yes."

"Sound check," one of the tech men said from the floor. "Have her speak into the mike."

"Okay, Lisa," Sgt. Terrell said, "I want you to read me the first line of the script."

Slowly she held up the paper. "Hi, Randy. Do you know who this is?"

"Good," the tech called. "We're hot."

The nurse closed the cubicle door from the inside and leaned against it with her arms folded.

"All right," the lieutenant said. "Thanks to the generosity of the charge nurse, we have five minutes to make this happen." She glanced at Magnus as she raised her headset. "This is a mono feed," she said. "Swivel that earpiece and hold it against your ear and we can both listen."

Magnus moved so close to her that their shoulders touched. He could hear her breathing and smell the same delicate fragrance he had scented in her car.

"Okay, Lisa," Terrell said, "we're placing the call."

There was a crackling, static sound in his earpiece, then the musical tones of a telephone number being dialed.

Magnus glanced at the lieutenant from the corner of his eye. She was completely focused, intent on the little black disk she pressed to her ear, oblivious to anything else in the world.

He heard two slow clicks and then a ringing sound. A second

ring. There came an airy noise and muted laughter, and Magnus saw Lisa jump. He wondered if she could go through with it.

"Hello?" It was an adolescent's raspy voice.

". . . Hi, Randy." Her voice cracked. It was so soft even Magnus himself could scarcely hear her. "Do you know who this is?"

"Excuse me?"

"I said—" her voice grew stronger "—don't you know who this is?"

"Well—no."

Lisa's cheeks turned bright red. "You don't?"

"Uh, no." His tone was flippant.

"Well I guess I sound different without a pillowcase over my head."

There came what seemed to Magnus an interminable period of silence. The boy did not speak. Lisa did not speak. And then he saw her take her eyes from the script and lower it slowly.

"Do I sound different to you, Randy . . . when I'm not taped up in the floorboard of your backseat, with your little boyfriends stomping me and threatening to kill me if I screamed?" Her voice quivered.

". . . I don't—know who—"

"You know exactly who this is, you goddamn bastard. And I know exactly who you are."

"We—I thought you were—"

"Nope! Alive and well. Looked dead, didn't I? Amazing how much weight that soft sand will absorb." She lifted the script and glanced at it. "Now, you football career on the other hand, your scholarship—that's deader than hell."

Magnus could hear her breathing over the earpiece. It was a ragged but fierce sound. Her cheeks were fiery red and tears were streaming over them.

"You want me to call the police, Randy?"

"Police? No. No."

"You have one chance," she said, "to make this right. I want you to come by yourself this evening. Six o'clock."

"I can't—"

"The hell you can't! One minute after 6, I call 9-1-1. Just like I found you, they can find you."

". . . Where?"

"You know where. Where you left me for dead. Don't be late."

Lt. Stipling was making a motion with her hand. The sound died in the earpiece. Magnus let go it and faced Lisa. Here mouth was open and she was panting, tears still flowing. She was looking at the nurse.

"Can you help me? I—I—I had a—"

Magnus glanced toward the nurse, who was weeping, biting her lip and trying not to break into sobs. He was stunned. Somehow it never occurred to him that nurses would ever cry.

"Come on, everybody," the lieutenant said quietly. "We'll come back and get our equipment in a few minutes."

"Magnus."

He had started toward the door and stopped abruptly, looking back to the bed.

"Will you wait in the hall? Will you come back in after she fixes me?"

"Sure I will, sweetie."

As they left the cubicle, the other officers made a swift, little line, exiting the ICU. Lt. Stipling held back, and drew near Magnus just outside the closed door of Lisa's room.

"I need one more thing from you."

He was surprised at how close she was. He could feel her breath on his face as she spoke.

"Just one more thing," she said, "and then I think we can conclude your official business with the Aberdeen County Police Department."

He studied her face, the proportions and skin tone he already knew so well. "And then I get back my things?"

She straightened. "I didn't say that," she said. "In half-an-hour when your visit with the girl is over, you need to call me. I want your help with this rendezvous."

With that she turned and walked away.

Just as he had been told to do, Magnus stood at the spot where he found Lisa Faucet. His hands in his pockets, he gazed out at the gentle waves. The tide was coming in and there was only the softest breeze from the gray-green water. Crabs popped up from holes in the packed sand, scurried sideways and disappeared into the next wave that washed over them.

He glanced at his watch when he heard the car pull onto the gravel lot. Ten minutes he had been waiting. He had known it would be that long because Lt. Stipling told him so when she showed him where to stand. And she knew because the police had the boy under surveillance and knew every moment exactly where he was, exactly how close he was drawing to Scotch Bonnet Beach. They had known within a few seconds how long it would take him to get to the spot where Magnus was standing.

He heard the car door close. He felt himself sigh. What had the kid thought when he saw the parking area empty, deserted? How would he respond when he saw Magnus standing there?

He was staring straight ahead to where the ocean began when, from the corner of his eye, he saw Randy Plank again, this time walking out of the passage between the dunes. The boy stopped when he saw Magnus standing motionless at the infamous spot of now smoothed sand. As casually as he could, Magnus turned toward him. They stared at each other, twenty yards between them.

"I'm the man you want to see," Magnus said, "if you want this to go away."

Plank held his ground. He was lean and fit looking, his neck and shoulders thick beneath his knit shirt. He was almost as Magnus had remembered him. When he slowly began to step closer, Magnus realized he had a small mole on the left side of his chin that he had not remembered. Apart from that, he thought the likeness he had drawn had been quite close. The boy's expression this day, though, was less one of dread than apprehension, extreme caution.

And then there was the sound of another automobile pulling onto the gravel parking area. The kid jumped and turned around. Standing at the mouth of the beach access was Officer Miller, who had emerged from where he had been concealed on the far side of the dunes. Miller's drawn weapon, held in both hands, was pointed at the sand before him.

Plank turned back toward Magnus, as if to find a route of escape in the opposite direction. There he saw Lt. Stipling, who had been hiding in the dunes near where the attack occurred. She held an automatic pistol as well, pointed also at the sand before her.

"Going somewhere, Randy?" she called softly.

For an instant his eyes grew wide with panic. He looked out toward the ocean. Magnus wondered if he would have to help the

71

officers subdue the boy. Then Plank's expression changed. Magnus could see a calmness come over him. His escape cut off, he seemed to turn his thoughts to what other alternatives remained. What had the young artist said about him that morning—he had "mad skills in the backfield." The kid had determined to hold his ground, Magnus decided. He was waiting to see what was going to happen next.

"Put your hands behind you, Randy," the lieutenant said.

She was continuing to walk toward him. As the boy lowered his hands and extended them backward, Officer Miller holstered his weapon and produced handcuffs. He slapped them around Plank's wrists with practiced ease. And Lt. Stipling slid her pistol into a small holster beneath her jacket that Magnus had not seen.

"You are under arrest," Miller began in his quiet baritone. "Anything you say can and will be used against you in a court of law."

There was the crunching sound of more cars pulling simultaneously onto the gravel parking lot. Magnus and the kid raised their faces, listening. These were surely police cruisers, surrounding the boy's car, blocking it in.

"You have the right to an attorney. If you cannot afford an attorney, one will be provided for you."

Several more officers, led by Sgt. Terrell, appeared from the parking access. Their weapons were drawn, but they holstered them quickly when they saw Plank's hands cuffed behind him.

"Do you understand these rights as I've explained them to you?"

Plank snaked a look over his shoulder at Miller. It seemed to Magnus there was a recognition, a look of acquaintance he gave the officer.

"Yeah."

The police—half a dozen of them—slowly gathered around the boy. His head was down. His shoulders stooped.

Magnus, hands in his pockets, kept his distance as he waited to see what was going to happen. Would they take him to the police station? Would they try to take advantage of the moment and the setting and question him as he stood at the beach?

"Randy, I'm Lt. Stipling, Aberdeen County Chief of Detectives. I guess you know why we're all here."

". . . I guess I don't." His voice, shaky and fearful, also had a resolute defiance to it.

Lt. Stipling nodded, not impatiently. "Then let me spell it out for you, young man. These are the charges you are currently facing: attempted murder, kidnapping, first degree sexual assault, attempted vehicular homicide, hit-and-run, group violence—that's a new one instituted to curb gangs. Looks like it will come in handy. And, driving your car across the dunes in violation of county ordinances. That's the only misdemeanor in the bunch. The rest are felonies."

He was shaking his head. "What about you cops hiding in the dunes? Ain't that against the law?"

"We don't leave tracks." She glanced at Terrell. "Sergeant, did I forget any charges?"

"Yes, ma'am. The federal charges."

"Federal?" Plank raised his head.

"Oh that's right," she said. "Kidnapping is both a North Carolina and a federal crime. And since you kidnapped her in South Carolina and brought her across the state line, that's a second federal felony."

"No parole on federal crimes," Terrell added with a shrug.

Plank shook his head with an exasperated expression, as if a referee had just blown a call that cost his teach a touchdown. "I don't know what you all are talking about. I haven't done a thing."

"Yes you did," she replied. "We have overwhelming evidence against you. We have a security video of you taking your grandfather's car from storage yesterday. And do you see that man over there?"

She motioned toward Magnus, who sheepishly lifted a hand.

"That's Mr. Thorsen. He saw you driving off this lot in the car with all your friends. We have photos of tire tracks on the beach and on various parts of your victim that match your grandfather's car. We found sand that originated on this beach in the wheel wells of the car. And of course there's the DNA evidence we're processing even as we speak."

"You can mix DNA all together," Sgt. Terrell said, "and we can still sort out everyone who donated some."

"And, the lieutenant added brightly, "then there's your confession."

"Confession?" He smirked. "I ain't confessing nothing."

"You already did, son." He stared at her as she continued. "When you came out here—to the scene of the crime, you as much as admitted your guilt."

He straightened, leaning back. "I came out here because some girl called and told me to."

She shook her head. "No, Randy. We have it all on tape. And four of us were listening. She never mentioned where you were supposed to come. You came here because this is where you raped her, ran over her and left her for dead."

Magnus watched the boy's eyes flutter and his mouth fall part way open. Even in the lengthening shadows, it was clear his face grew pale.

"Now," the lieutenant said, "here's what I can do for you, and maybe we can help each other. I can keep you from doing federal time. We can handle everything here in Aberdeen County. We can avoid a trial—and all that goes with it. That's assuming you will help us. . . . We know you were not in this alone. We want the names of the others. That's very important for us and for you. For you, it's the difference between you spending your life in prison or having a future to look forward to."

The boy lowered his head again. He seemed to be searching for something in the sand before him.

Terrell spoke up. "You know we're going to find them all anyway."

"Well then find 'em all," the kid said.

"There were four or five of you, son," the sergeant continued. "Think about who they are. Ask yourself which one is going to roll on the others. He's the one who gets the deal. Only maybe he was the real culprit and he's going to get off easier than the rest of you."

Lt. Stipling said, "Randy, do you see how much trouble we went to, to arrest you without incident? Even so, it was in your eyes. When you saw us, you were thinking about running. Some of your friends may try that if we don't get the chance to stop them first. When a young person tries to run, the danger to that person as well as to the police is magnified greatly. With your help, we can put this all to rest tonight. Quickly. Nobody else needs to get hurt."

He was thinking, deciding. At length he raised one side of his face and glared at the lieutenant from the corner of his eye.

"I just want to talk to my dad. He's got a lawyer. They'll tell me what to do."

Magnus saw the lieutenant flinch and shake her head. It was her turn to look down at the sand. He knew she believed she had failed.

The possibility of an easy confession, the swift arrest of the other boys, was slipping away.

"Do you know who I am, Randy?"

It was Officer Miller. He had been standing silently behind the boy, listening to the conversation. It seemed to surprise all the other officers—even the lieutenant—when he stepped in front of the suspect and spoke.

"Well sure, Spike. I've known who you were since I was, like in the sixth grade. The year you made all-state—my eighth grade year—I didn't miss a single one of your home games."

To Magnus it was jarring and strange. In the middle of being arrested for attempted murder, suddenly the boy wanted to start talking about football. And what about the deputy? Was his name really "Spike?" Why had he interrupted?

Miller nodded. "And the last couple years, every Friday night that I wasn't on duty, I went to all the Osprey games. Wherever they were. Even the one in Sanford. You all had a better team than any of the ones I played on. Even better than the one that beat us in the semis my senior year and won state. . . . Randy, do you not understand how you're ruining lives?"

"Oh, no." He shook his head. "The girl lived. I heard her voice on the phone."

Lt. Stipling and Sgt. Terrell exchanged a glance. Again, without being away of it, the boy had implicated himself, had implicitly confessed. Terrell pulled a small, flat rectangle from his breast pocket and held it by his side. It was, Magnus realized, a digital recorder.

"Surviving doesn't mean her life isn't ruined, Randy. After all the operations she has to have, she's going to have to learn to walk again," Miller continued. "She'll probably never have children, if she ever let's a man get near her. And do you think there will ever come a day she can be out in public and have someone touch her from behind without having a flashback of what you all did to her?"

The kid stared at him.

"Only, I wasn't really talking about the girl. I meant the lives you've ruined besides hers. I mean all of us who drove all over the state to watch you play and dreamed about seeing you in college—maybe even the pros. And the coaches who brought you along. Taught you to believe in yourself. To play with confidence and pride. And your teammates who all looked up to you. Especially the ten in the huddle with you who respected you and trusted you enough to do exactly what you told 'em. That respect was why you won."

The boy's eyes widened. His mouth was nearly closed. He was transfixed by Miller's words.

"But mostly I was talking about your family, Randy. Your folks have been so proud of you, son. We have all been proud of you. But nothing compared to what they must feel. . . . Now, in a different way, you've raped them too. And your little sister? This fall she's going to be a junior, isn't she? She's going to walk those same halls over at North that you walked. Only when people whisper behind her back now, it will be for a different reason.

"And you think maybe a lawyer can get you out of this? So you're going to go to trial. You're going to sit in the courtroom and make that girl's family listen to what you all did to her. You're going to make your mother and your father listen to what you all did to that girl. You're going to make all of them look at the pictures of her, naked and busted up on the beach. I took those pictures yesterday, Randy. I wouldn't want anybody I cared about seeing 'em. . . . As if you hadn't caused enough pain." He shook his head. "This isn't the way you were taught, son."

Plank's head drooped forward. His mouth was open now and tears were streaming down his cheeks. His body quivered with each breath he drew.

"I can't believe," Miller said, "this was your idea. And, whether it was or not, it's totally disgusting to think you would protect someone who would do something like this. Whoever did this has no pride. If you have any respect for yourself, your parents, your team, your school or the way you were taught that made you a champion, you have one chance right now to do the right thing."

The boy was crying. The little crowd surrounding him watched in silence. Not moving. Waiting.

". . . It was—" his voice broke "—Garrett."

"Garrett Toliver?" Miller asked.

"Yes." He sighed deeply. "He was pushing us. He was after us for a couple weeks. He dared us. He said we were cowards. . . . I told him I could get some money. We could just pay one of those Ukrainian whores to do us all." He sniffed, wiping his nose on his shoulder. "He said they have diseases. We'd be safer and better off just finding an American girl. . . . Finally, I guess, we just gave in."

"Who else?"

"Len Massey. Bob and Joey Carter. But, really, it wasn't Joey. He's just a kid. He's only fourteen. He didn't want any part of it. He sat in the front seat and wouldn't even watch. He didn't rape her. And I didn't rape her either. I couldn't bring myself to do it."

"What happened?"

He took a deep breath. And another. "Garrett knew about my grandpa's car. We used it before a couple times when we wanted to go out drinking without being recognized. And he said nobody ever came to this end of Scotch Bonnet. We should go down to Myrtle and talk some chick into the car with us and bring her up here and take what we wanted if she wouldn't give.

"We had a little to drink, maybe, and cruised around for half an hour. And Len saw the girl at the bike stand. He said, 'Ah, I seen her before.' So he and Garrett hopped out. I thought they were going to talk to her. . . . But they just went up behind her and covered her head and dragged her into the back. God, by then the damage was done. I took off. They taped her up and kept her in the floorboard. . . . And we came here. Mostly, while it was happening, I just kept telling Joey it would be okay.

"When we all got back in the car, Garrett and Len pulled out a baseball bat. I swear to god, I didn't know they had it. I never saw 'em put it in the car. I knew right away what they meant to do. So we started having this quiet argument. Garrett said we couldn't leave her to identify us. I said, she hadn't seen us and we needed to go while we could before somebody came along. Garrett said, if I tried to drive off, he was going to jump out and kill her anyway. Somewhere in there I realized he meant to kill her from the beginning.

"Then Len yells out that she got loose from the duct tape. She was looking at us. . . . It was just like a reflex. I started the car and threw it in reverse and backed over her. I wasn't thinking when I put it in first and pulled forward that I'd run over her again. . . . It made the most sickening sound. I pulled up a few feet and stopped and raised up to look out the back. She was . . . squashed like a bug. And Garrett says, 'Hell, she's dead. Let's go.'

"The strange thing was, as I drove along the beach, I was thinking how I backed over her to save her from Garrett killing her with the

77

bat. I was so distracted as we were leaving that I pulled up crooked to the driveway on the parking lot. And this man—that guy, I guess—had to wait for me to move. I realized he saw us. But I was hoping that he wouldn't find her body, 'cause it was close to the dunes. And if he did, we were in the old Chevy that no one knew about."

His head hung low and his shoulders were stooped. Nothing was said after he finished the story. Finally the kid wiped his nose on his shoulder again and Lt. Stipling motioned to a couple of the officers who had been standing back and listening. They put their hands on Plank's back, turned him toward the beach access and walked him away.

Magnus watched Sgt. Terrell turn off the recorder. He took out a small notepad and began to write.

"I trust you have those names, Sergeant?" the lieutenant asked.

"Yes, ma'am."

"They're all athletes over at North," Miller said. "They won't be hard to find."

"I'd like them picked up immediately." Lt. Stipling's voice was insistent. "I mean before we notify Plank's parents or in any way let any word of this get out. I want the boys kept in separate rooms at the station and we'll speak to them individually. Let's make sure all the parents are apprised of what's happening and are present with them. We'll give them all a chance to call their lawyers. We'll tell them that Plank confessed and that everyone we arrested is going to be charged with attempted murder and first degree sexual assault. Then we'll ask if they want to share their sides of the story. The last one we're talking to is this Garrett Toliver kid. I want to see if any of the others confirms Plank's account of him as the instigator."

"Yes, ma'am." The sergeant nodded. "What do you want to do about his car? Shall we impound it?"

Her eyes widened. "Let's have forensics check it out before we give it back to his parents. Make sure there isn't a baseball bat in it. Speaking of which, let's see if we can find that bat. And the duct tape. Let's see whose fingerprints are on them."

"Yes, ma'am."

She turned to Miller. "Officer," she said, "that was excellent work. What you did benefited everyone involved."

Miller showed no emotion—nor any movement—as he responded. "Thank you, ma'am. Everything I said to Plank . . . it was true."

She nodded. "Yes. I know it was."

Miller turned and walked silently toward the parking area. Absentmindedly, Terrell—still making notes—followed slowly behind him.

Lt. Stipling glanced over her should at Magnus. "I guess we're through here, Mr. Thorsen. Are you ready for me to drive you back to your gallery?"

One of the officers had brought her cruiser back to the parking area. As they got inside, the only other police car remaining was Miller's. He sat inside it impassively, apparently waiting for the tow truck that would deliver Randy Plank's Pontiac to the investigators.

At length, as they came to Hwy 17 and drove north, Magnus spoke. "I have a whole new respect for your job."

". . . How's that?"

"It was seamless, the way you did this." He shook his head. "In the matter of a few hours you built an iron-clad case against the kid. You cut off every possible escape route—physically at the beach, but also legally. So he had no recourse. It was amazing to watch."

She considered his words. "This is an unusual case. It was fortunate for us in several respects. First, the girl didn't die. It ramps everything up when you're charging people with capital murder. It was good—" She glanced at him "—that you found her when you did. There was a very small window of time for that, I'm told. Less than an hour to save her, given the extent of her injuries.

"Second, we had an eyewitness who could indisputably identify the perpetrator."

"And draw a recognizable likeness of him."

She smiled. "Well, Mr. Thorsen, with your gift you really don't need the camera in your phone, now do you? And third, we had the ability to put this case together before the boy knew we were looking for him. Most times we're chasing after someone who knows we suspect him. . . . So often it feels as if we're grasping at straws. This is a situation where everything held hands."

"And I helped, huh?"

She turned toward him again, her expression suspicious. "Yes, Mr. Thorsen. You helped a great deal."

"So you owe me a favor?"

She ignored his question. "Then there was Officer Miller. He was the only one of us who could make contact with the boy that way."

"You mean all that 'pride-and-respect football code of honor' bullshit?"

"It's not bullshit if it's what you believe. It's a way of looking at the world that Miller and Plank were taught to have faith in. Plank violated the code. Miller called on him it. . . . This was a catalytic event for Miller too."

"You mean 'Spike?'"

"His name is Martin. They started calling him 'Spike' because of the way he played football. He was an outside linebacker. When he tackled someone, it looked like he was sticking them in the ground. People in the stands would yell, 'Spike!'"

He gazed at her. "You went to all his games, did you?"

She smiled, shaking her head. "I make it point to know all about the people who work for me. Miller is a pretty straight-up-and-down guy. Tonight he broke down one of his own. It had to be done. He recognized it as part of his duty. Still, he's got to be feeling really bad about it." Lt. Stipling starred down the four lane, divided road. "This case isn't done. Not by a long shot."

"Why do you say that?"

"Well . . . the investigation and arrest aspect is almost complete. Within the hour we'll have all five of these young men in custody. Then the DA and parents—and their lawyers—all get involved. Essentially what we've done to this point is give the district attorney's office a very strong case to prosecute and some real leverage to get those boys to plead out."

"What's going to happen to 'em?"

She exhaled slowly. "Hard to say exactly. If it goes the way I think it will and the others confirm Plank's story, I figure the fourteen-year-old will probably get five years in juvey as an accessory and they'll suspend it, so he probably won't do any actual time."

"Five years for refusing to participate in a gang rape?"

She leaned toward him. "Five years for witnessing what he thought was a brutal murder and not reporting it. There are a couple ways they can go with him. Accessory after the fact. Gang violence. The main thing is, he doesn't just walk with no consequences. If he keeps his nose clean until he's twenty-one, they'll expunge it so he won't have a record. With the others—they'll probably end up getting sentenced to double digits. They'll likely plead out to one or two of the more serious felonies they're charged with, and then combine the other charges. Twelve to fifteen years each, I'd guess."

"It won't be more for that Toliver kid?"

"Probably not. We will make clear to the prosecutor that he was the instigator—assuming Plank's story holds up. So whatever punishment gets handed out, his will be certain."

"Yeah." Magnus shrugged. "But if it weren't for him, none of this would've happened. There wouldn't have been any crime. Doesn't seem fair that he won't suffer more than the others."

She made a low chuckling sound. "Mr. Thorsen, if I don't miss my guess, Toliver is one of those who doesn't suffer at all." She looked at him, studying his curious expression. "This young man is most likely a sociopath. He doesn't feel things the way others do. People like him are motivated only by excitement, pleasure, rage and fear. Those are the only things they feel.

"I wouldn't want you to get the idea that, once his sentences is over, the criminal justice system will be finished with him. In seven or eight years he'll be out on the street again, with a whole new bag of tricks he learned behind the wall. Somebody like me will end up arresting him again. And it will happen repeatedly until the bitch kicks in."

"The 'bitch?'"

"Habitual criminal. He'll end up getting life at some point. I'm not being cynical, just realistic. It was strange to me this afternoon to watch Randy Plank struggle with his grief and guilt and conscience. He feels bad about the victim, and about turning in the other boys. Toliver, on the other hand, may be enraged. But does he feel guilt or remorse? Not a chance."

". . . So what will happen to Plank? The DNA tests will prove it if he was telling the truth about not raping Lisa."

"That is true." They pulled over the big Cape Fear River bridge and back into the outskirts of Wilmington. "In one sense he was a bystander. Maybe, like he said, he didn't even intend the kidnapping. Unfortunately he did facilitate the crime by driving and he was the one who ran over the girl—twice. The way he described it may be completely accurate, but running over someone with a car to prevent them from being bludgeoned is not a defense against attempted murder."

They turned onto Business 17 in Wilmington, headed toward the riverfront arts district and his store.

"And now the media will have their turn."

Magnus nodded. "I was wondering about that. This morning Lisa asked if the police were guarding her. I told her that the boys probably assumed no one had found her because it wasn't on the news. That surprised me. I thought reporters and TV people had scanners and stuff. I can't believe none of them showed up."

"Oh they did," the lieutenant replied. "Just after you left for hospital yesterday, Anika Brown showed up with a cameraman."

"The little girl from Channel 7?"

"Yeah."

"Well—"

"I talked her out of it. I told her she could have an exclusive with me after the arrest, but if the news got out before we apprehended our suspects it would make it a lot more difficult to bring them to justice."

He wondered if his expression revealed the admiration or the incredulity he felt as they exchanged glances. "I didn't think news people did that kind of thing. I guess I thought the relationship was more . . . adversarial."

She grinned. "It sure can be. . . . Anika is a young, black, professional woman. I guess we—empathize with one another."

The cruiser pulled into one of the half dozen parking spaces in front of the black and gold lettering that read, "Magnus Thorsen, Fine Art and Portraiture." His car was parked there. Molly Stephenson, the retired accountant who ran the gallery for him, had closed the studio already and gone for the day. Magnus reached for the door latch and the lieutenant spoke up.

"What was it you were asking?"

"What?"

"You said we owed you a favor. I assume you want your jacket and things?"

He traced the symmetry of her face with his gaze. "That wasn't what I was talking about, but since you brought it up, when do I get them back?"

They stared at each other. For the first time, he was aware of the low rumbling sound of the Interceptor engine and the gentle hum of the air conditioner.

"Not yet. . . . That wasn't the favor?"

"No."

". . . Well?"

Slowly he smiled, not a mischievous or treacherous smile, but warm and open. "I told you when you came to my studio I wanted to do a real portrait of you."

Her forehead tipped toward him just slightly. "A 'real portrait?' What was it you did this morning?"

"It was just a quick pastel charcoal and chalk. I want to use a different medium. And take the time to make it a real work. . . . And, I want to do a semi-nude."

She straightened. "What is a 'semi-nude?' A naked woman painted on a tractor-trailer?"

He laughed. "You'd be draped with clothing or fabric. Covered as much as you want. And it would be very discrete."

". . . Discrete. You mean the portrait, or who see it?"

"I mean both. I have my own, private selection of paintings to which I am extremely partial. No one sees them except me. . . . You. Your face. Your form. You are art. You deserve to be on canvas."

She looked at him strangely. She was wrestling with something, some question or decision. Yet, oddly, he didn't think it was about whether or not to pose.

"You don't have to decide now," he said. "Why don't you think it over? Tomorrow morning I've got to come over here to do a charcoal at the gallery. Then after that, I'm going to see Lisa at the hospital and do her portrait. If you decide you're willing, you can come to my cottage in the afternoon sometime."

". . . In the afternoon? Don't you need the 'east light' of the sunrise?"

He grinned. "East light is just the direction of the light on the canvas. Any time of day, I can create just the light I want for a special piece."

Her eyebrows arched. "I have no doubt."

He pulled the latch and the passenger's door opened. "Well, think it over. I hope to see you."

She spoke as he started to get out, "You were wrong about one thing, Mr. Thorsen."

He stopped. "What was that, Lt. Stipling?"

"You said, if the Toliver boy had not instigated the kidnapping and rape, there would not have been a crime at Scotch Bonnet Beach yesterday."

"Yeah?"

"But there would have been. There would've been a suicide."

His expression changed, his eyes widening.

"As you're wondering about the random, thoughtless evil perpetrated by those boys against Lisa Faucet yesterday, perhaps you should figure into the mix the way that, if she hadn't been raped, run over and left at the beach, you'd be dead." She cocked her head. "Isn't there something in your A.A. program about the intervention of a higher power?"

He pushed open the door and got out.

Chapter 5

"What's your mommy's name, Cheyenne?"

Like her mother, the daughter of the Lumbee nurse had jet black hair, eyes that were sparkling dark pools and the same single dimple that appeared when she smiled—which was not often. Unlike so many six-year-olds he had encountered, she was obedient and still.

"Alison," the child responded.

"Oh. Alison. I think I can remember that." He had roughed in the shapes of their two heads on the heavy paper and was using twig to find their features. "Has anybody ever told you that you two look an awful lot alike?"

The nurse smiled. The little girl, sitting on her lap, nodded.

"And you don't have any brothers or sisters?"

She shook her head, her lips pressed tightly together. Magnus decided his questions annoyed her. The mother's gaze kept flashing past him toward the great clear glass window that served as the front wall of his gallery. He knew she was looking at the people on the sidewalk who were stopping to watch him create the portrait. Working in his "window studio" was something he had done a lot more often fifteen years before when he had first opened the gallery, when he had charged a lot less for portraits and when there had been long, dry periods with little work. Lining up friends who were willing to sit while tourists gawked at them inevitably jumpstarted his business.

"Just out of curiosity," he said, "why did you want me to do Cheyenne's portrait rather than yours, Alison?"

She thought it over. "Well. If I had to choose between us, I'd rather have hers. She's not going to be my baby forever."

"Okay. But it's not because you're 'canvas shy' yourself, is it?"

She laughed. "'Canvas shy.' I never heard that before."

Magnus was adding shadow below their faces and highlighting their eyes and hair as he decided on the right background tone. The mother would be surprised, he knew, not only to see that it was a portrait of both of them, but also that he had changed the color of her clothes to match the girl's lacey dress. He added folds to her

85

sleeves with navy shadows and an ivory sheen that made her blouse appear to be silk. He needed the child to smile one more time.

"Whatever you do," his eyes grew comically wide as he leaned around the edge of his easel, "don't tickle her!"

An expression of delight filled the girl's face. The dimple and small white rows of teeth momentarily appeared. The mother smiled and caressed the girl's hair.

"It's so nice of you to do this. For a long time I've wanted one of your portraits. . . . But even the charcoals like this one are a little expensive for me."

"Well," he said slowly, "what you did to help me the other night was so nice. This is the least I could do."

On many past occasions, Magnus would've paid an excessive compliment to an attractive woman who came to have a portrait done and thanked him profusely, as the mother had thanked him. He would've said something flirtatious or even outright seductive: "I only charge big money to keep homely people away. For a beautiful lady like you, we can negotiate the price." When it was clear that an attractive woman wanted to upgrade to a more expansive medium or to have an additional portrait painted, he would subtly hint that perhaps some mutually suitable arrangement could be achieved. And when an agreement had been reached, the women with whom he contracted—even those who seemed reluctant or unsure—almost always consummated the bargain.

He asked himself why, with this particularly lovely and grateful young woman, he was not willing to pursue his advantage. Was it because he didn't want her to be stigmatized afterwards by his imminent suicide? Was it that, at long last, in proximity to own demise, he was no longer willing to do anything coercive to another person? Was it a side effect of his one hundred plus days of sobriety, a condition he had unaccountably become eager to escape? Or was it more because he really wanted to be with Dot Stipling, that he obsessed himself with her visage and drew her repeatedly in his imagination?

"You know . . . I've been thinking of not doing this anymore. Of giving it up."

"What? You mean not doing any more portraits? So you would do, like, ocean scenes or landscapes?"

"No. I was thinking—" He added the faintest touch of rose to the edges of their foreheads and the outlines of their cheeks "—of maybe giving up on art all together."

The mother drew a sudden, surprised breath. "Quit art? Completely? Why? She had an almost desperate look. "Have you done so well that you don't have to work for the rest of your life?"

He nodded. "Actually that's pretty close to accurate."

"I'm sorry. I guess that was sort of a personal question. It just popped out. I know it's none of my business. "It's just that . . . with talent like you have, I'd hate to think you'd just quit drawing all together."

"Hey, it's not so bad. Just think, with this charcoal, you could have one of the last two or three pieces of art I will have ever done."

He had hoped to impress her with his comment, make her feel fortunate. The effect seemed to be exactly the opposite. Her expression was silent dismay. Magnus decided to change the subject.

"So did you work last night?"

"Yeah."

"Did you hear anything about how Lisa's doing?"

The nurse's face brightened. "She's doing real well. They're moving her out this morning to a regular room."

"Oh. No more ICU, eh?"

"She's basically a very healthy young woman. Someone like her gets well pretty quick. Of course," she said reflectively, "she's going to have a couple emotional jolts today."

"Emotional jolts?"

"Yeah. I guess her mother and sister are coming."

Magnus had finished the shading. He leaned around the edge of the easel again. "Why would that be a jolt? That's a good thing, right?"

"Depends on her mother and sister. On how well they cope with her being in the hospital. Lots of times people don't know what they're seeing. Miss Faucet is still going to have a couple IV's. She'll still have the halo on her leg, so she'll be propped. Her arm will be in a sling. Lots of times patients are doing really well, but their families freak anyway because they don't get what they are seeing. . . . And then there's the news."

"The news?"

"Yeah. You know about the boys who attacked her. You saw that, didn't you?"

"Uh." Suddenly Magnus felt stupid for not watching TV or picking up a paper. He had been avoiding anything that strengthened the fleeting world's tenuous hold on him. "Guess I haven't today."

"Last night at 11 they started showing scenes of the Aberdeen County police chief on the news. He was talking about arresting five boys. We realized in the ICU that those were the guys who attached Lisa Faucet. But she never has asked to watch TV, so we just leave hers off and don't mention anything to her about the news. We figure that today she'll see it. It caused quite a buzz in the unit because one of the boys they arrested was an All-State quarterback."

"Randy Plank?"

"Um hmm."

Magnus picked up the can of spray fixative and shook it. "Did my name come up on TV?"

She thought it over. "No, actually. Not that I remember."

He sprayed the portrait in nice, even strokes. Rolling his stool to one side away from the easel, he smiled at the little girl.

"Cheyenne, hop up and tell me what you think of this picture."

The little girl came right around and stared up at the easel. She pointed at the charcoal. "That's just like Mommy."

"Mommy?"

The mother got up and came around to look. Magnus watched their faces as they studied the portrait. He knew the likeness was precise.

"I hope it's okay if I did you both."

A tear ran down the smooth, taupe cheek of the Lumbee woman. Reflexively she wiped it away with the side of her finger.

"I don't know what to say."

He stood and picked up a cardboard cylinder. "You don't have to say anything, Alison. This is my 'thank you' to you." He unpinned the paper from the easel and began to roll it up. "I sprayed this with a fixer, so it shouldn't smudge or anything. Just keep sticky little fingers off of it."

She waited patiently as he slipped it into the cardboard and capped it. As he handed it to her, she stretched up to buss his cheek.

"I'm going to take it right now and get a frame." She looked into his eyes. "You shouldn't give up on your talent. You bring so much joy."

She took her little girl by the hand and walked out of the

window studio into the entry. Magnus followed her. Molly, the receptionist—bookkeeper, appointment secretary, dispenser of sage advice—was sitting at the desk, opening mail. She and the Lumbee exchanged smiles as the front door opened. And then mother and daughter were gone.

"Molly," Magnus asked, "do you have today's paper?"

"Always. Front page is what you're looking for. She pulled out a quarter-folded section and handed it up to him. "I assume that's your girl they're talking about."

He shook out the paper. There was a banner headline: "Aberdeen Police Arrest Five in Attack." Beneath were two photos. One was of the police chief, Rex Hardt standing behind an array of microphones. The other was a team photo of Randy Plank wearing his football uniform, his helmet under his arm. Magnus began to read:

Aberdeen County police announced the arrests Friday evening of four local men and a juvenile on charges including attempted murder, rape and kidnapping. Among those taken into custody was Randy Plank, starting quarterback of last year's state semi-finalist North Aberdeen High Ospreys.

According to Police Chief Rex Hardt, the charges were related to an attack against Lisa Annette Faucet, a senior at UNC-Wilmington. Faucet was reported to have been abducted from Myrtle Beach and taken to Scotch Bonnet Beach where she was sexually assaulted, run over with an automobile and left for dead. A passerby from Fraser Beach discovered her shortly after the attack.

"Wonder why they didn't name you?"

"What?" he asked.

"You're the hero. You saved the girl's life. You IDed those boys. Why aren't you getting the star treatment?"

Magnus smiled. "Well, Molly, sometimes things just work out the way they're supposed to."

Setting his leather case down by his left leg and leaning his collapsing easel against his right leg, he pushed the button marked "4." The elevator door rolled shut and Magnus drew a breath. He had a sense of being almost back to where he had been on Thursday when his crazy adventure had commenced.

The night before he had begun working on the canvas stowed

in the case at his side. It did not take long—just creating a contrasting seascape with a space in the left center in which to paint Lisa Faucet.

He would finish the painting swiftly and present it to her. He would kiss her goodbye and, when he left that afternoon, be done with her. Magnus would have saved her life, helped arrest her attackers and fulfilled his promise to reveal and capture her prettiness. And finally, after the extended interruption, he would be free at last to pursue his own ultimate concerns. He assured himself that he had more than satisfied any obligation to Lisa.

What else was left to distract him, he wondered. What concern or event had the potential to defeat his single purpose? Who, apart from Lisa, had the ability to prevent his demise, either intentionally or unintentionally?

Grady, for all his wisdom and persistence, would not be able to stop him. Magnus had ignored the two phone calls Grady had made Friday evening—one before the A.A. meeting and one after—as he prepared the canvas for the girl's image and then went about restoring his cottage to its pristine state. Grady was his conscience. Magnus appreciated and admired him. Only, Magnus for decades had successfully ignored the voice of his conscience.

The elevator stopped with a jolt. There was a ding and, as the doors opened, a disembodied woman's voice spoke without inflection: "Fourth floor." He picked up his gear and started down the hallway toward room 436.

Dot Stipling was another story. She was clever and resourceful. If she suspected Magnus meant to do himself in and decided to intervene, she had the ability to make his suicide a difficult undertaking. On the other hand, she likely assumed that having possession of his pistol—his only registered firearm—stymied his self-destructive intentions. Magnus smiled. What she had no awareness of, on the other hand, was his stash of Phenobarbital. A three month supply. Carefully concealed from before he went into treatment. He kept it in the event he could find no preferable manner of death.

He wondered as well if she had any real reason remaining to be concerned about his living or dying. According to the morning paper, she had gotten confessions from most of the boys. She no longer needed testimony from Magnus. So would it matter now to the prosecution of Lisa Faucet's case if he killed himself? And, anyway, based upon her reaction he had determined that asking her to pose nude had emotionally driven her away. He was sure his request had terminated their relationship, dashed any possibility of future contact. Much as he regretted the end of their dealings, he recognized that it had opened a door for him. Now he could fulfill his prior intent.

"Mr. Magnus?"

A woman had walked up to him. She was a small, thin person, about his age, wearing casual street clothes, her dishwater blonde hair drawn back in a ponytail. She seemed vaguely familiar.

It doubly surprised him when she stepped in front of him, blocking his way. Typically he was completely attentive to everyone around him. He had learned to distinguish the expressions of strangers who recognized and wanted to engage him—as if he in turn should know who they were and be willing to talk to them. This woman, who had come straight down the hall toward him, had totally taken him by surprise. It was the cost, he thought, of dwelling on his own demise.

"Thorsen," he said. "It's Magnus Thorsen."

She smiled in an open, almost childlike way. "I'm Ellie Peters. I'm Lisa's mom."

"Oh. Oh." He set his equipment down and took her hand. "How are you? So good to meet you."

She dropped his hand and reached her arms up for him, weeping. "You saved my baby." Her voice was breaking.

"Oh, Miss Peters." He patted her on the back. "That's all right. I just happened along at the right moment."

"Thank God. Thank God you did." She backed away from him, pulling a tissue from her left hand with her right. Dabbing at her eyes.

She had to take the tissue from one hand with the other, he realized, because she was also holding cigarettes and a lighter in her left hand. Magnus had scented the nicotine on her when she was pressed against him. He noticed as well the red undertone of her complexion—what one of his counselors referred to as "treatment face." Lisa's mother, he surmised, was an active alcoholic.

"She said you were going to paint her picture. She had her roommate fix her hair."

91

"Oh my. Katie Magpie."

Ellie Peters laughed. "You have been as good as your word with my baby."

"Well. I've tried."

She nodded earnestly. "That's so important." She studied his eyes, seeming to search for something. "She loves you, Mr. Thorsen."

He looked down at the linoleum floor. "May I call you 'Ellie?' Ellie, the police tell me that, when I found her on the beach and phoned for help, I became her 'safe person,' the one she could trust—until her family got here. Now that you all are here and they've arrested the boys responsible for what happened, she's not going to need me for a safe person anymore."

She smiled. "I know what you say is true. I also know Lisa. I probably wouldn't underestimate what my baby feels for you, Mr. Thorsen."

It was Magnus' turn to search the woman's face, to try to understand what she meant and what she was assuming about him.

"Mrs. Peters, I hope you know I would never do anything to hurt Lisa. I have nothing but the best intentions."

"Oh I know that." The woman shifted, moving her cigarettes from one hand to the other and dipping her hips with her legs together in a way that was almost seductive. She smiled at him coyly and, rising on her tiptoes, kissed his cheek. "You're a very good man."

His eyes widened. Twice in one morning he had been kissed by women who overestimated his virtue.

"I know that you know," she said, looking past him, "she's been hurt enough already. More than one person can stand. Well, I'm going out to smoke a cigarette. Would you believe you can't smoke anywhere in the building? I have to go out to the parking lot."

He nodded. "Who would've ever thought? And in North Carolina."

She pointed down the hallway. "It's the last room on the left. Katie's in with her along with my older girl, Dana. I'll be back in a few minutes."

Magnus picked up his easel and carrying case again and walked down the hall to the last room. The door was part way open. He sat down his easel and knocked.

Katie's voice responded. "Come in."

There was a fairly narrow entry that opened up into a large, square room. A floor-to-ceiling curtain, designed to bisect the room if two beds had been present, had been pushed all the way back against the wall. And against the wall in the corner farthest from the window, her feet beneath her as she sat in a reading chair was a plump, plain young woman. This, Magnus decided, was Lisa's sister—older, quieter sister—Dana. She made scant, momentary eye contact with him and then looked quickly away.

Katie, sitting in a plastic chair at the head of the opposite side of the hospitable bed, had begun to talk the instant he entered the room.

"Hello, Mr. Thorsen. So you found the room, huh? You just missed Lisa's mom. She went to smoke and you have to go outside."

Katie's appearance was notably different from the day before. Her hair, short and dark, was fixed neatly. She was wearing makeup and clothes that were just a little nicer than any college student would wear to class at UNCW, if she weren't trying to get someone's attention.

It was an old story to Magnus: friends and family who accompanied someone to get a portrait often came dressed better than the subject to be painted. Sometimes, he had decided, they did so consciously. And sometimes, as with Katie, they weren't consciously aware of what they had done.

"Well you're really going to draw her, aren't you?"

"Hi, Katie."

"Hi. That's Lisa's sister, Dana."

"Hi," he said.

Dana gave no audible reply. If she acknowledged his greeting in any visible way, he wouldn't have noticed, because he was looking at Lisa in her hospital bed.

Lisa Faucet was propped—almost seated and slightly to her left—with two or three regular bed pillows—not hospital pillows—behind her. Her hair, straw blonde, had been washed and dried and set, and it flowed about her face radiantly. And on her face she wore makeup, expertly applied, along with a slightly triumphant smile. Her hospital gown had been replaced with a pajama top, Carolina blue, that buttoned up the front. A sheet covered the rest of her, including the metal halo over her right leg, up to her waist.

93

Three images came to Magnus as he stood staring at her. Lisa reminded him, first, of a stately monarch, a princess finely adorned, attired to impress and waiting for a particular subject of her with a particular purpose in her mind. She reminded him, second, of a seductive, aggressive young woman waiting with some impatience in her bed for her intended paramour to find his way through all the other rooms of the house to where she reclined. Third, she seemed to him like a little girl, intending to surprise her daddy—one she knew would find delight in her. He understood clearly now what her mother had meant.

"Hello, Magnus."

"Hi Lisa. You look like you're ready for your portrait. How are you feeling?"

"I'm okay. I still have my pump." She nodded toward the little device on an IV pole at the head of the bed.

"Good old morphine," he said.

"They're taking it away tomorrow," Katie chimed, "if she keeps doing good."

Magnus looked at the roommate and smiled. "I'm sure she will. Katie, I have a job for you."

For an instant she seemed flustered. "I'm not going for sodas."

He grinned. "No, no. Nothing like that." Magnus unfolded the easel and locked it effortlessly into place at the foot of the bed, making sure to leave space for a nurse or doctor to walk behind him. "Can you move your chair right over here by the edge of the window, dear, and turn to face Lisa?"

"Uh, yeah." She picked up her chair and carried it over to the right side of the artist. Sitting down in it, she asked, "Like this?"

"That's about perfect."

He opened his kit and took out two clamping lights with collapsing bellows. One he hooked at the top of the easel, pointed down. He walked to the head of the bed and clamped the other onto one of Lisa's IV poles. She watched him closely as he turned it on.

"Hey," Katie said, "battery operated."

"Lot of places I paint don't have outlets." Gently he moved Lisa's face away from him and toward her roommate. He stepped back and examined the angle. "Watch her when we get started, sweetie. She's all dressed up for you."

It took only a minute or two for him to create his workspace.

The three women watched him with a curiosity approaching awe. When he uncovered his wet pallet and attached it to the easel, Katie craned her neck to see.

"Are those oils or watercolors?"

"No. Neither. Watercolor is the most difficult medium for a lifelike portrait. I think so, anyway. And oil it too finicky. Takes too long to dry. This is acrylic." He opened the wide, flat satchel and slid out the canvas. "Acrylic is the best of both worlds. Fast drying, like watercolor, and easy to work with. It gives you what you need where you need it. You can paint light over dark with it. And it has the nice rich texture of oil."

"Hey!" Katie exclaimed. "You already started on that. You've got the ocean and the shore painted on there."

Securing the canvas to the easel, he leaned toward the roommate. "That was going to be a surprise."

Her cheeks shot bright pink. "Oh. . . . Oh, I'm sorry."

"I'm glad for you to watch as I paint, Katie. Only let's let Lisa see it for herself."

"Okay. Sorry."

He adjusted the light atop the easel, sliding it down to the right upper corner of the canvas. Picking up a brush, he glanced at his model on the bed and roughed in the shape of her face and hair, then body, with light gray paint.

"Lisa, will you look over at Katie? She's going to talk to you and make you laugh."

Lisa, a childlike smile on her face, rolled her face slightly toward Katie. Dana, to Magnus' great surprise, got up from her recliner and walked around behind him. She stood apparently pressed against the wall—unmoving, unspeaking, watching him paint.

When he knew he had the proportion of her form right, he went to a blue—a shimmering turquoise—to shape in her blouse and then a white—just a little bit brighter than the canvas itself—for the Capri slacks he meant for her to wear.

"Does she have that?" a voice behind him asked.

Magnus started when the sister spoke to him. "What?"

"Does she really have a shirt that color?"

He glanced over his shoulder and winked. "I don't know if she does. But she should. It's her color."

"Dana?"

It was the little woman he met in the hallway, back from smoking her cigarette. A nurse or patient aide, hands on hips, was standing beside her.

"Why are you pestering Mr. Magnus while he's working?"

"She's just fine, Ellie," Magnus answered. "She doesn't bother me at all."

He looked back to the canvas and finished roughing in the girl's form. As he painted, the two women in the doorway quietly approached Dana and stood beside her watching.

Magnus had begun first developing the image of Lisa's body, leaving her face for last. He was painting her atop windswept dunes, gazing over her left shoulder toward the sea. Her loose-fitting turquoise blouse seemed to be pushed inland by the ocean breeze. Her hair would appear to be blowing as well by the time he finished. Her posture, beneath the quick brushstrokes of his hand, was casual and limber, creating for Lisa an attitude that was relaxed and peaceful.

The nurse quietly walked out the door. From the corner of his eye, Magnus saw Ellie draw closer to Dana and loop her arm through the girl's. They leaned on each other as they watched him paint.

"I can't wait to see this," Katie said. "Where you hanging it, Lees?"

"Don't know. Yet."

"It would look so good in my living room," Ellie called out softly.

"No one in Ohio knows what the ocean is, Mom."

Magnus stopped painting to blend a paler blue. He intended to pull the water around behind her in the portrait so the beach disappeared and the ocean began at her form.

"You want her to come home to recuperate, Ellie?" he asked.

"I could take good care—"

"Never going to happen, Mom. I'm already signed up for my fall classes."

"Baby, will you even be walking by then?" Ellie asked. "How are you going to go to class? In a wheelchair?"

Lisa looked away from Katie toward her mother. "First of all, if I withdraw from school, I lose my health insurance."

"You can sue the boys who ran over you."

96

"Shut up, Katie," she continued. "Second, in this age, when you can't go to class, class comes to you through an internet video hook-up."

"What can you learn off a computer?"

"Mom, I already take most of my tests on the net. I do research and submit my essays on the net. . . . Do you even have a computer?"

". . . You know, baby, we could get one. If you're doing it on a computer like you say, you could come back here once the semester starts just long enough to get your assignments and then come home and finish all your work from your bedroom."

"You mean Dana's bedroom? Now she's finally got me out, do you think she wants me back?" Lisa's voice was tinged with well-aged, refined, unresolved bitterness. "Anyway, I'm not leaving Wilmington until Magnus takes me on the Riverwalk for supper."

He flinched. He leaned over his pallet and ran the brush across it as if he were changing colors. Supper on the Riverwalk. He had forgotten. It was the one promise he had made to Lisa he would not be able to fulfill if he ended his life that night.

"Isn't that right, Magnus?" she asked.

"Yep," he answered quietly.

Now she was looking at him. "You didn't change your mind, did you?"

"Of course not. Look back at Katie. . . . How come you're so quiet, Katie?"

The nurse who had walked out of the room appeared at the door with a gaggle of other women dressed in nurses' uniforms. They whispered among themselves.

"It's hard to talk and watch you paint," Katie said.

"So," Magnus said, blending the tone for Lisa's face, "if you close your eyes, Katie, do you automatically start talking?"

"I don't know about that," Lisa said absently, "but I know that for the past two years as soon as she opens 'em she starts."

Katie giggled.

The nurses formed a silent phalanx and, pressing themselves against the wall, moved to where they could watch him paint. For Magnus it was just like sitting in the glass studio at this gallery with a crowd outside gazing in while he worked. One of the nurses was wearing a little too much perfume. And another smelled of laundry detergent.

Lisa's face flowed out of his hand. It was just the look he had wanted: an alert, serene expression as she searched the pale, distant waves. Strands of hair hung across her forehead. Her lips, parted, suggested she was about to speak.

He mixed a silver gray to create the shadows around her. As he applied them, Lisa's form seemed to step forward on the canvas, and the earth and sea retreated behind her. It was just what he intended, he thought, painting "Magnus" in the lower left.

From the corner of his eye, he could see Katie leaning out of her chair, studying the portrait, her mouth open. He glanced at the bed. Lisa was staring at him. Her eyes were tired, but she smiled expectantly.

And then the nurses behind him began to move. Several of them spoke in low voices. It so surprised Magnus that he glanced over his left shoulder at them and saw a young woman standing in the doorway—and a tall young man beside her with a large video camera under his arm. Magnus and the woman—a petite, immaculately dressed, lovely black woman—stared at each other silently.

Her eyebrows arched and she said, "May I come in?"

"You're asking me?" Magnus replied.

The nurses behind him, who had been edging slowly toward the door, began to giggle as they suddenly picked up speed and the whole little flock of them squeezed past the couple in the doorway and disappeared.

"I'm through with all I can do for now," he said. He dropped his brush on the pallet. "I'll come back later and finish up."

"No," the woman said, taking a step into the room. "I want to talk with you too."

"I'm not family," he said. He cradled his easel and maneuvered it toward the wall behind him, forcing Ellie and Dana to step aside. "I'm just a friend and I was just leaving." He nodded toward the bed. "This is Lisa Faucet." Coming out from behind the easel, he eased it back until the canvas was too close to the wall to be seen.

"I'm Anika Brown," the woman said.

"Oh my god!" Katie exclaimed. "Channel 4?"

"Channel 7," Brown responded. "And you're—the artist."

"Magnus Thorsen," Lisa said.

"He's a famous painter," Katie added.

Ellie still pressed against the wall—and still hanging onto Dana—called, "He saved my baby's life."

"Let me slip out," Magnus said insistently. "You need to interview Lisa."

He felt himself being pulled back into the world he had almost escaped. He feared he was losing control of his life again.

"But I want to talk to you too."

"No, no. I'm not part of this."

"I heard you were," the reporter's voice was insistent also. "It was you who found Miss Faucet after the attack."

"Saved her life," Katie said.

He shook his head and muttered, "I just called the police."

"He did save my life."

"I heard," the reporter continued, "you were responsible for identifying her assailants."

He saw Lisa look away from the reporter and toward him. "You did?" she asked.

"He drew a likeness of the driver that was so good all the police recognized it immediately."

He smiled cynically. "And let me guess which policewoman told you all this."

"You did that?" Ellie asked. "You drew that boy from memory?"

"Oh, he's like a genius," Katie said.

"Look I got to go."

"But wait," Brown said, stepping closer to him. "Surely you don't mind if we tape a few comments from you and Miss Faucet."

"You're already taping," Magnus retorted. "Like I don't see the red dot on that camera?"

Discovered, the videographer lifted the camera to his shoulder and looked through the eyepiece at Magnus.

Brown raised her chin. "They're saying you're a hero."

"You believe everything the police tell you?"

"It's true, though," Lisa said slowly. "Dot told me you'd probably get some recognition for what you've done."

"'Dot?'" There was more anger in his voice than he intended. He turned back toward the bed. "Are you 'girls' with her too now? Were you in on planning this 'surprise' interview with her?"

When Lisa's face darkened, he spoke to her softly. "I was only

99

interested in protecting you, darlin'. I want no recognition. I just want you to be okay."

"Lt. Stipling also said," the reporter interjected loudly, "they never would've gotten the assailants to confess if it hadn't been for you."

Magnus went to the side of the bed and grasped her left hand with his. "Do you even know what's happened, Lisa? About the boys?"

"We been watching it all morning," Katie replied.

"They arrested them all," Lisa said. "No bond. I'm safe from them."

"And the arrests were made possible by Mr. Thorsen," Brown went on, authority in her voice. "He identified the driver and the car and confronted the chief assailant yesterday at Scotch Bonnet Beach."

She searched his face. "Why didn't you tell me you did all those things?"

Magnus shook his head. "I didn't think it was the time to talk about it yet." He straightened and faced the reporter. "And it's not time to talk about it. I'm sure Lt. Stipling told you there were things that can't be discussed for legal reasons."

"Actually she told me the case is settled. The last of the boys, Garrett Toliver, made a guilty plea this morning. She said you could tell me all you want."

He stared at her. "Or tell you nothing?"

"I can't understand why you're such a reluctant hero," Brown said.

Katie spoke up. "Me neither."

"I've been told you talked to Lisa on the beach to keep her spirits up. You promised to take her out to eat fish when she's able to walk again."

"He did." Katie nodded.

"You told her you were going to paint her portrait so she could see that she is still a very pretty young lady. At least you could let us see that," Brown implored. "What a great human interest story: 'local artist paints rape victim in hospital.'"

"'Lisa Faucet,'" he said slowly, "not 'rape victim.' What the hell's wrong with you?"

"It's beautiful," Ellie said. "Looks just like her."

100

"Yeah, it's beautiful," Katie agreed.

"Has Lisa even seen it?" the reporter asked. "Let us have a look."

"I'm a little self-conscious about my work before it's finished," he said. "I don't let people see what I'm doing until it's ready."

"Like those six nurses?" Ellie asked. "And Dana and me?"

"Or the mob of people who stand outside your gallery when you're painting in the window?" Brown said.

"Anyway, you must be through with it," Katie said brightly. "You signed it."

Magnus glanced back at the easel, forced against the wall. To his surprise, Dana made and held eye contact with him.

"Why are you so shy?" she asked.

He jumped. He felt his shoulders sag.

"*Et tu*, Dana?" he said. "Then fall, Magnus."

He pointed, indicating the videographer should go to the other side of the hospital bed, and waited for him to comply. Brown crossed over as well and stood with her back to the window. Magnus picked up the easel and carried it to the corner where Dana had been sitting opposite the window. He turned the canvas toward the Lisa and stepped away so it could be seen.

Someone gasped. The cameraman rolled a peg on the camera lens, zooming in on the portrait. And on the bed, tears began to roll down Lisa's cheeks.

"Do I really look like that?"

He nodded. "Pretty close. Only it really doesn't do you justice, sweetie."

Magnus went to the end of the bed and packed up his kit swiftly. He caught a glimpse of the camera turning toward him. He didn't look up.

"Your art speaks so eloquently for you, Mr. Thorsen," the reporter said, "but we would sure appreciate any comments you'd like to add."

He fastened the leather satchel. "As I told you, the person you need to speak with is the beautiful young woman in this bed. She has many grand hopes and dreams for this coastal area, which she has come to love. And now those of us who live around here have an opportunity to show her that—despite the awful thing that happened to her—her affection for this community is justified."

He started toward the door, leaving behind the painting, the easel and the portable lights.

"Magnus," Lisa called.

He looked over his shoulder.

"Will I see you tomorrow?"

He put his hand on the threshold and sighed. "Maybe not tomorrow, sweetie. I will be thinking of you, though. You're doing great."

"Yeah," Katie said, "except she has to have surgery next week."

Magnus drew a breath. "Katie, do you talk when you make love?"

The roommate's eyes rolled upward. Her mouth dropped open.

He smiled. "I didn't think you'd know."

Chapter 6

When he had finished writing, Magnus dropped his pen on the table and held the paper up to read.

Dear Officer Miller,

I'm told you are an extremely dependable person. I have observed that you are honorable as well. That's why I'm asking you to do this favor for me. I believe that you are the sort of person who would not neglect to fulfill a dead man's final request.

Please use the enclosed $100 Blue Pirate Café gift certificate to take our mutual acquaintance, Lisa Faucet, for a meal when she is physically able to go out to supper. Because you were at least as responsible for saving her life as I was, you deserve this reward as well.

By the way, I suspect I have given you something of a bad time once or twice about your professional demeanor. I'm sorry for that and I hope you won't hold it against me. At least you know I'll never do it again.

Yours,

Magnus Thorsen

He smiled and folded the note, sliding the gift certificate inside it. He wrote "Officer Martin Miller" on the outside of the manila envelope, sealed it and placed it on his little stack of farewells.

Magnus checked his watch. Almost 6:30. The large combination pizza he had ordered would arrive soon. He would eat it and drink most of the pitcher of sweet tea he had brewed. It was a full two-and-a-half hours before the sun went down, but he was already prepared for what was coming.

He opened the screen door to the lower deck and walked out. Brisk sea breeze in his face filled his lungs. Looking straight down to the beach, he watched the waves sliding up and petering out a dozen feet from the dunes behind his cottage. By 9 p.m. the tide would be all the way in and the sun would be down.

As he had done on Thursday sitting in the parking lot at Scotch Bonnet Beach, Magnus went over his mental checklist. He had cleaned the place thoroughly, including putting fresh sheets on his bed and new towels in the bathroom. He had taken the sturdy, yellow, wooden Adirondack beach chair out of the ground level storage unit and left it on the cement parking pad under the house. He had pulled out the medium sized canvas beach bag with the flat vinyl bottom and placed in it the unopened pint of blended whiskey he bought at the ABC store that afternoon, along with three full prescription bottles of Phenobarbital he had taken from their hiding place among his art supplies.

When the pizza was finished, he would carry the box it came in out to the trash along with the small amount of perishable food remaining in the fridge and wash out the tea pitcher. Then, when darkness came, he would carry the chair out to the end of his wooden walkway to where the steps descended to the sand. And he would sit down in the darkness and open the whiskey and pills. With his stomach full, he would swallow the barbiturates and wash them down with the liquor and lean back in the comfortable chair. No one would bother him. The tide would go out and come back in, the sun would rise and Magnus would still be in his chair overlooking the beach, apparently asleep. His neighbors had seen him in the same place many times. Those who knew him best would just assume he had fallen off the wagon and gotten drunk. Most likely it would be noon, or perhaps midafternoon, before it occurred to someone that he wasn't asleep at all.

Magnus gazed up and down the beach. It came to him—though he pushed away the thought and the wistful feeling that came with it—that he had seen the east light of sunrise for the last time.

The doorbell rang.

"Oh true pizza man," he muttered, walking off the deck and through the house, "thy delivery is quick."

When he opened the front door, his sponsor stood staring at him, arms folded across his chest.

"Grady!"

"I'm glad you remember, Mag-man. And I'm glad you're sober. You inviting me in?"

He stepped out of the doorway and Grady pushed past him into the house.

"Make yourself at home."

Grady walked into the kitchen. He looked in the trash as he spoke, "That's three straight meetings you missed. As of tonight."

"You think I lost count?"

He opened the refrigerator, then the freezer. "And you ain't returning my calls."

"I been busy, Grady. It's nothing personal."

"'Specially you never said why you needed to buy a gun."

"Who said I bought a gun? The only thing the paper lists is gun permits."

"Why do you need a gun or a permit?"

Magnus leaned against the threshold of the kitchen. "I don't know if you've been keeping up with current events, man, but my favorite beach has gotten sort of dangerous."

"It's dangerous as hell if you're packing a piece. But you got that permit before your girl got run over anyway."

"Grady, I'm pretty sure there is nothing in the program about not buying a gun. And if I were going to drink, I'd have my whiskey upstairs in my workshop."

"I'll make it up there." He pulled a chair out from the kitchen table. "Saw you on the TV."

". . . Channel 7. Anika Brown?"

"They showed the picture you painted. Nice job. Girl really look like that?"

"She will. When they get her put together and she learns to walk again." He hung his head. "Isn't there something in the literature about avoiding notoriety?"

"Yeah."

"I tried real hard to keep out from in front of that camera, man."

Grady smiled. "I could kind of tell. Why haven't you been returning my calls, pigeon?"

"Well why have you been giving me such a bad time? I don't need to pick up a starter chip. And I never heard of any sponsor being as intrusive in a sponsee's life as you are in mine. I'm not in treatment. And this is no halfway house."

He leaned his chair on its back legs. "I treat you like I do because it hasn't worked with you yet, Mag-man. I see you listening at meetings. You're taking it in. You're giving it a go. But no awakening moment. No peace of mind. I keep waiting."

"That's all that matters to you, isn't it? I save a girl's life. Help the police find and arrest the kids who tried to kill her. I keep my promises to all of you. And what do I get? The cops either treat me like a suspect or a commodity. The goddamn news people, when they found out about me, were on me like white on rice. And all my sponsor wants to know is if I picked up a drink."

"Now there's your problem, Mag-man." He sat his chair flat and put his arms on the table. "All I hear is that 'poor little me' shit. If a guy was really working his program, he'd be telling this story with gratitude. . . . Four months ago, could you have gone through something like this without drinking? The whole world will open up for you eventually, Mag-man, if you'll just 'don't drink and go to meetings.'"

The doorbell rang.

"Well, aren't you Mr. Popularity?"

Magnus looked over his shoulder at his sponsor as he walked toward the door, leery that he might nose around the canvas beach bag on the deck where his pint of blended whiskey lurked along with his deadly stash of pills. The pizza would be large enough, he thought, for the two of them to share. He would assure Grady that he wouldn't miss another meeting and they would part on good terms and he could follow through with his intentions.

When he opened the door, he found Dot Stipling standing before him.

"Lieutenant. Guess I didn't expect to see you."

She was gazing at the table by the door. "I bet that's true in several ways, Mr. Thorsen. May I come in?"

"Surely."

As she stepped past him, Magnus glanced down to his gravel driveway. Beside Grady's old Taurus there was a yellow Chevy Cavalier. The lieutenant had not driven her police cruiser.

When he heard their voices, Grady got up and came out of the kitchen. He stood, transfixed by the tall woman, his eyes alive with mirth.

"Uh, Lt. Dot Stipling, this is my—friend, Grady Stinson. Grady, this is . . . this is the hot police lady you were going to turn me in to."

The lieutenant's eyebrows arched. Grady began to laugh, his head dropping forward.

"He's blushing," Magnus said. "You just can't tell it."

"Hey, Lieutenant." Grady held out his hand. "Good seeing you."

106

"Charmed." There was mocking distance in her voice. She turned to Magnus. "So it appears I've come at a bad time."

"No, no," Magnus said quickly. "Old Grady, he was just leaving. Weren't you, Grady?"

His sponsor stared at the officer. "I was?"

"Grady came over here looking for something to drink. Since all I got is tea and coffee, he didn't find what he was looking for. So he lost interest and decided to leave. Didn't you?"

"I guess I did. You all have some more official police work to take care of, do you?"

"There is some unfinished business, a few loose ends we have to tie up. Yes," the lieutenant replied.

"Hmm. Well in the interest of public safety, Miss Lieutenant, I have to warn you about dealing with Mag-man here."

"Really?"

Magnus wondered what Grady was about to say. His sponsor seemed much less interested in him and his sobriety, however, than about continuing his conversation with the woman.

"There is more to him than meets the eye."

"Well," she responded, "I would certainly hope so."

"I don't mean that in no good way," Grady protested.

Magnus found it strange listening to the two of them discussing him, each insulting him differently, cleverly.

"Well what should I watch for, Mr. Stinson?"

"He's a bigot to start off with. He's a complete racist."

"Really. How do you explain him having a black A.A. sponsor?"

His hands folded casually across his chest, Magnus silently stood listening.

"Oh. You know about that. . . . Deception, I reckon. He don't want people to know he hates black folks."

"It's a good thing you see through him, Mr. Stinson. He's never been anything but courteous and respectful to me."

"He's sly like that," Grady nodded. "And he tricks mostly women. He's always making a play for unsuspecting women."

"Really?" Her eyebrows arched regally. "I personally had taken him to be gay."

Grady chuckled. "Well he might be. He's full of surprises." He tilted his head. "You aren't that way, are you, Lieutenant?"

"You mean, am I gay? You're asking if I'm gay?" she replied. "Not at all, Mr. Stinson. Here I am dealing with a man who's a secret bigot and a womanizing homosexual. I find no reason whatever for levity."

Grady missed the joke, but Magnus laughed at it, and then broke into the conversation. "Okay, I've had enough. Have you two had your fill of ripping on me? I haven't done anything to disappoint either of you for as long as you've known me. Either of you. I haven't take a drink. And I helped you solve your crime. For my trouble, all you all want to do is play 'make fun of the white boy.'"

"See, here's another problem, Lieutenant. He has no gratitude whatever. Always he's feeling sorry for himself."

"Yes. So I see. And what was it he meant a moment ago when he said you were going to turn him in to me?"

"Oh no!" Magnus exclaimed. "You were here, Lieutenant. You heard his message."

"A gun permit. I just don't know why the boy needs a gun permit."

"A gun permit?" Lt. Stipling said with feigned surprise. "Do you suppose that was for the .38 snub nose revolver with one bullet in the cylinder I confiscated from him on the Thursday?"

"One bullet?"

"Enough! I doesn't matter now, Grady. She has the goddamn gun and I'm not going to try to get another. And as far as meetings, you have my word, I won't miss another. You're leaving now and you don't need to know what other business I might have with the lieutenant here."

"All right! All right! I'm going." He turned his attention to the woman. "Now if you need me to rein him in somehow, you know I will. You need my number lieutenant?"

"I'm sure I can get it from Mr. Thorsen."

"I'm not sure he has it. He never will call it."

"Goodnight, Grady." Magnus stood at the door, holding it open.

"I'm gone. I'm gone."

Magnus closed the door as his sponsor left. The lieutenant stood staring at him. He pressed his back against the door, his arms folded across his chest.

"To what do I owe the pleasure, Lieutenant?"

She smiled, a more relaxed smile than he had experienced from her, as if she thought something were truly funny. "You forgot?" She nodded toward the pile of manila envelopes on his entry table. "Your outgoing mail stack seems to have grown. You having trouble getting to the post office?"

"I take it all down to my gallery and meter it. It's all business mail."

"Really? What if I guessed there was an envelope to Lisa Faucet in that stack?"

"What if you did?"

"Is there an envelope for me?"

"Just keep watching your mail."

"I have a hunch that everything in that stack is going to be hand delivered. And not by the mailman, but by some poor cop like me."

He gazed at her silently, absorbing the familiar appearance— dark blue suit and white blouse, small purse hanging primly off a shoulder—he had assumed he would never see again.

"I thought we had a sort of deal," he said. "Once you got your confessions and the case was closed and you didn't need me anymore, you would butt out of my life."

"Just because I'm in your living room, Mr. Thorsen, doesn't mean I'm in your life."

"Do you think you could call me 'Magnus?'"

"Well. My name is 'Dot.'"

The doorbell rang.

"Damn it, Grady."

He turned and yanked open the door, which thoroughly startled the pizza delivery boy.

"Oh, dude!" Magnus exclaimed. "I'm sorry." He fished the twenty out of his pocket. "Here you go. Keep the change."

"Thanks," the kid said, his eyes still wide under the blue and yellow baseball cap with the round logo on the front. "And thanks for calling Panini's Pizza."

Magnus closed the door and turned toward Dot Stipling, holding the great, flat box in front of him. "Hope you like pizza."

"Actually I'm starved."

"Me too." He nodded toward the kitchen. "Good thing Grady left. I'm not sure there would've been enough."

"Left? You practically threw him out the door."

"I brewed some sweet tea."

109

He dropped the box on the little kitchen table and went about pulling out plates and glasses. She sat down and watched him with a curious expression.

"That was big tip you gave that young man."

"Well, you know, I think I scared him, opening the door all-of-a-sudden like that." He set a glass of tea before her and pulled out a chair for himself. "I have a little bone to pick with you."

"Really?" Her voice was mocking.

"Yes. Really. You set me up today."

"Set you up?"

"Don't be coy. You sicced that Anika Brown girl on me."

"Good pizza. How do you figure?"

"How do I figure? Anika Brown knew Lisa was out of the ICU. Nobody else seemed to know that. And when she walked into that hospital room, she knew everything that had happened on the beach."

"It's all public record." She took a drink from the big tumbler he had set before her. "Once the case was closed, everything became subject to common knowledge."

He shook his head. "She was ready with a comeback for everything I said. Like maybe you prepped her."

"What kind of tea is this?"

"Sweet."

"No, no. This is different. It has some kind of flavor in it."

"Don't change the subject," he said precisely. "The tea has blackberry in it."

"Blackberry juice?"

"Blackberry tea."

"I've never seen any blackberry tea in the store."

He sighed. "I order it in by the case. You brew two family size bags of regular tea and two small blackberry bags. With a cup of sugar, it makes half a gallon. Now, like I said, you set me up with the girl from Channel 7. Why?"

She studied him closely. "Why not? That's the real question. It's like one of the folks asked you this morning in that hospital room: why are you such a reluctant hero?"

"You know what was said? You bugged Lisa Faucet's hospital room?"

"No, Magnus. Anika showed me the video."

"Why would she come back to you to show you that? She'd already talked to you. You told her everything. You even told her what to ask."

"I asked her if I could see the video of the interview with you and Lisa in the hospital."

". . . You asked her? Why?"

"Because I wanted to see how you would respond when she tried to talk to you, to ask you what had happened. . . . I never saw anybody try so hard to get out of a room as you were trying to get away from that camera. You acted like a whore in church."

"What of it? Why would you care?"

"Because—" She picked up another piece of pizza and took a bite. "—as soon as I saw it, I knew what you were going to do."

"Do tell. And what's that?"

She drank from the tea glass. "Just what you've done. You went right back to planning your suicide. You came out here and cleaned the place up. You wrote more goodbye notes and sealed them. You pulled your yellow beach chair out and left it downstairs—although I'm not exactly sure what you intend to do with it yet."

"So I take it," he said slowly, "you did not really come out here to let me paint you in the nude."

"Oh. So you didn't forget after all." She pushed back from the table and stood. "Where do you want to do this? I certainly don't want to delay your plans any longer than necessary."

It was strange, he thought, as he sat staring at her standing before him. This woman was so beautiful. So different and alluring. She was willing to take her clothes off and allow him to paint her. Why wasn't he leaping to his feet and leading her upstairs?

"Are you sure?"

"Let's do it, Magnus. Unless you're all talk."

He chuckled. "Then come up to my studio."

Magnus stood and walked toward the stairs. Dot followed him silently, several steps behind. She stopped at the door to the studio and watched as he moved about, wordlessly preparing to do her portrait. He closed the floor-to-ceiling blinds on the windows facing the ocean and turned on a series of ceiling and wall lights that illuminated the area where Dot sat on Friday morning when he drew her in charcoal. Light—bright but not overpowering—shone down around his easel. Magnus opened a series of case and set out paint

111

tubes, brushes, sponges and spreading knives. He set a large, clean canvas on the easel.

"You have this down to a routine, don't you?"

He did not look up at her.

"Yesterday you could talk while you worked."

He nodded. "Yesterday I wasn't about to see you naked."

"Is this your first time then?" she asked.

Spontaneously he almost blurted out, "No. But it will be my last." Instead he shook his head and said simply, "No."

"Look, if you don't want to—"

"I do. I do. Very much."

"Then why are you so glum? Where's that sarcastic, irreverent, womanizing misogynist I've come to know and love?"

He stopped arranging his paints and looked at her. "You know, we're not going to do this. I just don't need you busting my chops anymore. I haven't done anything but help you. I caught your goddamn rapists. I helped you put them away without a trial—less than forty-eight hours after they attacked Lisa. I don't know, maybe you think letting me paint you nude is returning the favor in some way. But honestly, I don't need it. It was never about a payback for me."

She stood staring at him. "I have two questions for you. The first one is, what on earth made you want to pain me in the nude? I'm sure you're not lacking for lovely young models."

". . . Why? Because you are spectacular," he said slowly. "You are completely unlike any person I've ever known. I can't put into words how beautiful and different you are. I can't even understand it really. Sometimes, though, the quality I cannot apprehend about somebody flows out of my hand onto the canvas when I paint them. . . . I wanted to try that with you."

Dot seemed to sigh. She slipped off her blue jacket and stepped out of her low-heeled shoes.

"So, do I sit over there?" She motioned toward the chair she sat in the day before.

"Yes."

She began to unbutton her blouse.

"Let me get you a hangar for your clothes."

"They'll be fine here on the carpet. Don't bother."

Magnus sat down. He watched in disbelieving stillness as she took off her blouse and slipped out of her navy skirt and black slip. Dressed only in her bra and panties, her limbs appeared lithe and long to him, her skin silky.

She made no eye contact as she unclasped her black brassiere and pulled it forward over her arms. Her breasts, small and perfectly round, crowned with dainty, dark nipples, transfixed him. And then, unashamed and with no hesitation, Dot pushed down her lacey, black panties and stepped out of them. Magnus gazed at her vagina and felt himself becoming aroused.

Dot went to the chair and sat down. Only then did she look at him.

"I think you said you wanted me to wear a robe or something."

"A drape? No how. No way in a million years do we conceal your charms."

"How do you want me to sit then?"

"Um. So cross your legs and turn away from me just slightly. Now look back at the back of my easel. . . . No." He started to stand. "May I?"

"You are the artist."

The emotion in her voice was different from any that he had heard her express, almost seductive. Magnus had heard her angry and icily distant, casual and even jovial. He had never, though, heard her sound this way.

He went to her. He put his hands gently on her shoulders, positioning them. Her skin was supple and smooth. She moved easily, not resisting his touch. He put a hand beneath her chin and tilted her head slightly away from him.

"Put your far hand on your knee. Right. And your near hand on your hip. Yes. Like that. Can you sit comfortably in this position for a few minutes?"

"I can sit as comfortably in this position as is possible when I'm naked in front of a strange man. Am I supposed to look at you?"

"No. The back of my easel. Just like that. And now open your mouth, as if you thought of something you wanted to say, but you haven't said it yet. . . . Perfect."

He sat down and picked up a number 3 pencil. Swiftly the shape of her head flowed from his hand onto the blank canvas. He stopped for a moment, trying to decide on the basics of the backdrop. When he started to draw again, he glanced up at Dot. As he was roughing in the shape of her body sitting in the chair, he suddenly recognized that her nipples had become erect. Magnus sat, turning the pencil in his hand as he gazed at her. For an instant her eyes flashed to his, then looked away.

He mixed tones of yellow oils until he achieved the color he wanted and used it to create negative space along the left side of her form and in the crook of her arm. For the right side negative space, he blended a still paler yellow that invaded the outline of her face, following the contours of her eyebrow, cheek and chin.

Magnus painted the chair upon which she sat into the image, transforming it to an eggshell white, the color darkening as it moved away from the east light. At the bottom left side of the painting, he created her discarded blue suit, looking used and unneeded. On the floor at the right side, he painted in her navy purse, part way open with her badge sliding out—the exposed portion of the gold shield shining in yellow light.

He paused when he had finished, gazing at his subject again. He blended the tone for her skin and painted her seated form, aware that he was working more slowly. When he painted her breasts, he felt himself becoming aroused again, almost as if he were touching her. He went back and added rich shadows of midnight blue and vermilion.

"Can you sit for a couple more minutes?" he asked. "I'll be finished soon."

"Yes."

Magnus painted her upswept hair, the left side of her head and the shadows beneath her chin. When he formed her face, as he had anticipated, the image flowed from some deep source of recognition within him. It captured the facet of Dot Stipling that lay concealed from her fellow officer and civilians and the media and casual acquaintances. It was the inner morsel of intimate soul that Magnus' inward being had somehow seen, and sought. When he finished her hazel and chocolate eyes and highlighted her lips, he leaned back from the canvas. He had unclothed Dot Stipling in more than one way.

He blended a magenta tone and signed his name in the lower left corner. Immediately she realized that he was done.

"Is it finished?"

He pushed back from the easel in his chair. "Come and see."

114

Magnus closed his eyes—and he didn't know why—when Dot stood. He heard her walk around behind him. There was the delicate aroma he smelled whenever she drew close to him. And then, in her breathing, he heard the same halting sound he had heard the morning before when he had drawn her in charcoal.

"Is that how I look?"

He opened his eyes and sighed, gazing at the portrait. "It doesn't really convey your beauty. . . . Only, I think it does have a little of your essence. I achieved what I wanted to, the most I could, with it."

Then he felt her hands on his shoulders, gently sliding forward down his chest. And the unmistakable, marvelous, maddening feeling of her breasts against his back.

"For someone to paint a woman—me—like this, and say it doesn't equal my beauty, is the finest compliment I've ever received."

Magnus began to stand and turn toward her, expecting that she would pull away. Instead she wrapped her arms around him and, clinging to him, pressed her face and body to his, forcing her tongue into his mouth. He put his arms around her, holding her to himself tightly.

"I want you," he said, taking a breath. "I've wanted you from the instant I saw you at Scotch Bonnet." When she didn't reply, but put her hands on his face and looked into his eyes, he continued. "I can't explain what it was like to see you. I didn't think I'd ever see anyone like you—or paint them—ever again. And the first thing I did that day was put my foot in my mouth."

"Better my tongue," she said, kissing him again. She put one leg, long and firm, behind his and pressed his hips against her. "Let me guess you have a bedroom on this floor as well."

He sucked in his lips, tasting her on them. "Two of them. The master bedroom—king size bed—is across the hall."

"Why don't you show me? I have a hunch about why they named you Magnus and I want to see if I'm right."

She took his hand and they walked around his painting equipment toward the door. Dot stopped and, without letting go of him, reached down for her purse.

He laughed. "Does this have something to do with handcuffs?"

"No." Her voice was as silken as her touch. "It has to do with

115

the condoms I brought along."

"Oh. We can use those if you want. I'll tell you now that I have no diseases. And my ex made me have a vasectomy seven or eight years ago."

She dropped her purse back to the carpet. "Vasectomy, huh? We better check and see if it's working."

Dot led him into the bedroom. Twilight made its way through the sheers on the windows. She sat on the bed, making him stand before her, and began to take off his clothes. And when she had exposed him and he had pulled off his shirt and dropped it on the floor and shed his shoes and socks and stepped out of his pants and underwear, she scooted to the middle of the great bed and watched him.

Inside his head a voice pleaded with him to remain silent, not to spoil this moment.

He leaned forward and down as he crept into the bed, pushing his head gently between her thighs. He put his hands beneath her buttocks, lifting them slightly, and kissed her wet vagina. He covered it with his mouth and tasted it, probed it with his tongue. He felt her tremble and crumple slowly back on the heavy quilt. Then he felt her hand behind his head, pressing him hard against her vulva as her legs opened farther. And she moaned softly, almost sadly.

For a time she moved against his face with a gentle, slow, maddening rhythm. Then she whispered softly, as if someone else might hear.

"Fuck me now, Magnus."

He raised his head and gazed at her, her arms and legs spread, her eyes closed. Magnus crept forward until his knees touched the bottom of her thighs. He raised up at the waist and put his hands on her hips, looking down at their weeping genitals. His member was bowed so hard he did not have to guide it. As he entered her, she made an assenting, whispered sound, like a distant cheer. And, though her legs were wide apart, he felt her inner walls close in on his penis.

Dot was moving, toward him and away, her grip sliding sweetly around the length of him as she whispered, "Make me come."

He leaned close to her, kissing her, one hand on her breast, and he moved against her, into her, in counter rhythm with her, watching the ripples of movement course through her as the orgasm slowly approached. He felt his member pulse and throb as her vagina tightened on it, stopping its motion for an instant. Then he felt the convulsion spread through her as she came—her limbs quivering, her breast and nipple growing hard beneath his grasp, her passage losing its tautness and letting his excited member surge forward. Urgently he put both hands beneath her thin buttocks and forced himself into her again and again. Her body seemed to sense the moment he came, as her inner lips sucked at him again.

She inhaled through her nose, a long, satisfied breath, and said, "Good."

He let himself down on the bed beside her. He studied her face—turned toward him—in the growing darkness, the only sound his ragged breathing.

"It was good, wasn't it," he agreed.

She nodded. "It was a good start. Let's see how you follow up after we finish the pizza."

As he quietly pulled on his jeans and a t-shirt, Magnus gazed down at Dot. Even covered by the sheet, the form of her dark, naked body thrilled him—both as a man and as an artist. He wondered if she would lie still and let him paint her this way. Softly walking down the stairs to the kitchen, he thought of Wyeth and Parrish, artists who repeatedly found beauty and variety in a single model. Dot Stipling, he imagined, could be that compelling muse for him.

East light from the rising sun filled the downstairs. He smiled. His assumption that night before had been that he would never see the sunrise again. Magnus stared out at the gray-green expanse of the ocean as he stood above the stove brewing coffee. He pulled out the sleeve of eggs and a half-pound of bacon, grateful that he had planned on waiting until the very end before trashing his perishables. He could even mix some biscuits, if Dot wanted them.

As the aroma of the coffee filed the kitchen, he headed back up the stairs to wake her and ask what she wanted for breakfast. He was surprised to see her with her clothes on and not in the bedroom but the studio, standing before her portrait.

"What's going to happen to this?" she asked.

He was surprised again—that she knew he was in the doorway watching her. "What?"

117

"You have to promise me that no one will ever see this."

". . . Okay."

"You keep your word, don't you, Magnus?"

"For you? Sure."

"Then say it."

"All right. No one but you or me can ever see your portrait."

She walked toward him and held out her hand, as if they had just negotiated an important contractual agreement. He was taken back by it. Everything about her surprised him this morning. There was a distance in her handshake that reminded him of her aloofness when they first met: touching without touching.

"Want some bacon and eggs? And biscuits? I'm making some egg coffee for you."

"No breakfast for me." The tone of her voice was business-like as well. "I guess I'd better be on my way."

"You working today, Dot?"

"No."

"Well—" He watched her as she took a final look at the painting. "—when can I see you again?"

She turned and walked past him through the door. "Anytime. Just pull out my portrait. There I am, naked."

"No," he followed along behind her. "I mean, when can we get together again? When can we be together, like last night?"

She stopped at the top of the stairs and looked over her shoulder at him. He recognized the professional, cool expression she constantly wore when she was on duty.

"We can't be together again."

". . . What do you mean?"

"Just what I said. It was clear enough."

"Why? But why? Did I do something wrong?"

She smiled and shook her head. "It's who you are. And who I am."

"I don't know what you mean. We're great together. At least I thought so."

"Where can you take me, Magnus? Can I go to all your shows and art extravaganzas? You going to take me home to your momma?"

He cocked his head. "My 'momma' lives in Wisconsin. And, compared to my crazy ex-wife, Mom would be delighted with you."

118

She laughed cynically. "Well I can't see my momma dealing very well with you. But the real question is, where could we be together besides up here? I don't fit anywhere in your world. And you sure don't fit anywhere in mine. We aren't high school kids rebelling against social norms. We're grown adult people who have made our own lives already. And neither of us belongs anywhere near the other."

". . . I thought lovers made their own world together. Doesn't 'love conquer all?'"

She leaned toward him, seemingly startled. Her expression was one of amazement and disbelief—as if he were a suspect in a crime who had just given her a totally absurd alibi. Abruptly she turned started down the stairs. Magnus caught up with her halfway down.

"Dot?"

"Is that what we are, Magnus? After one good fuck? Are we lovers?"

"Well." Despite himself he chuckled. "I'd say we got a pretty damn good start on it."

She had gotten down the stairs, past the kitchen and most of the way to the front door, and she stopped and turned back toward him.

"A start, did you say?"

"Well, yeah! If I didn't think it would make matters worse, I'd invite you back up to my bedroom and we'd lay a little more on the foundation of our relationship."

He couldn't tell what she was thinking as she stared at him.

"So you want us to be lovers?"

"Sure. That's exactly what I want."

"For a lifetime?"

"Yes. Whatever that means. I know we're different. I know we live in different worlds. But, yes, I want us to be lovers. For a lifetime."

"That shouldn't take long, should it?"

"What?"

She walked back into the kitchen, sliding the strap of her purse off her shoulder and setting it on the kitchen table. She leaned against the back of a chair. Magnus didn't understand what was going on with her. He hadn't grasped why she was angry, why she had almost stormed out. And now he didn't know why she had stopped. Apparently it wasn't because he had persuaded her.

"I think your coffee is ready."

The aroma of egg coffee permeated the cottage. Magnus turned off the burner and moved the pot.

"You want a cup?"

"No," she said quietly. She pulled out the chair and sat down. "You don't remember, do you? Last night I told you I had two questions for you. The first one was why you wanted to paint me in the nude. And you gave me this sort of acceptable, Bohemian-artist kind of an answer to that."

"I told you the truth."

"I suppose. It sounded better than just saying you wanted into my panties."

"Well, that would've been true too."

". . . So, Magnus, what was my second question?"

He lifted his empty hands in exasperation. "How should I know?"

"You say you want us to be lifelong lovers. Why would anyone want to be the lover of a man who spends his free time elaborately planning his suicide?"

Magnus straightened. "That's the question?"

"No. I'll get to the question. First I want to know if you think I'm stupid enough to have a love affair with a guy who's trying to kill himself."

". . . I don't—"

"Don't bullshit me," she cut him off. "You have not one but a whole stack of suicide notes on your table by the entry. If I don't miss my guess, you've made detailed instructions for how to divide your estate and provide for your survivors. And you love this beach house. So I'm guessing you don't want to kill yourself inside it. You want your family to feel comfortable in here where you're gone. That's why you went down to Scotch Bonnet. And I'm betting that's why you pulled out that yellow beach chair. You plan to sit on the beach and kill yourself.

"Only I got your .38. And your lucky bullet. So I'm guessing you have a backup plan. Like maybe squirreling away a few dozen of those Phenobarbitals your doctor was prescribing for you before you went into treatment."

He gazed at her in silent astonishment—and no small amount of admiration. She had sleuthed out his intentions almost precisely.

". . . How did you—"

"Oh, come on, Magnus. I may have wandered out of a tobacco patch, but it wasn't yesterday. I do this for a living. And I have to be good at it. There is something I haven't figured out, though. This is my second question from last night. And I want you to drop all pretense and answer it."

"What?"

"Why? Why do you want to die? Why are you so intent on killing yourself?"

His head drooped. At length he stepped to the kitchen cabinet and found a cup. He poured it full of coffee.

Without looking at her, he said, "I did what they told me in treatment. I sobered up just like I was supposed to. But when I did, turned out I was still Magnus Thorsen."

She did not reply, so he continued.

"Magnus Thorsen is a fraud. I went to school and studied art. I learned what is art and what is not. I learned how to create art. . . . And then, I sold out. I'm not an artist. I'm a visual pacifier. A bromide for living room walls of the upper middle class.

"I make thousands of dollars by creating the images of children that yuppie parents wish their kids could be." He shook his head. "So many of my subjects are absolute little shits. Monsters. Under no circumstances can they sit still in a chair for five minutes. I'm lucky if I get them kind of still for ten seconds so I can take a goddamn photograph. Then I tell their moms, 'Okay. That's all I need. You want to come back to see, or shall I ship you the finished painting?'

"And you should see the business dicks and society sluts I paint. I take my time with them. I ask lots of questions while I'm setting up. Not to get the perfect angle, but to listen for their ideal perception of themselves. And that's the way I paint them. I pretend they're captains of industry. New age southern belles."

He blew over the top of the cup and lifted it. The coffee burned his lip.

"I do this all strictly to make money. I make a shit load of money. I'm the reverse Van Gogh. In his lifetime he sold one painting, but created a mountain of real art. In my lifetime I've sold mountains of paintings, but created very little real art. . . . What I did with you last night—before we got in bed, I mean—that's art. That's pretty much the real thing."

121

He sighed. "But I have this awful fantasy that one of my old art professors down in Charleston has a print of a Vermeer and next to it puts up some stylized portrait of some jerk-off I painted. And he points to the print and says, 'Now this is art.' And he points to my original and says, 'This is a hack just paying the rent. Even Norman Rockwell was more invested in art than this guy.'"

He looked at her sharply. "I know how that sounds. It makes me seem incredibly egotistical. But I really did have talent. I really understood and I could create. I could do innovative things. I would have, too. If I had stayed with the gift and developed it instead of selling out. . . ."

She waited for him to go on. "So why did you sell out?"

He shrugged. "Because it was easy, I guess. It was the path of least resistance. There's always somebody willing to pay to see themselves on canvas, especially when I make them look better than they look in real life. Impressing those people. Getting into their billfolds. And lingerie. That was definitely an easier path than trying to create something magnificent—and then hoping that somebody notices, and recognizes it for what it is. . . . Over time, though, taking the low road makes you need to drink. And then, when you can't drink at your own unworthiness anymore, what are you going to do? You get a gun permit and a pint of blended whiskey and go down to Scotch Bonnet.

"Incidentally. You said to me day-before-yesterday that I should be grateful Lisa Faucet was there when I arrived. You said it was probably God's doing because it saved my life."

"I believe I said 'Higher Power,' that maybe your Higher Power was at work. But, yes, I don't see how you can escape the idea that God was behind that coincidence."

"Then God must sanction suicide," he said with a little grin. "If I hadn't been suicidal, if I hadn't been about to blow my brains out, I wouldn't have been there. And Lisa would've died."

She shook her head slowly. "Circular reasoning at its best. So that's it? That's your whiny, pissy reason for wanting to blow your brains out. Your sponsor was right about you. You are a master of feeling sorry for yourself. Totally self-absorbed. You're the largest, slyest, horniest six-year-old I know. With you, even killing yourself is an over-the-top act of selfishness.

"And you're right. You aren't any different. You aren't special.

I've seen so many sad little fucks like you, with educations and careers and the whole world at their feet, who end up feeling sorry for themselves. Then they take pills or they drive into a pylon or they jump off some high structure. They permanently wreck their families and they leave a big-ass mess for poor assholes like me to clean up—all the while thinking they are so clever and cute. I bet every one of those notes is smug as hell."

". . . Not really. A lot of them are sentimental."

Dot scooted back her chair and stood up.

He didn't know what to say to keep her from leaving. "Yeah, you're welcome for the tea and pizza and the entertainment last night, for what it was worth. Not the beginning of something, I guess. I love you too."

She cut her eyes over to him. "That's another thing. You're hell-bent on taking your life, but you say you want a long-term relationship."

"When I'm with you," he replied, "I don't feel like killing myself."

"Well that's a real comfort to a girl, Magnus." She slipped the thin, blue strap of her purse back over her shoulder. "As long as you stay interested in me, I don't have to worry about you shooting yourself. Or poisoning yourself. Of course, if were a thing and I broke off our relationship or we got really mad at one another, there would always be the chance you'll do yourself. So how stupid would I have to be to get into a relationship where, from the very beginning, I'm being held an emotional hostage?"

Magnus stared at her. He had the intuition that she was playing him, that he was wandering into some kind of trap she had cleverly constructed. Only he couldn't yet grasp where she was leading him.

"If I commit to you that I won't kill myself, I won't."

Dot nodded. "Like you committed to your sponsor you wouldn't miss another A.A. meeting? Deals like that are only good as long as the person who makes them doesn't change his mind. Do you think that I think you're not sneaky enough to quietly kill yourself?"

"You've been around me long enough to know that I'm as good as my word. I keep my end of the bargain. Always."

"What about your agreement to take Lisa Faucet for a fish dinner?"

123

"I provided for that," he said indignantly. "I've set aside a gift certificate for Officer Miller to take her to the Blue Pirate. That's the nicest restaurant on the river."

"And how are you going to explain your cop-out suicide to Lisa? This will be a preview of the note you'd leave for me if we were lovers."

". . . I just wrote that my death had nothing to do with her. It was planned before I found her on the beach. I told her I was going to have Officer Miller fulfill my promise because I couldn't be there. But I always do keep my word, Dot. I'll always keep it with you."

She pushed in her chair. "I believe you. That's why you have to destroy my portrait."

"What?"

"You see, you promised me you wouldn't let anyone see it. If anyone did, it would immediately destroy my career and my life, particularly if the artist who painted it committed suicide right after helping me with a murder investigation. How do you think that would look?"

"I understand the position it would put you in. I'm not going to let anyone see it."

"That's because you're going to destroy it. You have to."

"You're crazy, Dot. That may be the finest piece I've ever painted. I'm not destroying it."

She had started toward the door and stopped, looking over her shoulder at him. "Think about this, Magnus. Suppose somebody—anybody—sees that painting. And suppose you're dead. How am I going to explain that?"

"I don't have to have a nude model to paint a nude," he protested. "I paint figures all the time from memory. Like the quarterback kid. There's nothing that says you posed for me. Just that I admired you and imagined what you look like without clothes."

She chuckled. "My portrait is anatomically correct, Magnus. You're very observant. You caught the size and shape of my breasts perfectly. Even my nipples. Suppose I get investigated? 'Lt. Stipling, what kind of relationship did you have with this witness? How did it effect his testimony? What in your interactions contributed to his suicide?'

"Suppose I say you imagined how I look naked and the chief doesn't buy it—which, by the way, he won't. They send some female detective to compare my tits to the painting. I'm humiliated. I'm out of a job. I have no career. Not to mention, having your death on my conscience. I can just hear Anika Brown asking me if there was anything I could've done to prevent you from killing yourself. Of course you wouldn't be there to console me because your ass would be dead."

He had a weary, winded feeling in his chest. "You knew all this before you took off your clothes. . . . Why'd you do it?"

"You put me in bind, Magnus. I just returned the favor." She shook her head. "I watched how you were with Lisa. Sure, I knew you were a womanizer, a chauvinist, a big momma's boy. But I also knew you were softhearted. That you wouldn't intentionally hurt Lisa. And I knew you wouldn't intentionally hurt me. So now you know you can't kill yourself unless you destroy that wonderful painting. You won't hurt me, love. And I'm gambling you won't destroy that portrait. This is my best hope of keeping you alive."

She turned away and walked toward the front door. Magnus followed her.

"If you walk out of my life, if you refuse to be my lover, why should I care what happens to you? I will be dead, like you said. What will it matter to me if someone sees the painting?"

He could see her smiling ironically. "You see, you aren't willing to destroy it, are you? And if you really felt like hurting me, you wouldn't tell me about it. You'd just do it. You said that to try to sway me." She put her hand on the doorknob. "You know, Magnus, you sound like someone who has a lot to live for."

The phone rang. They both gazed toward the kitchen silently. It rang a second time.

"You going to answer that?"

He shook his head. "That's Grady. He wants to tell me what meeting to attend today." There was a third ring. "Then he wants to ask about you. How long you stayed. Did we talk about him."

After the fourth ring, the answering machine clicked on and they listened to Magnus' outgoing message. Then came the live sound of someone quietly listening on the other end, and the distant beeping, busy noises of a hospital room.

"Magnus? This is Lisa. Sorry I'm calling so early. I hope I'm not waking you up. Are you coming today? I know you said you weren't, but I really need someone sane to talk to. When Katie and my mom get together, I just about go crazy. . . .

"Did you see us on TV? Did you see the picture? All the nurses have been coming in from all over the hospital to look at it. Some people I don't even know came in and they want to know how much you charge for a family portrait. You know you left a bunch of your stuff here. Do you want to come get it? Or I can have Katie take it to your studio. Can you call me back? They want to do another surgery on me tomorrow. Can you come over if it's not too far?"

The phone in the hospital room was hung up slowly and the answering machine clicked off. A red number "1" began to flash.

"Sounds like somebody needs you. How conflicted you must be. Poor thing." She grabbed his chin in her right hand, immobilizing his face and kissing him fiercely, forcing her tongue into his mouth and then pushing him away. "I crave you, you bastard. But I'm not stupid. Don't let me interfere with your personal decisions, Magnus. You do what you have to. You have to die with the consequences." Dot pulled the door open. "As for me, I can't be the lover of a guy who hasn't decided for himself whether or not what we had last night is better than self-pity."

Dot pulled the door open and walked out, leaving it ajar. He followed her out, standing at the top of the landing, listening to her steps on the wooden stairs. Then he heard her walking on the gravel below and, gazing down, he watched her emerge from the shadow of the cottage and into the east light.

Charlie Cherry's Ninth Step

Chapter One

So, like a child at last allowed a longed-for privilege, on the last Wednesday of May at 6 in the morning—his rebuilt gun barrel gray Mazda RX7 loaded with a duffel bag of clean clothes, two dozen country music cassettes and his least tool box—Charlie Cherry drove across the Mississippi River bridge from Memphis into Arkansas.

The red, early sun emerging behind him cast brilliant, oddly hued shifting beams of light down Interstate 40 as Roseanne Cash sang love songs above the hum of the old Wankel engine. It seemed to him that the day was made for driving and the car wanted to run.

A farmer plowing in the delta had stopped his ancient Massey Ferguson tractor just south of the highway. As he gunned the engine, jets of black smoke blew open the exhaust cover and drifted across Charlie's path.

"You got a clogged intake, buddy!" Charlie said with a laugh. "You're burning rich. I can smell it from here." And he coursed down the highway without looking back. "You're on your own today."

The miles melted away in the changing of tapes and the climbing sun. He had looped south of Little Rock before he pulled off the interstate for something to eat. When he started south on I-30, he reached into the tape box and pulled out a cassette without looking at it. It slid smoothly into the tape deck. An old George Jones standard began to play:

"He said, 'I'll love you till I die.'

She said, 'Oh, you'll forget in time.'
As the years went slowly by
She still preyed upon his mind."

The rest of the song was lost to him. His thoughts were filled with memories of Madelyn and the little hometown he had not seen in fifteen years.

He saw her on the very first day of school. Madelyn's family had just moved to Melanna at the start of his sophomore year. Watching her became his immediate project. Whenever he went into a class for the first time or walked through a place where a number of kids were gathered, he would look all around for her. His interest was partly from the novelty of having somebody new in a school with less than 300 students who had known each other all their lives, but mostly because he was really drawn to her.

Madelyn was not beautiful, but she was pretty. Her face was a distinctive heart-shaped oval, graced with a small, up-turned nose and surrounded with strawberry blonde hair that cascaded in thick ringlets nearly to her slight shoulders. Sometimes, when the afternoon sun came through the window of Mrs. Tyler's world history class and played upon Madelyn's curls, Charlie could not tell where the sunlight ended and her hair began.

He found himself standing behind her one day in the cafeteria line. For some reason, she turned all the way around toward him. Charlie was already over six-one and her gaze rested just below his adolescent Adam's apple. Her eyes climbed up to his and stopped.

What he said to her, at the moment he had asked and even years later, caused him to cringe with embarrassment. "Is your hair really like that?"

Her eyes blinked, then made a wide, disbelieving circle. "Do you think my mother would ever let me change it?"

In that instant their relationship was set. He was seized by great desire to savor and protect her giddy, frightened innocence. He wanted to touch her, to know how her skin would feel to his fingers. And already he began to dislike her mother. As he watched her short, thick legs scurry away from the food line, the way she slowed as she glanced over her shoulder at him and then giggled as she pressed her head against a girlfriend's shoulder in virginal glory, he knew he was hooked.

128

Charlie Cherry's Ninth Step

Unlike infatuation or lust, feelings with which he was acquainted already, the passion he had for Madelyn was fixed and unchanging. Charlie was bound to her as much by his paternal instincts as by his raging hormones. The series of brief, enticing, frustrating encounters with her that followed caused him to push his feelings back, but also intrigued him and made him all the more determined to capture her attention and affection in some way.

Several weeks after they first spoke, his buddy Gary convinced him to call her and ask her out on a double date. Charlie dialed the number, his hand palsied, hoping his voice wouldn't break when he began to talk. He shouldn't have worried. Her mother answered the phone.

"Hello. May I speak to Madelyn please?"

"Who is this?"

"Uh, Charlie Cherry."

"Well what do you want Madelyn for?"

"Oh. Well," he stammered," I was going to ask if she could go out on a double date with me and—"

"She can't date until she's sixteen." The phone clicked.

Charlie stood dumbly, the receiver still against his ear as if her hanging up called for some response from him. Gently he put the phone down.

Gary asked, "Did you talk to her? What did she say?"

He shrugged, his expression matter-of-fact. "She said she can't go out because her mother is a bitch who chains her to the bed on Friday night."

The next year, when her magical sixteenth birthday arrived, Charlie was dating someone else. He was not the first to take her out. Yet he sensed there was a feeling between them, an unspoken emotional covenant. He was almost afraid to draw too near, to speak too often—as much as one watches a chick hatching from an egg with anticipation, but distance. He had an awareness that a time for the two of them was coming.

In the spring of his junior year his entire class loaded onto two school buses and took a field trip to the Dallas Museum of Fine Art. Charlie and Gary followed the gaggle of girls containing Madelyn onto one bus. As she sat down in a window seat, Gary pushed the girl who started to sit with her back one row and Charlie slid in beside Madelyn.

129

"Can I sit here?"

She didn't say anything. For a moment she didn't even move. Finally she looked over her shoulder at her friend. She covered her mouth, suppressing the giggle he had come to know so well, and blushed crimson. Charlie started to laugh himself and looked away.

He was sitting on the outside edge of the seat as the bus began to move, his long frame as taut as a cocked spring and held in place by the death grip he had on the seat in front of him. Only occasionally did he glance at her. He could not tell by her expression if she were thrilled or mortified, but he was fairly sure that the kids sitting in front of him could feel his heartbeat passing through his arm into their steel bus seat.

They had passed Plano and were almost to Richardson when she said in an almost conspiratorial voice, "Aren't you uncomfortable like that?"

Charlie turned toward her, wondering what she wanted him to say. She pushed herself against the side of the bus to give him as much room as she could. Relaxing his grip, he eased into the seat.

They had not gone another half-mile down Highway 5 when the bus lurched and he was suddenly pressed against her side. As they straightened themselves, Charlie realized that their legs were still touching, from hip to knee. He waited for her to pull away. But she didn't. Neither did he pull away. They sat staring straight ahead, electrically magnetized at their thighs. And all around them the packed, raucous bus was oblivious to the delicious sin they shared.

When the bus pulled onto the lot at Fair Park in Dallas and jostled to a stop, kids started rising immediately, their loudness competing against the teachers at the front trying to quiet them with shouted instructions. Madelyn and Charlie did not move. He wanted to sit there for the whole morning while everyone else went to the museum.

He turned toward her when it became apparent that they would have to get up and leave the bus. Most of the kids were already gone. She stared back at him silently.

"Will you go out with me Friday?"

She nodded. "If my mom will let me."

"She's crazy if she does," he said, "'cause I'm crazy about you."

She smiled. "You're just crazy, Charlie Cherry. Can we get off now?"

Coursing down Interstate 30 toward Texarkana sixteen years after the bus ride, Charlie winced. Most of the memories he had of their relationship after that were painful ones: memories of goofy adolescent mistakes and false macho statements he had made. There had been embarrassing, confusing encounters with Madelyn's mother—whom he could never please under any circumstance. And there had been tears. Madelyn cried when she was angry, sad or afraid—which was a fair bit of the time. She even cried when she was happy. The constant tears always made him feel responsible, if somewhat powerless, and they stirred within him the emotions of grief and guilt.

Charlie wondered if this trip at long last could really exorcise the ghosts of those last days in Melanna. Assuming that he could find Madelyn and atone for what had happened, would he be able to remember those events without hearing the mocking voice of self-reproach that always accompanied them?

Was it the *Big Book* or the *Twelve and Twelve* that Desmond, his sponsor, kept quoting? There was a promise that, if you kept working the program, eventually you would be able to look back on the past and feel no regret. The promise seemed impossible to believe. Yet so many good things, beginning with his being able to put aside the bottle, had happened to him since the first A.A. meeting that it had become almost impossible for him to not be optimistic. He reflected for a moment. Charlie had no idea what to expect on this trip.

Little Rock and Texarkana had changed some, as he had expected. But Dallas was the real surprise. The city sprawled out the interstate to meet him, disguising itself as the few little towns it had swallowed in its bloat. The jarring billboards and businesses and condominiums and housing developments grew progressively thicker and closer the further he drove.

Charlie recognized none of it.

Highway markers, it seemed to him, had become signs pointing to the crime scenes, the place where the locations and sweet history of his youth had been gobbled. Nothing but Lake Ray Hubbard was familiar to him. Giant, gravestone-like apartments had crowded even to the water's edge.

He saw it as desecration and asked himself silently why no one had done anything to stop it. Almost immediately the irony came to him: this was prosperity, progress. Lots of local folks, as well as quite a few outsiders, must've made money off this swelling. And after all, it was no concern of his. Certainly not his business. He didn't even live around here anymore.

"Grant me the serenity to accept the things I cannot change. . . .

He followed I-30 toward downtown Dallas, watching for an exit that would put him on old US 75 headed north toward Melanna. By the time he saw the oddly shaped Dallas skyline, the traffic had slowed him to the point that he was driving in third and often second gear. Inching up each hill, around each curve, slowly seeing each new vista, he expected to arrive at the wreck or construction that had the road back up so badly. But he never came upon it. Eventually it dawned on him that this was a normal flow, the way things always were. By the time he passed Fair Park, something that seemed at least remotely familiar to him, and he saw the sign for the exit ahead and he had been reduced to stop-and-go traffic.

The traffic eased as he exited onto the Central Expressway North ramp. He was able for a moment to get the Mazda back up to fourth gear. Within a quarter mile he was back to creeping along.

Charlie began to feel impatient. When he realized it, he experienced an immediate surge of joy. He had been crawling through bumper-to-bumper traffic, heavy exhaust fumes, blasting horns and rising heat for miles—and only now was he getting impatient.

"Shit. I guess the program does work," he muttered.

He had seen the barbeque sign and decided to exit half-a-mile— two minutes—before he got to the ramp. The car zipped off the roadway as if newly freed. He pulled onto the parking lot and got out, unfolding slowly to six feet and four inches.

"Lord, that's a long ride in a squatty little car."

The inside of the barbeque house was dark, cool and deserted. He could tell from the sweet, strong smell of the sauce that the meat would taste good.

A man wearing an apron was sitting alone, reading a newspaper. He lowered his paper only slightly and looked over the top at Charlie.

"You open?"

"Sure." The man, who had a thick, Middle Eastern accent,

hadn't moved. "What do you want?"

"Uh. . . . You got ribs?"

"You bet."

"A rib plate. Cole slaw and pinto beans. Iced tea. And extra sauce on them ribs."

"You bet."

Charlie watched the man scurry behind the counter. He was young, in his late twenties.

"How 'bout pecan pie?" the cook called out. "A slice for after the meal?"

"No thanks."

Charlie started toward the cash register at the end of the service line, but the man waved him away.

"Naw. Sit down. I'll bring it to you. What do you want in your tea?"

"Nothing."

He sat down at a table facing the blaring plate glass window. The mid afternoon sun, presiding over the skyline, made the inside of the restaurant dark. Charlie looked down on the Central Expressway traffic sliding past him in unbroken flow, then glanced at his watch.

"Why are you having rush hour traffic when it's only 3:30?" he asked.

"What rush hour?" The cook was picking up the tray and carrying it to him. "That's all the time. Three in the morning, still bumper-to-bumper." He set the tray in front of Charlie.

"Hey, man," Charlie said. "I told you I didn't want no pie."

He gave him the same waving-away motion. "You don't like it, don't pay for it." He sat down at the nearest table. "The traffic is really better today than usual."

"Better?"

The ribs had a lot of meat on them, he thought, and the flavor was as good as the aroma had suggested.

"You bet. Less honking today?"

"Honking?"

He nodded vigorously. "Sometimes sounds like geese."

"Well," he said around a mouthful of slaw, "sure has changed."

"You from around here?"

Charlie shrugged. "I used to think so. Lived here until fifteen—

sixteen-years-ago. But nothing is the same."

The cook pursed his lips, his shaggy black eyebrows making a vee. "Too many Yankees."

Charlie laughed. "What are you talking about? You aren't from around here. I'm guessing you're . . . Lebanese."

The cook straightened. "My god. Yes. I'm Lebanese. You are the first person who ever knew. How did you know that?"

Charlie shoveled in a mouthful of beans. "In the Navy we had a Lebanese guy on the ship. Something about the shape of your face. A little rounder, maybe?"

"Everybody here thinks I am Iranian or Iraqi. God at the insults I get. 'Go back to Baghdad, camel jockey.' Some guy down at the grocery store calls me a 'diaper head' every time he sees me, as if I didn't understand what he was saying."

"So why do you keep going back and taking it?"

"Because I get even. I tell him in one of several languages he does not understand that he is an ignorant son-of-a-bitch. His mother whored with a goat." He held out his hand. "Bobby Hadad."

Charlie raised his hand to show it was covered with grease from the ribs.

"Aw, come on," Hadad said. "I work in this all day."

Charlie shook his hand. "Charlie Cherry."

"Pleased to meet you. Welcome back to Dallas."

He laughed. "Well, really I'm from Melanna, little town north of here."

"Yeah, I know. I go by it when I go to Lake Texoma fishing for stripers."

"You do, huh?" He dug at a string of meat wedged in his jaw teeth with a fingernail. "How long does it take you to get there? Hey, isn't old Highway 5 right around here?"

"Five?"

"Yeah. The old state highway. What'd we call it? Greenville Avenue."

"Greenville? You bet. About maybe two blocks east." He waved toward the back of the restaurant.

"Good. Well, I'll just take it."

"You taking Greenville Avenue all the way to Melanna?"

"Still goes through, don't it?"

"My god. I guess."

134

"Well. . . . Maybe I'll see some familiar terrain. I've got lots of history up and down that road." He studied Hadad's dark, foreign face. "It's strange, isn't it? I'm from around here, but I don't know this place at all. You know all about it, but you're from the other side of the world. If you don't mind me asking, what brought you here?"

Hadad smiled. "A little death in the family. My wife's brothers say they are going to kill me."

"No shit. Why's that?"

"I, on one occasion, knocked the hell out of their sister," he smiled, "my wife."

"They wouldn't let you say you were sorry and you wouldn't do it again?"

"Sorry? Hell, I wouldn't apologize. The bitch. She had it coming. So damned spoiled. Baby of family. Little princess, she thinks. 'Give me this. Give me this.' Finally I got tired. 'Grow up,' I say. She hit me. I hit back."

"You hurt her?"

"Not bad enough! She ran to her family, screaming, yelling, crying. My god, they came after me to kill me. Assholes meant it too. So my family got money together. They sent me here."

The tea was bitter. Yesterday's.

"How long you been here?"

"Six years."

"Ever think of going back?"

"No." Hadad shook his head and dropped his chin. "Assholes. Just try to kill me again."

"Yep." He smacked his lips inadvertently. "It's easier to keep going forward with a grudge than to back out of it. So, you miss her?"

He lifted his head, his eyes bright. "My wife? You bet. She was as beautiful as anyone you ever see. Why she married me who knows. So her brothers would have convenient person to hate, I guess."

"Well." Charlie wiped his fingers on a paper napkin. He dropped it and reached for another. "Did you ever think of bringing her over here? You know? Get her away from her family. Have a second chance at life."

Hadad thought about it. Slowly he shook his head.

"She would never leave. She would be too afraid. Over here, she would not know how to be."

"Not if you don't give the chance."

He looked up at Charlie. His eyes narrowed and the suspicion in his voice overwhelmed the community between them. "Why are you so concerned about my wife? Maybe for the same reason you guess I'm Lebanese?"

Charlie eased back in his chair, sitting on his tailbone like a teenager. "Get a grip on reality there, Lebanon. I don't give a shit what happens between you and your old lady. It's sure as hell none of my business. I could care less whether or not you ever see her again. What I'm getting at is, anybody can see that you ain't ever going to get on with your life 'til you get over her."

Slowly Hadad's expression became conspiratorial. He wagged his finger at Charlie.

"That's why you came back, isn't it? History with a girl. A score to settle, maybe."

Charlie pushed the plate of spent ribs away and pulled the pie toward him.

"Am I right?"

The pie was good. There were plenty of pecans and the ones on top had a smoky flavor. He cleared his throat and took another swallow of the bitter tea.

"I'm to a new place in my life, buddy," he said. "I don't bullshit no more. You was straight with me, so here's my deal: I'm coming back to find the girl I married when I was a teenager. There was a— misunderstanding, and we got separated. I got to find out if I'm still married. A month ago only two people in the whole world knew that. Now I'm telling short-order cooks. And, yeah, I got a couple scores to settle."

"Her brothers?"

He laughed. "Her uncle. And I want to tell you something, buddy. You do a little thinking yourself about how you got treated before you came here. You go back and it'll be interesting to see whether it's you or her brothers who have reason to be afraid."

Hadad was thinking again. He took a big breath.

"No. I have to let the past go. The past is only ghosts. Not life."

"Yeah?" Charlie made a fist in the air. "I've found that sometimes the past has got you by the balls." He dropped the fork onto the plate and stood up. "And if a ghost is real enough to grab your privates, it's real enough to kill you."

Hadad got up and started toward the cash register. "Yeah. Sure. Good luck killing a ghost." He rang some numbers into the old-fashioned register and the drawer rang open.

"Seven fifty-seven. No charge for the pie."

"Ah, go ahead. Put it on there. It was good."

"No, no. Good conversation—good pie. Good swap."

He gave him a ten. "Fair enough. Keep the change. You say Greenville Avenue is a couple blocks East?"

"First light. You bet. How long you staying here?"

"Oh, a week or two." He stretched and started for the door. "Depends on how long it takes me to find everybody I need to."

"Good. Come back. Show me your ghost skin."

Charlie smiled as he opened the door, but he didn't look back.

Chapter Two

Highway 5 still ran contiguously all the way from Dallas to Melanna. Only, to Charlie, it's meandering, stop-and-go path through northeast Dallas, Richardson, Plano and Allen was a maddening tour of once known old parks, intersections and landmarks wearing the disguises of time and change.

McKinney was less altered. The county courthouse and jail he had unwillingly toured when it was new seemed to have settled and shrunk, but were still familiar to him. The squatty buildings and pitted streets gave him a good, familiar feeling. The red light on the highway, just a block east of the old cotton mill and the railroad tracks, still took forever to cycle through the colors. And sitting there waiting and looking around, he didn't particularly want it to change. He might have been in high school again. If the light became green, it seemed to him, it might allow the metastases of the big city to corrupt the heart of the little county seat as well.

But, inevitably, the light did turn green, and he went slowly through the intersection. Half a mile down the road he came to the tiny motel where he and Madelyn had gone on the afternoon they had gotten married. Charlie was amazed to see that it was still in business. He pulled onto the parking lot and stopped the Mazda in front of the cottage marked "2," a place of great historical value to him.

That night he did what he and his young wife had never done together: sleep through the night in a motel room. And since there was no phone in the room—no television or radio—he slept without waking until 7:30 on Thursday morning, two hours longer than was his custom. Oh well, he shrugged, he was on vacation.

Pastor Werner had continually thumbed the pliable edge of the small, black book he held. Charlie had wondered if it were a Bible, or perhaps some sort of prayer book. Throughout their hour together, the pastor had seemed the slightest bit nervous and ready for Charlie to be finished sharing his Fifth Step.

Toward the end he asked, "Is there anything else?"

"Well, Pastor," Charlie said. *"I've told you about almost everything. All that leaves is the big thing."*

The minister's eyebrows arched above his gray glasses before he smiled and chuckled. "The 'big thing,' eh? That sounds important."

"Yeah." Charlie looked down and nodded. "I guess that's why I saved it for last. I have this feeling that this behind a lot of my drinking. This is what started it all for me."

He slid down in his chair until he was sitting on his tailbone, his long legs bent double and his knees pressed against the underside of the table between them. He leaned his head back and studied the white acoustic tiles of the ceiling.

"You remember me saying that I went to high school in a little North Texas town?"

"Mel—"

"Melanna, yeah. Well, in the middle of my senior year, my dad took a job up in Kansas. Wichita. Since I was on the baseball team and only needed a semester to graduate, we made arrangements for me to stay in Melanna. I mostly lived in the back of the service station where I worked. You remember about the guy I stole the $20 from?"

"Your boss? Tommy?"

"Yeah. Tommy Thomas. He was my boss. He had a room in the back of the station. I usually went to the café for breakfast and, when I wasn't working, I had supper with my buddy Gary. His mom could take me or leave me, so I tried not to wear out my welcome.

"About that time—" he cleared his throat, "—I was dating a girl I was pretty attached to."

"Yes," the minister replied. "I expect you were."

He glanced at Pastor Werner. "Why do you say that?"

"Well, because she's the first woman you've told me about besides your mother who you didn't refer to as 'chick.'"

"Oh." He laughed easily. "Well, she was special to me. Her name was Madelyn Stewart. She was as cute as a button, and we just sort of gravitated to one another. Her folks were real controlling people. Especially her mother. She just scrutinized the hell out of Madelyn. So she had a kind of miserable home life. And of course mine was non-existent." He shrugged. "We found a lot of comfort with each other.

139

"I realize now it was, what do you call it, a 'co-dependent' relationship, you know, kind of immature. But at the time, it was the deepest thing I've ever felt. The best thing I could imagine. I remember just aching for her."

"Puppy love is real to the puppy, eh?"

"Yeah. Well, in the natural order of things, we got to the point in the spring of my senior year where we wanted to make love. And it wasn't just me pressing her, either. We both wanted it. Madelyn was a very moral person. God knows I was trying to be too, but we could both see where things were going. We wanted to be responsible. So Madelyn went to a girlfriend's doctor in Allen, just south of McKinney, and got some birth control pills.

"So we held off for a month or so and then we made love," he said slowly and sighed. *"Afterwards she was really torn up. What would her mother think? She should've waited and got married. And so on. So I said, 'Good Lord, Madelyn. I love you. Let's get married.'"*

Charlie shook his head. He scooted his chair back and stood up. Pushing his hands into the pockets of his jeans, he turned away from Pastor Werner and looked out the window of the study onto the church playground.

"I don't remember exactly how we pulled it off. It was a Wednesday, I remember, and somehow we got out of school in the morning and went way over to a little county seat town called Rockwall. Somehow we got a marriage license." He shook his head. *"Hell, it's something I'd never even try in a million years now that I'm grown. But we went down the hall in the courthouse to the J.P. and got married. Then we went to the motel in McKinney—to make it official, I guess. We were back in Melanna just after school let out."*

It was raining outside. The playground was deserted. Through the wrought iron fence, Charlie could see the white sign by the street: *"Redeemer Luther Church, LCMS, Lawrence Werner, Pastor."*

"We went the next two months without telling a soul. Madelyn would cry. Oh, what had we done? How could she ever tell her mother? Her parents would get it annulled. And I would stand up, real macho, and say, 'I'll go tell you folks, Madelyn. I'm not afraid. I'm proud we were responsible enough to get married.' But I'll tell

you, Pastor," he turned back toward him, *"I never argued too much when she said to keep it a secret, because her old lady was crazy. I was a little afraid of her. There was no reasoning with her. Her dad, now, he was just sort of fat and quiet, like an old house cat. But her mom—that was one loony woman. She had the strangest, strictest rules you ever heard. Madelyn could only see me twice a week, for one hour. Well, naturally, we got around that. But it wasn't easy. Her old lady was the momma-dog-from-hell, and she checked up on Madelyn all the time. It was just something you had to anticipate.*

"Eventually, about graduation, we figured out a plan. I was going to go into the service while Madelyn stayed with her folks. Then, after I got stationed somewhere and got a little money together, I was going to send for her. She was just going to come wherever I was, then write her folks and tell them that we had been married all along." He leaned against the wall, gauging the minister's expression. *"Not too grown up, huh?"*

"So her mother found out?"

"No." He shook his head. *"Nobody ever found out. To this day, you are the only person I've ever told. I haven't even told my sponsor."*

"What happened to Madelyn?"

Charlie pulled out the chair and sat back down.

"Pastor, we got tricked. Both of us. See, there was this girl in our graduating class named Arletta. She was sort of a—semi-bimbo, I guess. She went around seducing guys. Any poor sucker who caught her eye, she'd go for him. Then, two weeks or a month later, she'd ditch him like a used rub—uh, like a dirty shirt."

"I know the type," Pastor Werner nodded.

"About the only thing we could figure out that attracted her to a guy was if he had a girlfriend already and had never shown any interest in Arletta."

"Oh yes, I definitely know that type."

"Well, unfortunately that was me. Right after—and I mean the day after—I graduated, I went down and signed up for the Navy. They had this deal where I was going to leave for boot camp in a couple weeks and eventually I'd be stationed in Virginia. Madelyn was excited and scared. I was excited and scared. It looked for all the world like our plan was actually going to work. What was weird: my buddy Gary had also signed up for the Navy. We were going to

boot camp together, but he still had no idea that Madelyn and I were married. We had all these people we were going to tell.

"So it gets down to about three or four days before we're supposed to leave. It's a Saturday afternoon early in June and Arletta pulls into the service station. In those days we still gave full service. So I go out and she asks me to fill up her car. So I fill it. Then she asks me to check the oil. I check the oil. It's fine. 'Check the air in the tires.' I check the air in every one of her damn tires. Seems like there was something else she wanted me to do, but by this time I suspect that she's jerking me around. I just don't know what she's up to.

"So she sort of leans back from her window and says, 'Charlie, could you look at this.' I go over to her window. She keeps looking out the passenger's window, I remember. And she says, 'What is this red light on my dashboard?' I think, well, why would she have a red light on her dashboard, since the car's not even running? I bend down to look in and she wraps both arms around my neck and gives me a big old kiss—I mean tongue and all. I pushed her away and backed up and asked her what she thought she was doing. She gives me a little grin and says, 'Call me later, Charlie.'

"About an hour later—" something was in his throat. He coughed, trying to clear it away. "—You know, in a little town like that, gossip travels at the speed of light. Couldn't have been an hour later my buddy Gary calls me. All hell is breaking loose over at Madelyn's house. She or one of her girlfriends saw me making out with Arletta.

"Damn it to hell! The minute I heard it, I knew what Arletta had done. See, right across the street from the service station was this mom-and-pop grocery store. Somehow Arletta tricked either Madelyn or one of her friends into going over to that store to spy on me. Then she just waited until they pulled up and gave me a big kiss. She wanted to break us up! She wanted Madelyn to think I was fooling around on her."

He cocked his head, like a dog hearing an unfamiliar noise. "Why did she do that, Pastor? I mean, I'm sure I've done a low-down thing or two. You just heard my Fifth Step. But I've never heard of a guy doing something like that. Seems like only chicks do that sort of stuff."

Pastor Werner nodded. "Charlie, I've done many, many Fifth

Charlie Cherry's Ninth Step

Steps since we began having the program here at Redeemer. I've heard a multitude of unexplainable wrongs, and I think you're onto something there," he said. *"We have a lot of teenagers here in the church too, and never a homecoming or a prom goes by without me hearing gossip about a young lady who's just heartbroken because another girl has been passing rumors about her, saying she's pregnant or that she's giving sexual favors to a whole gang of boys."*

He nodded. *"Why? Why do they do that, Pastor?"*

"Well, I don't know. Always has seemed to me that adolescent boys go to break your head and girls go to break your heart."

He nodded. *"When Arletta did it to me, I just freaked. I had to go see Madelyn right then and tell her what had happened. I begged Gary to come to the station and take over for me. He worked there too. I just needed half-an-hour.*

"He came right then. I jumped in the service truck and tore off to Madelyn's house. When I pulled up in front and stopped, Madelyn's uncle came out." He turned his gaze back to the window. *"He wasn't really her uncle. He was married to her sister. The guy was named Sloan Witt. I tried to walk past him. . . . He was just looking for a reason to start a fight, Pastor. He was high or drunk, or both. He beat me up pretty bad. Yeah, I tried to fight back, but he was just too much. I ended up crawling back to the truck. The whole time he's yelling at me, 'We know what you did! She don't want to see you! Get outa here!'"*

Charlie sat silently, contemplating the table between them. "I was hurt pretty bad. Six years of football and a lifetime of fistfights, but I'd never been hurt that bad. I got back to the station and Gary took a look at me. He locked the door right away and drove me down to the emergency room in McKinney. And when they saw me down there, they called the sheriff and sent deputies up to arrest Witt. He was already gone. Back to Wichita Falls, I guess. Later . . . I found out he had taken Madelyn with him. I didn't know it, but I had seen her for the last time."

The minister waited, listening for Charlie to continue. Finally he said, *"You know she didn't want him to do that to you, don't you, Charlie? That seems rather extreme for one kiss."*

He smiled. *"I know that. Witt was an extreme guy. I figure he was just taking advantage of her being upset. It gave him a chance to let some of his natural meanness out. . . . Still, it has bothered me all these years that I never set the record straight with Madelyn. All this time and she must still be thinking that I was carrying on with that two-bit whore."*

"You never wrote her or—"

"Pastor, I went into the Navy. Just like I was. Broken nose, sprained butt, cracked ribs, concussion, black-and-blue. Navy loved me. I don't remember much about the next few days. Gary loaded me up on the day I was supposed to join just to take me down and show them I was too busted up. They took me anyway. Hell, I was a warm body and they didn't care.

"And I never saw Melanna or Arletta or any of them people again." He sighed. "I guess it goes without saying that my attitude toward the whole thing over the years has not been conducive to good mental health. This has been in the back of my mind ever since."

Pastor Werner thumbed the pages of the little book. *"Sure enough, Charlie, that is the big one. It's easy for me to understand how a situation like that—especially unresolved for so many years—can stay in your thoughts and contribute to your drinking."* When Charlie didn't respond, he continued. He began to sound as if he were reciting a speech he had given before. *"Events like these we have discussed are quite difficult for us to reconcile within ourselves. But I believe that sharing all this with another person— as you have with me today—has begun the process of healing and has given you the opportunity to forgive yourself and to put all of these episodes behind you. You will find, I believe, the past with all its regrets and wrongdoing has already begun to lose its power over you."*

Charlie eased his chair slowly forward until all four legs were on the floor. *"Put it all behind me? Tell me something, Pastor, isn't there another step—two or three on down the list—where you go back to anyone you've hurt and make it up to them?"*

He nodded. *"The Ninth Step."*

"Well, doesn't this sound like a 'ninth stepper' to you?"

The minister arched his eyebrows. *"Hmm. You want to make amends to Madelyn for never telling her about Arletta's trick. That's very understandable, Charlie. Perhaps it would help put the matter to rest fully in your mind. But how would you go about making*

144

amends? Do you even know what became of Madelyn?"

He took a breath. *"No. Not really. I know she never went back to Melanna. Gary kept writing his folks over the years and always kept me in touch with what they told him about the town and the gossip. It wasn't long after Gary and I left that her parents moved out of town."* He shrugged. *"I can't help thinking, though, that I could track her down if I had the chance. Somebody around there would know something. Or I could go over to Wichita Falls and look up Witt."*

"Uh huh." Pastor Werner smiled slyly. *"You feel as if you owe him a visit, do you?"*

Charlie exchanged glances with him. *"Let's face it, Pastor. I'm not a kid who can be taken advantage of by a drunk bully anymore."*

"So you want to repay him for the wrong he did you?"

He shook his head. *"My sponsor tells me I'm not supposed to lie if this program is going to work for me. I have to admit that on more than one occasion I've thought about getting even with Sloan Witt."*

"If you were going to turn this into part of your Ninth Step," the pastor said, *"a big question to ask yourself would be whether or not you would be doing it to make amends to Madelyn for the unresolved relationship, or if it were truly to pay this Witt character back for the beating he gave you."*

Charlie felt a slight drop of his jaw. *"Pastor, don't you get it? Sloan Witt aside, for all I know, I'm married. Somewhere out there I may still have a wife. How can I do anything permanent with my life until that's settled? If you were me, wouldn't you have to know?"*

Pastor Werner considered his questions. *"I suppose I would have to find out, yes. And find out how to . . . make everything right. My best advice, Charlie, is to talk this over with your sponsor. Who is your sponsor?"*

"Desmond. You know Desmond, don't you?"

The pastor nodded and smiled. *"Yes, I do. He should be able to give you some wisdom."*

Chapter Three

After all the revised places of his youth through which he had passed, Melanna was the least changed.

Not that it looked the same. The buildings seemed to him to be miniatures, little models of the houses and shops that were in Melanna when he left it, sitting in exactly the same positions their real-life counterparts once held. The streets were narrower and the blocks shorter. Even the trees were smaller.

In almost the same instant he entered the town he came to its heart: the intersection of a state highway and a farm-to-market road, with Melanna's one signal flashing red in four directions, as if to ward off the encroachment of progress. Was it worse, he wondered, to experience the cancerous sprawl of the big cities, or to endure the unchanging timelessness of his hometown?

And there on the northwest corner of the intersection was Tommy Thomas' Texaco Station.

Charlie pulled up the driveway and stopped beside the '78 Chevy pickup that he had driven down so many county roads—fixing flats, jumpstarting cars and trucks and tractors, restoring stranded motorists to their dead vehicles—with a five gallon gas can and the impatience of adolescence. He got out and stood for a moment looking into the dusty cab. Tommy still had not gotten a radio for it.

The acrid, rich smell of gasoline swelled his nostrils as he walked across the driveway to the portico. A black rubber bell hose was stretched in front of the pumps. Tommy still gave full service.

Beneath the overhang was an ancient Monte Carlo, the hood up and protruding beneath it were the voluminous green coveralls of Tommy Thomas. Even though all he could see was Tommy's behind, shifting from side-to-side with some unseen mechanical effort, still Charlie had no doubt it was his old boss.

"What are you working on, Tommy?"

The behind quit wiggling. A multi-chinned, frustrated face peered back at him. There was recognition and surprise.

"Why Charlie Cherry! I'll be damned."

Tommy dropped a socket wrench on the air breather with a clang. He shook Charlie's hand vigorously, repeating to himself, "I'll be damned."

"Tommy, how you doing?"

"Hand-to-mouth. Same as always. Haven't had any good help since you left."

In the daylight Charlie could see that Tommy's hair had turned completely silver. He great, round belly hung a bit lower.

"Is that right? I distinctly remember you telling me and Gary that neither of us was worth a shit."

Tommy gave a hearty laugh. "I did, huh? Well these boys today are worth a shit less. By god, it's good seeing you, Charlie. What are you doing these days? Where are you living?"

"Well." He looked down. "I'm in Memphis, Tennessee. Been there pretty much since I got out of the Navy."

"Playing and singing in a rock band, I guess."

Charlie laughed. Not until that moment had he remembered the way he had boasted during his high school years that he would be a rock star.

"Ah, geez. I completely forgot about that. No. No, believe it or not, Tommy, I run a shop that repairs and overhauls diesel engines."

"You're kidding," Tommy said, a note of good-natured disbelief in his voice. "Hell, I couldn't even get you to do oil changes for me. I don't think you ever did figure out how to use a wrench."

"Well, credit the Navy for that. They said they had no need for a guitar picker, but they had a shortage of diesel mechanics."

"So you're running your own shop."

"I'm the manager. Worked my way up. They tell me I run the best diesel house in Memphis."

Tommy gestured over his shoulder. "What do you know about fan belts on old eight-cylinder Chevys?"

"Is that what you're doing to it." He leaned against the grill of the car, his eyes adjusting to the darkness beneath the hood.

Tommy leaned over the fender, picking up the wrench. "Somebody told me that you could use the air conditioner belt for the fan on this engine, that they was the same size. But of course they're not. So I had to get a new one, and it's a tight fit. When I get the alternator pushed down, I need an extra hand to get the belt on."

147

Charlie took the tire tool lying on the breather and forced the alternator down. Wordlessly Tommy slipped the belt into place.

"Thanks."

"My pleasure."

Charlie pried the alternator away from the engine block as his old boss bolted it tight.

"You wouldn't want to take the air conditioner belt off anyway, would you? With summer coming on?"

"Shit. The A/C on this old derelict hasn't worked in years."

"Whose is it?"

"Old man Hubbard."

"Good god. Is he still living? I'm surprised he can still drive."

"He don't." Tommy grimaced, forcing a bolt as tight as it would go. "His niece drives him. But hell, she must be seventy-five herself. Not a lick of sense. They threw the belt off of this heap last evening about five miles out of town. Still drove it on in, though, car smoking and chugging."

"Probably cracked the block."

"I wish they would. Give me a chance to junk this bitch. I work on it once a week."

Charlie looked at the widespread engine, simple and wonderfully obsolete. "You don't see many of these big old V-8's anymore."

"Round here you do. Lot more of these around here than that slanty-eyed Datsun you whooped up in." He motioned over his shoulder toward Charlie's car.

"It's a Mazda."

"They're all Yokohama specials to me, buddy. What's worse is those European, high-dollar jobs. Once a week somebody comes in here with a $50,000 car needing a part for it. I have to tell you, I don't have much time for 'em."

"Now let me get this straight, Tommy. You waste all your time fixing these broken-down, piece-of-shit, falling-apart American dinosaurs, but you hate the foreign jobs that'll last forever?"

Tommy finished tightening the last bolt. Without straightening, he said, "I can't work on imports, Charlie. I raise the hood and I just can't figure out what they're doing. I even invested in a good set of metric wrenches, and I still can't fix 'em." He stood up. "What about you, Charlie? What brings you back here? Just visiting?"

Charlie shrugged. "Yeah, sorta. I had a little vacation time saved up. I guess I haven't been back here since I joined the Navy. Thought I'd see what's happened. For a while I was able to keep up because Gary's folks wrote him all the time. Then they moved down to Dallas."

"Where is old Gary?"

"Uh—parts unknown. We got discharged about the same time, and we traveled to Memphis and both stayed there until about two or three years ago. Then we had a little falling out. I lost track of him."

"Oh. Sorry to hear that. You two were buddies for sure."

"Yeah." He nodded. "I guess folks change with time. Anyway, I been real curious about some of the people around here I knew. Some I'd like to catch up with. A little unfinished business here and there I need to straighten up. I was wondering if maybe you can help me fill in some of the blanks? Tell me what happened to different ones?"

"Will if I can."

"Well, uh," Charlie swallowed hard, something sticking in his throat. "Fact is, you're one of those folks I needed to see."

"Me?"

"Yeah. Tommy, whenever I was working for you, I was honest pretty much all the time. I never took anything that didn't belong to me from the station. I didn't pocket any money either."

Tommy squinted at him in the morning sunlight.

"Only one time—" he held up a single finger "—I messed up. John Barnes came in late on evening. I'd already counted the money and shut off the lights and everything. He begged me into unlocking the pump and filling both tanks on that four-wheel drive Ford of his. Then he wanted something else. Anti-freeze or something.

"Anyway." His nostrils seemed to grow tight and dry. "It came to nineteen dollars and odd cents. I was going to open the cash drop and get his change, but he told me to keep it. So I just put the twenty in my pocket. The next day I meant to ring it up and somehow I never got around to it. So I never gave it back. What it boils down to is, I took twenty bucks from you that I never repaid."

Tommy's curious expression—and his stare—had not changed. The feeling was growing in Charlie that their friendly reunion was at an end.

149

"Part of why I came back was to pay you back. I wanted to apologize and give you the twenty and make amends anyway I can."

Almost imperceptible flash of surprise crossed Tommy's face. "Amends?" He leaned forward slightly, studying Charlie as if he were seeing something amazing for the first time. "My lord! You're doing a Ninth Step."

Charlie felt the same shock seize him. "You're in the program too?"

" . . . I might be a friend of Bill W."

Once again, slowly, they shook hands. They stood at arm's length, their hands joined, silently studying each other. Charlie took out his billfold and produced a twenty-dollar bill.

"It doesn't have the fifteen years' interest on it, but here's what I stole from you."

Tommy reached out and covered the bill with his hand and crumpled it as if extinguishing a flame.

"If this is part of your Ninth Step, I'll take it. Now there doesn't need to be anything come between us." He nodded toward the glass windows of the service station. "Let's go in here and sit down."

They pulled two chairs side-by-side and sat looking across the highway intersection the way they had long before, when Charlie was a kid and Tommy told him stories of the US Army and Japanese brothels.

"Charlie," he edged his chair closer, "I've owned this station since 1962. No telling how many kids I've had work for me—some of them pretty good. But you were the best. And I'm not just saying that. If twenty bucks was all you stole, you were about the most honest."

"Well," he sighed, "it's been on my mind all these years."

"Now your buddy Gary robbed me blind."

"Gary?" There was disbelief in his voice.

"Oh yeah. He wasn't the worst I've had, but I did catch him several times. The only reason I didn't fire him the last time was that you all were fixing to go into the service. He didn't want to get into trouble with his parents and he was worried about what you might think of him."

Charlie shook his head. "What I thought of him? Always seemed like to me that he was the one of us who had his shit together."

150

"Things aren't always the way they seem with folks, are they?"

"Guess not. For instance, Tommy, it surprised the hell out of me when you said you were in the program."

He nodded, a little grin pulling at the edges of his mouth. "Same way I felt about you. How long you been in?"

"Nine months. You?"

"Eleven years."

"Eleven years. . . . Long time to stay sober."

He held up a single finger. "You do it one day at a time."

"Were you drinking when I worked for you? 'Cause I sure never knew it."

"Oh yeah. About a year after I got the station, my first wife, Loretta, left me. I always drank, but about then it hit overdrive."

"I never saw a bottle or saw you drunk or even smelled it on you."

"Well, I kept it together pretty good," Tommy said. "I was what they call a 'high functioning' drunk. About once a month I'd drive down to Dallas and buy a case of blended whiskey. Whatever was on sale. Mostly I drank after I went home in the evenings. I could hold out all day, as long as I knew I had a bottle waiting for me when I got home."

"How'd you get into the program."

"Short miracle." He settled in his chair. "Every weekend—as long as I had somebody running the station for me, I'd tie on a real bender. Get absolutely zipped. One Monday morning I was in here pumping gas, hung over, gritting my teeth every time the bell rang. I had the shakes bad that day. And in came this little old Baptist preacher from Weston. Brother Stan is his name. I used to work on his car—tune it and shit like that. Well, I notice that he's sitting back and watching me with a strange look on his face as I fill up his car. He followed me in to get his change, and as he's putting his money in his billfold, he says real quiet like: 'Do you want to quit?'

"I says, 'Quit what.' And I was being completely honest. I had no idea what he was talking about. He takes out a pen and writes his phone number on my wall calendar for that day. He says, 'If you decide you want to quit, call me.'

"It was on my mind for the rest of that day. I kept wondering what he was talking about. Late in the afternoon, I got to thinking that maybe he was talking about drinking. 'No,' I thought, 'can't be drinking. He wouldn't know anything about me drinking and, besides, I don't drink that much.' I went home after work, opened a new bottle and right away I knew that was exactly what he was talking about.

"Without taking a drink or saying a word to my wife, I went straight out the door and back to the station. I took his number off the calendar and called him. The minute he answered I said, without even saying who I was, 'How'd you know I drink? Who told you?'

"He says, 'Cause I'm an alcoholic, same as you. You want to quit?'

"That next evening I went to my first meeting. It was up in Sherman. I've been sober ever since. I'm not saying it was always easy, but it damn sure works. I figure I've added, maybe, ten or fifteen years to my life. Good years. Sober years." He cocked his head. "What about you, Charlie?"

"Me, huh? This is just like a meeting." Charlie filled his lungs with air. "Well, I was drinking pretty steady before the time I got out of the Navy. Seemed like nothing in my life was working out for me. Things in Melanna had gone all wrong."

"Oh yeah. 'Specially with your girl. What was her name?"

"Madelyn," he said. "By the first Christmas after I got out of the Navy, I found myself in Memphis. I was working at a diesel shop. I was steadily making my way up the ladder. But gradually as I did, I was drinking more and more. Kinda like you, though, I was able to keep everything together. You had to know me pretty good—be around me a lot—to see how much I drank. I guess I thought I could rock along like that forever. It was getting worse all the time, but I wasn't letting myself see that.

"Finally, on Labor Day weekend last year, the owner shut the shop down on Friday and told us to take four days off. There were parties all weekend long and, being the boss, I was invited to all of 'em. It was constant. On Saturday, one of the trucking outfits we have a contract with threw a really big bash. It was in a company townhouse down by the river. Started about seven or eight in the evening. I was drinking all different stuff, trying drinks I'd never had before. I was finishing off other people's drinks if they didn't want 'em. I remember up until about 10:30 or 11.

"The next thing I know, I'm in my apartment—which is clear on the other side of town. I have no idea how I got there. Only, at first I didn't know where I was, because most toilets pretty much look the same on the inside. I woke up with my head in the toilet. I mean, inside the toilet," he said slowly. "My hair was in the water. The water was full of puke and piss.

"And, my god, the smell." He cringed, shutting his eyes. "It was like somebody had found a way to distill vomit. It was so bad I thought I was going to throw up again. So, real quick, I tried to pull my head out of the toilet bowl. I was so disoriented that I kept banging my head on the sides. I could not get my head out of the toilet! When I finally did, I just sort of fell over backwards and laid there for a while."

He sighed. "Eventually I just crawled back into my bedroom."

"Oh, I been there before." Tommy nodded.

"There was light coming through the window and the clock said 1:30, so I knew it was the afternoon and that I was home. I just sat against the foot of the bed for a while, trying to get some human feeling back in me.

"Then the phone rang. It was a mechanic of mine, an older guy named Gus. He starts giving me the business for missing his son's wedding. I was supposed to be an usher. I say, 'What are you talking about, Gus? The wedding's not 'til seven?' He says, 'The wedding was Sunday night, not Monday!'"

He leaned his chair back on two legs. ". . . Even like I was right then, I realized what had happened. Gus thought I had gotten the days turned around. But I had actually lost a day-and-a-half. It wasn't Sunday. It was Monday afternoon. For thirty-six hours of my life I had no idea where I had been or what I had done.

"You know, I've done lots of crazy, stupid kid stuff in my life," he said reflectively, "the kind of stuff that can accidentally get you killed. But for the first time, I was really scared. Really scared.

"I went back to work the next day trying my best to act like nothing had happened. And all the while I was hoping somebody would give me a clue about what did happen. I wanted somebody to fill in the blanks for me. . . . Nobody did. There were no remarks at all. It was like the weekend never happened."

He shook his head. "At first I thought, 'Well, good. Nothing did happen.' Then I began to have this fantasy that everybody knew some terrible something I had done while I was drunk. They were keeping it a secret from me until the boss fired me, or the police arrested me. I guess I stayed scared and thinking like that for two or three days."

It dawned on Charlie that he felt completely at ease telling his story to Tommy. It was something that, were they not both in A.A., he could never have done.

"On Friday of that week," Charlie said, "it finally came to me how paranoid I was being. So I went back to the bays that afternoon. I had a kid I'd hired about a year before that. I say 'kid.' He was twenty-five or six. When I took him on, he told me up front that he had had problems with drugs and alcohol, but that he was clean. I was a little leery, but I hired him anyway. He turned out to be one of my best workers. I mean, you can't give him anything he won't do—and he does it right.

"So I said to him, 'Lupe, how'd you know you were drinking and doping too much?' He gets this big grin on his face and says, 'So that's what's bothering you, man.' That night he took me to my first meeting. I didn't know you could do anything on Friday except get blasted. The program was whole new world for me."

Nodding, Tommy said, "You been in nine months?"

"Yeah."

"And you're already on the Ninth Step?"

"Already? Seems like it's taken forever. This is grueling."

Tommy laughed. "Hey, I was in two-and-a-half years before I could get past step four."

"Really? Do you think I going too fast?"

"No, no. You have to go at the pace that's right for you. Different steps are harder for different people. You just have to keep working 'em." He tilted his head toward Charlie. "You have more amends to make around this little town?"

"Yeah. The main person I'm really looking for is Madelyn."

"She left town before you did—and her parents not long after."

Charlie felt an anxious thrill. His search for her was beginning in earnest at long last.

"Any idea where they went?"

"No." Tommy shook his head. "Only one in that family I ever heard of again was that no-count brother-in-law."

"Brother-in-law? You mean Madelyn's uncle?"

"The one who beat the hell out of you."

"Right! Sloan Witt. What'd you hear about him?"

"He went to jail. Seems like he beat somebody to death when he was drunk. They sent him down to Huntsville on manslaughter."

Charlie leaned forward, his elbows on his knees. They looked at one another in silence.

"I don't suppose Witt was on your list, was he?"

He sighed. "Not for amends."

There was a burst of laughter. "No, he's on your shit list, isn't he? You hate that guy, don't you?"

"Well . . . when he tore me up, I was just a kid. Periodically that sort of runs through my mind."

"You know—" Tommy looked past the intersection and down the highway "—when you hate somebody for a long time, you kill them over and over in your mind. After a while you get to feeling down on yourself, like you're a murderer. What you have to do with that is let go of it. You can't change what Witt did to you. And I'm pretty sure he ain't going to come making an amends to you."

"Yeah. Well." Charlie straightened in his chair. "I imagine he's getting done to a turn down in Huntsville."

Tommy sensed he was about to stand. The two got up together and walked out of the office. They stood without speaking for a time in the shade of the canopy.

"What's next on your list?"

Charlie shrugged. "Thought I'd go over to the high school. Madelyn was real tight with some of the younger teachers. One or two may yet be working here. And if none of them are, maybe they have some records, you know? Maybe they sent her transcript to a college or a job."

"Harland Newman is still there."

"Mr. Newman? Lord, is he still the principal? He was ancient when I was there."

"Yeah, he's still there. He's up in his seventies, but he's willing to work for the district can pay. His memory's pretty good. Might be he knows where she ended up."

They ambled across the oil-stained concrete toward Charlie's car. It came to him in the brief moment of silence around them that he loved Tommy in a way, and probably would never see him again.

"Well, if Mr. Newman doesn't know, someone will. Somebody in this town knows what became of the Stewarts. And if it came to it, I might go down to Huntsville and look up my old buddy Sloan Witt."

"Well, that's been probably ten years or more. He's probably out by now—if they didn't kill him inside prison," Tommy said. He held open the door of the Mazda as Charlie slid in. "Say, uh, you got a sponsor?"

"Sponsor? Yeah. Smart aleck guy named Desmond. He's an ex-con. He got into the program while he was in prison himself. Stayed with it after he got out."

"Yeah." Tommy took out his billfold. He hand a worn, bent business card to Charlie. "Well, here's my number. Both work and home are on here. Some night you may not be able to reach him."

They shook hands again. Tommy was definitely going to start crying. He straightened and took a breath.

"Well, I'm proud of how you turned out, Charlie. You know, I really look up to you."

Charlie smiled. "Yeah. Tommy, when I left here I was already six-three. You've always looked up to me." The engine spun to life. "Hear it purr? I rebuilt this rocket myself. Just because I'd never seen how one worked."

He put it in first and drove away from Tommy's station.

Desmond had chaired the meeting and, when it was over, he came back and sat down beside Charlie.

"Charlie, my man, you didn't say two words tonight. You were acting like you weren't here, like sobriety is not your priority."

"Yeah it is."

"So what were you thinkin'?"

"About my Ninth Step."

"Ninth. Making amends. Finish making your Eighth Step list?"

"Yeah."

"So, let me guess: you have some tough restitution to make. Ninth Step was hard for me."

"It was?"

"Damn straight," Desmond said. "Hard to pay back folks for burglarizing their house when you don't remember what house you burglarized, what street it was on, when you did it and what you stole."

Charlie laughed. "Well, my main problem is the little bit of pussy I stole, and the heart I broke without meaning to."

Desmond considered him skeptically. "How you going to make up for that, man?"

156

Charlie Cherry's Ninth Step

Charlie was thinking about his words carefully. "Desmond, as my sponsor, I have a question for you."

"Oh, shit! Here it comes."

"No, no. This is real. I'm not in denial or anything this time. You remember a few weeks ago when I did my Fifth Step with that preacher?"

"Pastor Werner."

"We were talking about this thing that happened—really it happened to me, it wasn't something I made happen—and whether or not I could make up for it."

"Uh huh. Well if it happened to you instead of you being responsible for doing it, what is there to make up for?"

"Okay. I get it. I brought this on myself, as always. I am responsible. It's for decisions I made when I was in high school. It's like this: not long before I graduated, I secretly got married to this girlfriend of mine. I was fixing to join the Navy right away so we could get out of town. Then this crazy whore—who, I swear, I had absolutely nothing to do with—tricked my girl into thinking that I was fooling around.

"When I found out about what she did, I went over to my girl—my wife's house to explain that I hadn't really done anything. Before I could talk to her, her uncle beat the living shit out me and I never got to see her. She left town without me ever talking to her. I went into the Navy and never saw her or heard from her again. I don't know where she is exactly, but I feel like I need to set the record straight. Apparently she was really torn up about this, but I didn't do anything behind her back. And then—what's probably bigger—for all I know, I'm married and have been for fifteen years."

He paused and looked at his sponsor. "So what do you think? Should it be part of my Ninth Step to find her and make amends? Or should I just chalk this up to 'live and let live,' seeing how I have no idea of what happened to her?"

He had never seen Desmond think so hard. There was a strange clarity in his eyes when he spoke, "How you feeling about all this? Do you feel married?"

"Well," Charlie answered slowly, "over the years I've been with a lot of women, you know. I've shacked up a couple times. Some of them were pretty interested in me—maybe long term. But I've never had it in me to ask one of them to marry me. And I guess it's

because I always felt like I already was."

Desmond shrugged. "That sounds like unfinished business to me. I would have to resolve it, somehow. I think you should turn it over to your Higher Power—"

"I did."

"And."

"He said it's been a long time since I've been home."

Desmond's face creased in a broad smile. "So when do you think you can go?"

"I've got two weeks' vacation time I can take right now. There's nothing at the shop that somebody else can't handle."

"You talked to Bonnie about this?"

Charlie sighed. "No. The Ninth Step part, she won't have a problem with. The being married part . . . I don't know."

"Trust her. She's got good sobriety, and a lot more than yours. It's not like you all have some commitment." Desmond raised his hand and pointed it accusingly at him. "There's something else."

"Yeah."

"You planning to go see the asshole who whupped you?"

An almost childlike smile eased across his face. "Honestly?"

Desmond nodded. "That's the only way."

"I don't know where he is. I don't know that our paths will cross."

"Just see to it they don't."

Chapter Four

A scant two minutes after he left the Texaco station, Charlie found himself rediscovering familiar Melanna High School—freshly painted, complete with red and white Tasmanian devils. The school, like the rest of his hometown, had also been miniaturized. The little football bleachers seemed laughable to him and even the largest building on the small campus, the looming crimson gymnasium rising behind the vo-ag barn, was dwarfed by his memory of it.

He was perhaps only an inch or two taller than he had been where he graduated from MHS, but striding softly down the familiar hall toward Mr. Newman's office, he felt like a giant. And without looking, as he passed the open doors of the classrooms, he could feel the adolescent faces that were trained in wonder on the tall, strange man.

Charlie did not recognize the secretary who gazed over the top of her glasses at him.

"Hi. Uh, I'd like to speak to Mr.—"

"Charlie Cherry."

It was Mr. Newman: smaller, of course, and also an enfeebled version of what he had been; standing in the doorway of his old office, his hand extended and shaking with a slight palsy; his pink scalp ringed with a now pure-white band of angelic hair. There was something else. Charlie sensed it in his voice when he spoke.

"Welcome back, Charlie."

He smiled and took the frail hand in his. "Hello, Mr. Newman. How are you?"

"Just fine. Just fine. And how about you? Are you a rock-and-roll star?"

It was emphysema. The old man couldn't draw a deep breath. All those years of confiscating cigarettes and suspending kids for smoking in the restrooms, and the whole time he himself had smoked.

"Oh, no. Actually I run a diesel repair shop."

"It's just—" he breathed "—as well. I'd hate to think—you'd

159

make the kind of music I hear today."

He laughed. "You used to complain pretty bad about what we listened to back in the day."

"Didn't know—when I had it good. What're you up to, Charlie? What brings you here?"

"Well, can I visit with you in your office for a minute, Mr. Newman?"

He chuckled breathlessly. "That's a switch—when someone asks to see—me in my office."

Charlie wondered, as he followed the principal into his office, how a person so diminutive and fragile could possibly enforce discipline. He remembered his own seeming unruly insubordination, always on the edge of defiance and tempered by his defining need to be respectful, and wondered how the old man could control mid-teen boys in their wild, instinctive spring wildness.

Mr. Newman eased into his captain's chair and asked, "Now what can I do—for you, Charlie?"

"Mr. Newman, I'm trying to locate some of the kids I went to school with. In particular, I'm trying to find Madelyn Stewart."

He shook his head slightly. "That's a tough one, Charlie. We couldn't find either one of you."

"You were looking for me?"

"Ten year—reunion. About five years ago, I guess. Let's see—sixty-four in your—class. Found all but—five of you. No idea where you or Madelyn had gotten to."

"You didn't have any records? Like didn't you ever send her transcript anywhere?"

"Oh." His face seemed to darken. "You didn't—know about the fire. "Nine-years-ago—arsonist burned our old portable buildings where we—had home-ec in your—time. Records were all in there."

Charlie considered it silently. "My records burned up too, huh?"

Mr. Newman nodded. "Posterity will record—our first—graduating class was six-years-ago."

He stood up slowly, trying to understand how to proceed next. "And nobody ever got hold of Madelyn? You wouldn't have any idea of how I could locate, would you, Mr. Newman?"

"I don't, Charlie. We gave it—a pretty good—detective try."

"Well, thanks anyway." He opened the principal's door. "Sure was good to see you, Mr. Newman."

160

"Good to see you, Charlie. You—come back."

"Say, Mr. Newman," he said, leaning against the doorframe, "I have one more question. How did you recognize me so quick?"

It seemed to startle him. "Why—Charlie, you were always one of my fav—orites."

The moment after he had nodded and closed the office door and started back down the hallway toward the parking lot, he wanted to ask the principal why he had been one of his favorites. But he was afraid to turn back, afraid to go and find out about himself.

He paused at the ceramic water fountain and took a long drink of the tepid, late-spring Texas water. He was really buying time for himself, he knew. He was trying to figure out where to go next. The most discouraging thing was the reality that he was conducting a second search and the first searchers, people from the area who were familiar with its gossip and connected roots, had not been able to find Madelyn. Huntsville. An encounter with Sloan Witt, perhaps, was the only real possibility he had of finding her. And that seemed terribly remote. Maybe he should go to the Rockwall courthouse to see if she had ever filed for divorce or annulment.

He wiped his mouth with the back of his hand and walked toward the door.

"Charlie Cherry."

It was a woman's voice hailing him from a classroom. He stopped and looked in.

"I thought that was you a minute ago when you went by."

She was familiar: a short, dark-haired woman with an upturned nose and piercing green eyes amid an oval sea of freckles.

"Susie Amish."

"You remember. Only now it's 'Susan.' Unless you are a student, to whom I am 'Miss Amish.'" She gave him a quick grin and gestured toward the curious, silent teenagers staring at them. Turning toward the kids she said, "All right, young people, no one should be through yet. I'm going to be standing here in the doorway speaking to Mr. Cherry."

Susie stepped out into the hall, right up to him—beneath him almost. She smiled with obvious joy.

"A two-hour final exam. Today and tomorrow are the last days for tests. Then we're out for the summer. And the kids think they're excited."

161

He smiled broadly. "My lord. You're teaching here?"

"I'm finishing my fifth year."

"What do you teach?"

"Social studies."

Charlie tilted his head. "Susie—ah, Susan, you said, 'Miss Amish?' You never got married to old Carlton?"

"Yes, I married him." She took another step away from the class and leaned against the lockers on the wall. "We were married for seven years. I was Susie Homemaker and he was Peter Pan. Finally I decided to rejoin the real world. So I got my teaching degree and my name back. And here I am."

"This is the real world? Melanna High School?"

"Hey, I pack as much of the real world as you can get into thirty-six weeks a year. So what about you? I keep expecting to hear your name singing on the radio some day."

He laughed, his shoulders dropping forward. "You know, you are the third person to ask me about that today. To tell you the truth, I forgot all about that rock star business years ago. I run a diesel shop in Memphis, Tennessee."

"Well that ought to be rock-n-roll heaven. What are you doing back in this burg?"

Something rose in his chest. There was a feeling of hope, of possibility.

"Susan, maybe you can help me out. I came back here to track down Madelyn Stewart."

"Track her down?"

"I know she wasn't, like, your best friend. But you all were in the same group of girls. I'm trying to figure out some way of getting in touch with her."

Susan had a peculiar look on her face. Curiosity, and with it something else—resignation or disappointment.

"So you two never did get back together?"

There was a shuffling sound from the classroom and she turned away from him, looking inside. All the faces were down, intent on their tests. She turned back toward him after a few seconds.

"I heard some of what happened," she said quietly.

He nodded. "She left town, I left town and we never talked again."

"Don't you think—" she was glancing at her students "—after

162

all these years that she probably got married?"

Charlie smiled. "I wouldn't doubt it a bit. Maybe more than once. But I needed to clear up some old business with her. There was a real misunderstanding—"

"Arletta." She spoke with solemn quietness. "'Arletta the Slutta.' How could anybody be tricked by her?"

He gazed at her curiously. "You knew about all that?"

"I'll tell you what I know," she said. "Maybe it will help." She was looking at his feet. "After she left here, Madelyn lived for a while with her aunt in Wichita Falls. Just for a few months. Her parents moved then. I'm not sure where. My friend Gloria was friends with Madelyn's best friend, and I know she ended up for a while moving back in with her folks wherever they went. Her mom had some kind of a breakdown after her aunt got killed."

"Killed?"

"Yeah." Her mouth was a thin line. "Her aunt's husband—same guy who beat you up—beat her to death one night."

"Sloan Witt. . . . So that's who he killed."

"Apparently he just got drunk one night and went into a rage. He threw her all over the house. He had a little girl who saw the whole thing and called the police. They sent him down to Huntsville."

There was the slightest taste of brass in his mouth.

"I wonder if he's still there?"

"No." She shook her head. "They paroled him. See, my grandma lives in Wichita Falls. She said it made the paper there when they paroled him. People were really outraged because it was such a brutal killing. So Witt didn't go back to Wichita Falls."

"Where? Do you know where he went?"

She drew a breath. "Mesquite? Or Garland, maybe." Susan cocked her head. "Are you interested in finding Madelyn or him?"

He looked down at her. He remembered her clearly: wearing her red-and-white cheerleader's uniform, her long hair flowing past her shoulders. Always the petite shadow of giant Carlton Cummings, with her freckled, knowing smile. Charlie had always been attracted to small women, especially those whose observant quietness seemed to hide some undisclosed feminine mystery.

"Why do you ask, Susan?"

An involuntarily quiver moved her shoulders. "You want to

Lazarus Barnhill

beat him up, don't you?"

". . . I admit it has crossed my mind."

"Well? Will you, if you find him?"

"No." He shook his head. "In the long run that would be just one more thing for me to have to explain to someone else—and myself."

There was motion among the students again. She stood in the doorway, her hands on her hips.

"All right, young people. Do not be restless and disturb others. Everyone is trying to do their best."

When she turned back to him, he said, "Well, I'm taking you away from your 'scholars' in there. I need to let you get back—"

"Oh, don't! Don't. Are you leaving?"

"Ah—"

"How long will you be here?"

He shrugged. "I actually don't have any definite plans."

"Why don't you stick around and after school is out I can call some people and see if we can figure out where Madelyn got to." She put her fingers around his wrist. "Come over to my house. I'll write down some numbers. Do you have a cell phone?"

He laughed. "I left that back in Memphis. Otherwise there was no point in taking a vacation."

"Well you can call from my phone if you need to. It's free. Hey—" she shrugged "—if you don't have plans, I'll fix us some supper."

"I don't want to impose. Don't you have tests to grade?"

"I have a week to do that. Besides, I already know what everybody's making."

He nodded. "Okay, then. I'd like that. It would fun to catch up on old times. And I promise not to run up your phone bill."

"Don't worry about it. I'll be through and home by 4 this afternoon. You know those little streets behind the feed store going toward Blue Ridge? Well I live on Oak. That's the last one. And my house is the little yellow one, last house on the left. You can't miss it. In fact, if you want to wait there, you can go over whenever you get ready."

"No, I don't want to do that. Somebody would think I was breaking in."

"Breaking in?" She smiled. "You've been in the big city too

164

long, Charlie. Nobody locks their doors in Melanna."

"You guys still have a chicken fried steak plate?"

"Yes sir."

"What are my vegetable choices?"

"Any three of tomatoes, mashed potatoes and gravy, corn, green beans, baked beans, squash, fried okra, lima beans or a salad. You also get rolls or cornbread."

"Okay," Charlie said. "I'll have the salad, okra, tomatoes and cornbread. And can I have iced tea?"

"Sweet or unsweet?"

"Unsweet."

"Yes sir. I'll have it right out."

The waitress was as tall and bony and homely from the back as she was from the front. Charlie tried to remember if she had been there fifteen years before when he used to come down to Lou's Café in McKinney for lunch with his buddies. Probably she wasn't old enough to have been there fifteen years before, but it was a dozen someones like her: efficient, cordial, distant and—in some creative way—unattractive.

At least once a month he and Gary and a few of the other boys from Melanna found the time and money to drive down for Lou's chicken fried steak. In the years away from Texas, the single thing he had missed the most was chicken fried steak with cream gravy. Once in a Memphis steak house he had seen it listed on the menu, but it had turned out to be a little piece of breaded veal with half a ladle of brown gravy on top.

The night before, as he had driven down Highway 5, he had spotted the old café. Across four lanes of blacktop and fifteen years of absence, he could still smell the cream gravy and the thick, hot breading on the round steak. Even if he didn't find Madelyn—a possibility that loomed over him more and more—he had at least rediscovered true lunch.

"Say, miss?"

The waitress, setting the glass of tea on his table, glanced at him. "Yes?"

"Do you think you all have a Dallas phone book?"

"White or yellow?"

"White."

"I'll see, hon."

"Thanks."

She was back in a moment with a basket of cornbread and a huge phone book. "Just let me know when you're through with it."

"Thanks."

Absently he sliced open a hot cornbread muffin and buttered it. The tea was stale and the anticipation, as he tried to feel relaxed, was like electricity.

Sure enough, Mesquite and Garland phone numbers were listed in with the Dallas residential numbers, and also separately in the back of the book. He flipped the phone book open to the Garland listings first.

There was no "Sloan Witt." He went back up the listings. There were seven or eight Witt listings with only initials, including "SA Witt" and "SH Witt."

He studied the last name. "SH Witt." "Sloan Herbert Witt." Wasn't that right? Wasn't Herbert his middle name? Madelyn had gone to her aunt's wedding about the time they first started dating and came back telling Charlie about the oddities of it. The preacher, she had said, used the full names of the bride and groom during the ceremony. He could still remember the way she rolled her eyes as she described it: "Do you Louise Kay? Do you Sloan Herbert?"

The listing in the phone book might be his.

The waitress plopped the plate covered with steaming food in front of him. He gazed up at her.

"You through with it?"

"Uh—can I borrow your pen? Then you can have it back."

He wrote the phone number and address on his napkin. "Is there a pay—"

"By the cash register. That steak won't stay hot forever."

"Thanks. I'll be right back."

He got up pulling out his billfold and fumbling for his long-distance card. As he picked up the receiver and stared at the number he had written, he wondered what he would say. Should he ask about Madelyn, or say he was coming down to Garland to see him, or not even let him know who was calling?

The computer tones spoke to one another and hummed happily as he punched in three series of numbers. Then came clicking and the hopeful silence that occurs just before a phone begins to ring.

166

One ring. Two rings. Someone picked up the phone.

"Hello?"

Damn. It was a girl. Wrong number. No, wait! There had been a child. Susie said that Sloan and Louise had a child.

"Yeah, uh," he said, "this is Charlie. I was calling to see if Sloan was there."

". . . Charlie who?"

"Oh. I'm a friend of his from back when he lived in Wichita Falls."

The girl spoke quickly. "He ain't here. You got the wrong number." She hung up.

Gently, easily, he set the receiver on its cradle.

He had found him, Sloan Witt. This was his connection to Madelyn.

He folded the napkin and slipped it into his pocket. Should he leave now to see him? He glanced at his watch. If he just finished his lunch and drove straight to Garland, it would be after 1:30 or 2 p.m. when he got there. He had promised Susie he would come to her house by 4 p.m.

Could he possibly find out what he needed to know and be back to Melanna in two hours? And what if he and Witt got into it. Charlie had no intention of leaving without finding out from Sloan what he knew about Madelyn. And in his truest thoughts, he fantasized that, if it came to blows, so much the better. But then what if somebody got hurt or if the police got involved? What if he found out that Madelyn lived nearby? Would he really drive all the way back to Melanna for supper when the whole reason he had made the trip was close at hand? Charlie sighed. Why had he promised Susie he would come over?

Then, with clarity, through the fog of all the uncertainties, he remembered the voice of his sponsor. What was it Desmond kept saying to him?

"Charlie, first things first. You keep trying to pack too much into every damn day, son."

He drew a deep breath. Desmond was right. Sloan Witt would be there tomorrow. If he knew today where Madelyn was, he would still know tomorrow. At this moment there was a steaming chicken fried steak waiting for him, the first one he'd eaten in fifteen years.

Charlie patted the napkin in his pocket and walked back to the table.

Chapter Five

"I hope chicken fried steak is okay," Susan said as she cleared the dishes off the table with an anxious sort of quickness. "It's nothing special."

"It was great. I love it, and you can't get it in Tennessee." Charlie pushed away from the table. "Here. Let me help with these."

"No, no. That's all right."

"Hey, I'm a bachelor. I used to this, remember?"

"Yes," she protested, "but you're my guest."

"Please?"

She hesitated. "Well, okay."

Susan leaned over and pulled the serving bowls toward her. She had changed from the high-necked blouse and jumper she had worn that morning at school into a pair of wide-legged shorts and a loose fitting sleeveless blouse, with no bra beneath it. Several times during the meal and even more now as she was cleaning up, she would bend over enough that a breast—small and exquisitely shaped—would dance into his view. Surely, he thought, she should know that was going to happen with what she was wearing. He tried not to stare, or at least not to be too obvious.

"Let's go ahead and wash them," he said.

"Aw, leave 'em. I'll do them later."

"No, seriously. It'll only take a minute and it'll be one less thing to think about."

Charlie knew she had put a lot of effort into the meal. She had tried to say that she had the food in her house already and hadn't needed to go to the grocery store, but he could tell that the greens were especially fresh and the meat was a bright red before she breaded it. She must've found a way to get out of school early, he thought. He had arrived just a few minutes after 4. The little frame house was neat-as-a-pin. She had changed her clothes and started supper, and fresh tea was already brewing.

All her obvious effort touched a sentimental, almost parental chord within him. She was trying so hard to be hospitable to him. He made sure not to tell her that he had already eaten chicken fried steak that day. After all, he thought, it might be another fifteen years before he had it again. Twice in one day might be a blessing. What was that saying in the Big Book? "Acceptance is the solution to all my problems today . . ."

Standing beside her at the sink, he also felt a little sadness toward her. In spite of all the cozy, clever, feminine touches Susan had made, her little cottage wore a distinct mantle of loneliness. He recognized it from feeling it in his own impersonal apartment in Memphis.

As he turned a plate slowly inside the dishtowel, he said, "You know, Susie—uh, Susan, we've talked about so many people. The one we haven't talked about is you."

"Or you."

She was quick. Charlie smiled.

"Okay. Me too. I guess I've told a lot of people about myself lately. What I'd really like to hear about is Susan Amish."

". . . Like what?"

"Well, if you don't mind me asking, how come things didn't work out between you and Carlton?"

She thought about how to answer silently. As she leaned forward to find another dish in the soapy water, a superb breast moved into his view again, all the more enticing because—like the rest of her visible flesh—it was freckled, and the nipple was shocking pink.

"Carlton wanted to be a coach, always. I wanted to teach home-ec." She sighed. "He won this football scholarship to East Texas."

"Yeah, I think I remember that."

"So, I signed up and went out to Commerce too. Then, in the middle of his sophomore season he hurt his—"

"Knee?"

She looked up at him and smiled. "Right. His knee. And he had to have an operation."

"Well, with those big linemen types, it's usually the knee. They're never quite the same afterwards."

Susan nodded earnestly. "The changes aren't just with your body either. He couldn't pass the physical for spring training. But he did stay in school so he could finish his degree and become a coach." She squinted, her gaze resting on some distant place out the window above the sink. "Carlton got real clingy with me after that.

169

He told me all this crap about how he only realized after his injury how much he loved me and how much I meant to him, that I was his reason for living."

"So, let me guess. He really wanted you to take care of him."

"Right." Her voice trailed off on a bittersweet note. "So when we finished our sophomore year, we got married. The next September, I didn't go back to school. I got a job as a secretary in the history department while he finished get his degree. The deal was that he would get his diploma and then I could finish mine.

"But . . . of course . . . it didn't work that way. You see, he was a coach." She looked up at Charlie. "What a wonderful thing it is to be married to a Texas high school football coach. First we ended up way out near Brady. Where was I going to go to school out there? A year later we were down in the valley. Two years later we were out southwest of Fort Worth. It seemed like we really weren't staying anywhere long enough to establish a household and for me to get started back to school, which was pretty much the way Carlton liked it.

"Carlton made me the most splendid promises. And he never kept a single one, Charlie." She pulled the chain of the sink stopper and dishwater began to drain noisily. She leaned against the sink, facing him as she cupped her hand beneath the faucet and splashed water on the soap in the sink, rinsing it down the drain. "When I hear women talk about being 'football widows' because their husbands watch it on TV, I just laugh to myself. Being a coach's wife is the true meaning of football widow.

"Finally, when he started two-a-days in August right after our fifth anniversary, I said to myself, 'This is enough bullshit.' I called East Texas and I managed to get into the fall semester. My folks loaned me the money for school. Honestly, they'd had a snoot full of Carlton too. I switched majors because I had gotten interested in history when I had worked in that department.

"We were married for two more years." She shook her head. "I never saw Carlton that whole time. He called a few times. He said he was coming to see me once or twice, but it was always going to be after the next big event he was working on—spring drills or track season. I guess I never knew how much he really didn't love me until we were separated. As soon as I got my degree and a job at good old Melanna High School and my first paycheck . . . I filed for divorce." Her petite, charming voice was full of sadness. "It was anti-climatic. I took back my maiden name legally then, but I had already been using it for eighteen months."

The tears were there, but she wasn't going to cry them. Instead she reached up and pulled the dishtowel off his shoulder and dried her hands.

"It's kind of neat," she said, nodding ever so slightly, "to think somebody would love you enough that, after fifteen years, he would come back looking for you. Not knowing whether or not he would find you, or whether you were married or cared anything for him still."

Charlie leaned his head back and smiled. "Well let me say that I never told a girl I loved her—if I didn't feel it for her—especially if all I wanted was for her to take care of me. I'm not that kind of jackass. But on the other hand, I don't want you thinking I'm some romantic bastard either. I want you to know right up front that I didn't come back to sweep Madelyn off her feet like some 'knight in shining armor.' Me coming back to Melanna is not about being in love with her at all. I came back to square the deal. You understand what I'm saying? This is really for my sake more than hers. I had to make sure she understood I wasn't fooling around with Arletta. I have to put that to rest." He looked down at his Nikes. "Hopefully I won't have to think about Madelyn growing old and going to her grave thinking I was two-timing her."

Susan shook her head, wearing a tight little smile. "Still, you must have really cared about her to want to make things right."

Charlie studied her face, trying to decide how much he wanted to explain to her about why he had come looking for Madelyn. "It's like I said, Susie, it's not about her. It's something I had to do to make my own life right. If I owed Carlton a debt, I'd be asking you how to find him instead of Madelyn."

There was a momentary look of skepticism, and then it was as if she were shifting gears. "Hey. Want to see some scrapbooks?"

"What?"

"I have a bunch of high school pictures in a couple scrapbooks. It's in here." She took his wrist—much as she must have with her students when she needed their immediate compliance—and led him into the tiny living room. "This ought to be a hoot."

Even though the sun was just beginning to fade, the room was fairly dark. She turned on a floor lamp and motioned for him to sit on the sofa. In a moment she reappeared from what must've been her bedroom with a huge leather binder. She sat beside him, curling her feet beneath her, one creamy, freckled knee touching his leg.

Susan opened the scrapbook and put it in his hand, but then yanked it away from him immediately and said, "Oh, wait! Here's one you'll like."

She found it quickly. It was a photo of him in his baseball uniform. His arm was around Gary and he was saying something to him. Charlie had never seen the picture before.

"Remember this?" she asked. "It was your junior year. This was the time Gary made the error in the last inning of the regional playoff, and we lost the game by one run. You were coming off the field with him and telling him not to worry about it."

Quietly he asked, "Where did you get this?"

"I took it." Her voice was bright. "I was on the yearbook staff. Remember?"

"How come you kept it all these years?"

She gave a jittery little shrug.

Charlie nodded and, looking down at the photograph, said quietly, "I had a major crush on you too."

When she didn't respond, he looked at her. Her eyes were on him. They were a warm emerald from which he could not turn.

She said, "Swear, as God is your witness, that you aren't lying."

He shook his head slowly. "I don't tell lies anymore. I was pretty crazy about you."

Susan lifted her hands and raised her face toward the ceiling. "Then why the hell didn't you tell me?"

". . . Susan, in every class in every school, there are special people. People who are too beautiful, too hip, too cool. When you aren't one of those people, you always know that they will never be part of your life—or at least you could never really be a part of theirs. You can dream about them. Fantasize about them. Pretend they're in the shower with you." He glanced down and laughed. "But actually being with them? Having a relationship with them? That's too good to be true. For me, you were that person during our four years at Melanna High School. I was, like, just an ordinary guy. I always recognized that you paid attention to me, treated me like I was a real human being. But I thought it was just because you were being nice—because you were always very nice."

He gazed back down at the scrapbook and began to turn the pages. "Anyway, besides, you always had that big jockey strap Carlton hovering around you like a moth around a flame. Some goofy football stud always gets the prettiest girl."

"You played football."

"Christ, we all played football. There was barely enough to field eleven guys."

"You were all-district."

"Carlton was all-state."

She closed her eyes and shook her head in exasperation. "If I had known that you liked me, I would've ditched that guy in a minute. But I never would've believed you felt about me the way I felt about you. Know why? You were so devoted to Madelyn. . . . I think maybe you still are."

"It wasn't like what you're describing, Susie. There's no denying Madelyn and I had close relationship. It was based on need. Neediness. Like two people clinging to one another in a flood to stay afloat. I filled a place in her life that was empty. She did the same for me. I was really close to her and part of it, at that time in my young life, came from believing that what she and I had together was the best I could ever have. And maybe then it was. . . . Whatever we had, it's nothing that I'd recognize today as the sort of relationship a grownup would want."

He sighed. "The difference between the two of you was that Madelyn was so dependent. She was afraid. For her, life was a big, awesome question mark. She needed somebody to tell her that things were going to be okay. Her mother was crazy as hell and her father was a marshmallow with legs.

"Then there was you. You were never afraid of anything, so far as I could tell. You were always happy. Bubbly. You had the world by the tail. I didn't deserve you. . . . And you didn't need me."

Susan leaned back against the cushion, looking up to the ceiling again. "I'm not believing this."

"You mind if I ask you a personal question?"

"Sure."

"What was it you saw in me?"

She put her hand on the scrapbook. "That picture. That was you all over. You cared about people. You were always looking out for the people you cared about. Like Gary. He was always popping off to somebody because he knew, if it came to a fight, you'd be there with him. And Madelyn. As much as you could be, you were there for her." She squinted at him. "I guess I was a little jealous of Madelyn. I wanted you to care for me. Instead I was always taking care of my big moose Carlton. If someone was ever to ask me why I don't have children, I would tell them that I did—for the better part of ten years I had the biggest baby in Texas."

"Yeah." He nodded slowly. "I never knew you felt like that. This trip has been so strange for me. Today three people have told me how much they liked me when I was a kid. I never knew that. When you all told me, I didn't know why you liked me."

Susan uncurled her feet and leaned back. There was something going on with her, he sensed. There was that mystery.

"Now is it my turn?" she asked. "Can I ask you a personal question?"

"I guess."

"How come Charlie Cherry, the guy who always takes care of damsels in distress, never got married?"

He had come to their class photo in the scrapbook: all sixty-four of them in a narrow band of bleachers, squinting in the spring sunlight, a day just like this day had been. Charlie ran his finger over the glossy print until he came to the image of Madelyn, sitting with a crooked smile. She was three girls down from Susan, who was wearing her cheerleader's uniform.

"I did get married." He tapped the photograph. "I married her."

Leaning forward, Susan looked at the tiny face framed by curly hair. She said nothing.

"We got married a couple months before graduation. I was supposed to send off for her after I finished boot camp. But then there was that whole Arletta thing and her parents sent her away. And so much happened to me so fast right then, I didn't know how to get up with her." His eyes lingered on her expressionless face. He wondered what she was feeling. "That's really why I need to find her. I assume that somewhere along the way she got a divorce or an annulment. I kept waiting for her to track me down all those years I was in the Navy and serve me with papers." He sighed. "I have no idea if I'm married or not. I guess I've really been waiting for fifteen years to find out. Until I do, I can't get on with my life." He studied

174

her delicate features. "So, do you feel different about me now?"

". . . You know, ninety-nine out of a hundred guys would've forgotten about that marriage. Or gotten their own divorce for abandonment. But you didn't. I guess there could be two reasons. One, you still love her. Two, you are just a very responsible dude."

He smiled. "Neither one. You can believe me on this or not, but the truth is that I have to reconcile this for my own personal mental health. I have to get my house in order or I can't—maintain. I want the sort of resolution that will only come when I seen her and find out what she did about our marriage. Then I can say to myself, 'Well, you're really free now.'"

There was the tight smile. "What if she waited all these years for you?"

"Right."

"But you waited for her."

He laughed sheepishly. "I didn't get married. Hell, I couldn't! But that's not to say I waited. I've just been real careful not to form permanent attachments. And all the while I've been kicking myself for not clearing up this teenage marriage crap."

His hand was lying on the scrapbook. She closed her fingers around it loosely.

"You said I was never afraid. But I am afraid. Right now."

"Afraid?"

"Afraid you don't want me as much as I want you."

He opened his hand then and covered hers with it. "A man would have to be crazy not to want you."

She tried to draw a deep breath, but it came in quiet starts, her eyes closed. He could feel her shivering, as if suddenly chilled.

"When I saw you walk down the hall today, I didn't believe it. I thought it was, like you said, too good to be true. I thought, 'Oh my god, after all these years, he's come back.' And to have you here, now, with me. . . . It is too good to be true."

He raised his fingers to her face and caressed the tender flesh that had teased him throughout the evening. He leaned forward to kiss her and she wrapped her arms tightly around his neck and pressed their lips hard together and forced the sweet warmth of her tongue into his mouth.

They broke apart. She rested her head on his shoulder. He touched her along her back and lifted her loose blouse from behind

175

and kissed her breasts, supple and eager. They kissed again and, in the motion of their bodies moving toward each other, he lifted her off the sofa and carried her into the bedroom.

Even in the dim light, Charlie could tell there was an elaborate quilt on her double bed. He held her easily with one arm and started to pull back the bedspread when her whisper stopped him.

"Don't wait."

Her loose clothing slipped from her as if melting. She was clinging to him, pressing herself against him, making it infuriatingly difficult for him to get his pants down. As he kicked off his jeans and underwear, she opened herself to him and put her hands on the small of his back, pulling him against her. He entered her and immediately, rapidly, she moved to and from him, hungrily, whimpering. Thrilled and surprised, he had to withdraw for a moment and wait so he did not come.

"Whoa, Susie."

His arms extended, he held himself above her and gazed down upon her. She was splendid to him, naked and longing in the sepia colored shadows of the fading yellow light. Then he recognized tears in her eyes, running down the sides of her face onto the quilt. He touched the wetness, as if to find out if it were real.

"Am I hurting you?"

"No." She shook her head, her eyes closed. "Please don't stop."

He began again. This time she did not move as quickly, but still it was maddening to him. He scooped his arms beneath her and pressed their bodies together tightly. Surprising soon, he heard and felt her come, and it was impossible for him to resist his own powerful climax.

For moments he supported himself above her, his arms extended. Because she was so petite, he did not want to put his entire weight fully on top of her. Finally, sluggishly, he rolled onto his back.

"Will you lay on top of me," he asked, "so I can feel you against me?"

"Uh, if I do, I'll leak on you."

"Correct me if I'm wrong, but that's me you're leaking, Susie." He pulled her onto his chest, comforted and excited by her bare skin against him.

Neither spoke. One of his hands was behind his head on the

pillow. The other was weighted against her small shoulder as if to prevent her from moving off him. She lifted her head a bit and looked at something beside the bed.

"Well, it's not even nine o'clock. I've fed you and conversed with you and made love to you. . . . How am I going to entertain you for the rest of the evening?"

Slowly he said, "Well, this is pretty damn good right here. Why don't we just major in laying here for a while and see what comes up."

Her face was near his, where he could see it clearly. It was girlish. She was the enticing Susie Amish about whom he fantasized so often—only real and pressed so tightly against him that he could feel her heart beating. She smiled.

"When I was married to Carlton and we made love—" She stopped abruptly. "Is it okay if I say this?"

"Sure."

"Well, we'd make love and he'd—I mean we're talking five minutes of sex once every two weeks, right—and he'd give me this little shit-eating grin like he had just ravished me, and say, 'Are you coming, Mrs. Cummings?'" She turned her head and laid it on his chest. "I would guess I had an orgasm about once a year, kind of like a birthday gift. And he thought he was such a great lover." Charlie could not see her face and wondered at her expression as she spoke. "Sometimes I feel like going back to him and saying, 'You know, you never could screw.'"

"Nope," he said in a paternal tone, "you don't want to do that. The only reason to go back to the past is to try to forgive the wrongs others have done you and to try to undo the ones you've done to them."

"Is that right?" Her voice dripped of sarcasm.

"Absolutely. A friend of mine a few weeks ago quoted some poet. Carl Sandburn."

"Carl Sandburg?"

"Yeah, I guess," he said. "You're the educated one. Anyway, he said that Sandburg once wrote, 'The past, I tell you, is a bucket of ashes.'"

Susan didn't say anything at first. He wondered if she had been genuinely moved by what he said, or if instead she were trying not to snicker at his attempted wisdom.

"You know what," she said, "I think I have read that somewhere. I think he did write that." She raised up again to look at his face. "You certainly hang out with a philosophical bunch of diesel mechanics."

Charlie heard himself sigh. It seemed the sound filled up the stillness in the little bedroom.

"Susie, I guess I ought to tell you this. I'm a drunk. . . . I've been sober for almost ten months. I'm in what's called a Twelve Step program with a lot of other people like me. We're helping each other to recover from alcoholism."

"Like Alcoholics Anonymous?"

"Exactly. Part of the process of recovering is to lay the past to rest. That's why I'm here. To sort of finally, once-and-for-all, resolve what happened between Madelyn and me." He shrugged. "If that changes the way you feel about me, I'm sorry. That's just what I am."

"Charlie." She leaned close to him so that they could see each other's face clearly. "I'm nobody to cast stones. Knowing you had a drinking problem doesn't make me feel any different about you." She smiled. "It certainly hasn't ruined your sex appeal."

He had a relieved smile. "That's good to know. See, I have lost friendships over my drinking."

"Oh really? If somebody was really your friend, it seems like they would stand by you and try—"

"I lost Gary over drinking."

". . . Gary?"

"Yeah." He stretched, putting both hands behind his head. "Gary and I were both discharged in San Diego within a week-and-a-half of one another. Between us we had four or five thousand dollars saved up. In those days I still played a little guitar. So the idea we had was to go to New York City and start a band or get into a band."

"Why New York?"

"'Cause it was on the other coast. Diagonally on the opposite side of the country. Gary and I bought these, like, bus passes. We had a certain number of miles on them and we could take any bus anywhere. Our plan was to stop in every major city from San Diego to New York. We were going to party and live it up and, when we got to the Big Apple, we'd get jobs while I started up my band.

"Well, our money held out to Memphis. By the time we got there, we were just about hoboing it. I got on as a diesel mechanic. Pretty soon Gary was repairing stereos and TVs. Electronics was the trade he learned in the Navy. We stayed there, living within a couple miles of each other for, I guess, six or eight years. We had been buddies all our lives. We played in some softball and flag football leagues together. Every weekend we went out and got blasted."

Susan straightened herself on top of him, her chin resting on the back of her hand, so she could look into his eyes. Their moist, sensitive genitals embraced teasingly.

"About five or six months before the last time I saw him, Gary fell in with his ideal chick. She was very 'upwardly mobile,' as they say. Diana was connected by family to a group of folks who owned a big chunk of the electronics market in the Memphis area: big screen TV's, computers, camcorders, mp3 players, microwaves . . . even electronic appliances like washers and dryers. Just by knowing her and being in with her people, Gary was able to cut two or three huge deals, bang-bang-bang.

"After a few months they got engaged. He bought a condo not far from where he been living and moved her in with him. Diana was a pretty girl. Knew what she wanted. Took an instant dislike to me. That only got worse the first time I showed up at Gary's doorstep all lit up."

"Oh. I see." She put head on his chest.

"In the old days I was only out-of-control drunk about once a month. Gary always lived closer to my favorite bar than I did. If I had had too much—way too much—instead of driving, I'd hike over to his apartment and crash out on the couch. After he bought his condo, I thought the only difference was that he had a nicer couch. Until Diana moved in.

"Now I want you to know I don't blame him," Charlie said earnestly. "Really, not either of them. I guess it was about the second or third time after they were living together that I showed up ripped on his doorstep . . . it all came to a head. I don't remember leaving the club or getting over to Gary's. Incidentally, that's called 'being in a blackout.' But I do remember laying on his couch and suddenly being aware that they were arguing in the bedroom.

"Man, she was yelling at him. She kept referring to me as 'that drunk.' Gary was trying to get her to calm down. Saying stuff like

179

we had been friends for years. Well, that just pushed her into overdrive. She started talking about him choosing. Was he going to move forward with her or give his life up for a pathetic sot?"

He paused, remembering. "Well. I knew what I had to do. I got up off the couch and staggered to the bedroom and walked on right on in. She was standing beside the bed just in her panties when I opened the door. Immediately she dives under the covers and Gary screams at me to get out. . . . But I just stood there.

"I'm not sure of everything I said, but I think that, for being blitzed, I was at least making sense. And I guarantee you I had their attention. 'Gary, buddy, I don't have anything else to offer you. Diana does. For a long time now I've been a burden on you. I've taken a lot more from our friendship than I've given back. So I'm going to do the only good thing I can do. I'm leaving. Right now.'" For some reason he felt as if he were about to cry. "'And I ain't coming back.'"

When he didn't continue, she said, "So you left?"

"Yeah." He took a deep breath that elevated and then lowered Susan's slight body. "He sure didn't stop me. In fact, Gary didn't say a word. I just went out and walked home. For a long time I expected to hear something from him. I thought he might drop by the shop or give me a call. . . . I'm kind of disappointed that he never did. After a year or so, I quit expecting to hear from him."

"He never got in touch with you?"

"No."

"Jesus!" She shook her head. "You did it again."

"Did what?"

"Helped him out. Saved his ass."

He could feel her stretch and move forward. She grabbed his shoulders and pulled until her face was directly above his, only inches apart.

"You let him off the hook," she said, "again. All those years in high school. How many times did you save his bacon? A dozen at least that I can remember. And after all that, when his chickee girlfriend didn't like you, you drew all her anger onto yourself, and then split. And your great buddy Gary never came around even just to say 'thanks.'"

"Well I—"

"Save it, Charlie. Don't defend that guy to me. You were

180

hurting and down and he's the one who ditched you."

Her face had a new, girlish defiance to it. He smiled.

"You're just saying that because I made you pop."

"Yes you did. And I want more."

He kissed her and pulled her, firm, against himself. "You know what's worse than being hooked up with a Texas high school football coach?"

"Nothing."

"Wrong. Being hooked up with a drunk." He nodded. "You can say all the things you want about Gary, but having an alcoholic in your life is like setting a tornado turned loose. They tear up everything."

"You know how you've been going around to people and making things right?"

"Making amends. It's called the Ninth Step."

"Right. So I take it you haven't gone to Gary yet?"

He considered her question. "Well, he's not really on my list. Technically what I said to him standing in his bedroom that night was an amends, even though I drank for years afterwards. And, even if it weren't, the second half of the Ninth Step says that we're not supposed to make an amends that would harm another person. It was pretty clear to me that Gary just wants to be left alone."

"Son of a bitch. It's all about you taking care of Gary."

"No it isn't," he protested. "It's not about him, it's about me. It's about getting rid of an unfinished business that can cause you to drink. You remember what we were saying about Carl Sandburn."

"Carl Sandburg."

"Whatever. What I was trying to say is, you have to find a way to let the past go. The regrets and unpaid debts of the past rob us of the joys of the present. For instance, feeling you against me right now is a damn sight better than feeling sad because of all my past drunken disasters."

Something flashed within her eyes. She looked away instantly.

Charlie touched her face again. "What?"

She turned, avoiding his gaze. "'The present' is certainly fleeting, isn't it? 'Now' doesn't last very long. Us being here like this is just, at most, a little while. I don't even want to think about how long it will last. Then you'll go and fix your past, and I'll go back my wonderful life."

"You're doing it again," he said. "You've lost yourself in the future. The past is ashes—that sometimes need a good funeral. The future is a haze of hopes and fears. The only solid thing we have is today. Right now. And we don't have that if we don't live it."

Susan put her hand on his face gently. "I'm sorry if I have trouble staying in the present. Most of my 'present' moments are not as special as this."

He drew another deep breath. "I know what you mean. We can't stay in the present just because we know it's the right way to live. Nobody ever really escapes remembering past events or fretting over what the future holds. But . . . looking forward or back can sure can mess up a wonderful time when you have one."

"Don't I know it. Am I ruining tonight for you?"

"No." His expression was incredulous. "And I don't want to bullshit you into thinking that I'm free from anxiety about the past or the future. I'm not. There's a saying we read at ever meeting. Something like: 'None of us has obtained perfect adherence to these principles.' Something like that. I'm not where I want to be after a few months sober. Although I do have some moments of serenity. And the people in the program who know me say that I'm making progress."

"So. You do hang out with some philosophical people after all."

He laughed. "Well we aren't all mechanics. My sponsor, for instance, is an ex-con. He's a substance abuse counselor."

Susan shook her head. She pulled at the hair on his chest. "I sort of envy you having friends like that. I don't mean to be a downer. Right now I don't have a whole lot to look forward to in my life."

"Man, aren't you out of school for the summer starting the day after tomorrow? If I were you, I'd sure as hell be looking forward to that."

"Looking forward to what? Summer school starts in about a week-and-a-half and I volunteered to teach it this summer. I need the extra money. Even if I had the time and inclination to go somewhere, I couldn't afford it. Oh, my parents would give me the money. But I'm always getting stuff from them. I need to do things on my own."

"Well it could be a loan, you know. Save up and pay 'em back later."

She shook her head. "They won't take it. They won't ever really take it back. They just say, 'Well, eventually it will all be yours and your sister's anyway,' which just makes me feel guilty."

"I know guilt."

"And, anyway, if I had a few extra dollars, I wouldn't spend it on a vacation. I'd fix this place up a little. It's amazing how a little hole-in-the-wall like this can take so much care. Shoot, I don't even have enough in the bank to fix my car."

"Your car?" Charlie raised his head off the pillow, looking intently at her. "What's wrong with your car?"

"—Uh, Dad says he thinks it's the carburetor."

"Your car is too new to have a carburetor. What does it do—die on you?"

"Well, it never completely dies. It's sort of like I'm driving along and somebody puts on the brakes. Like magic, the car just slows way down."

"But never completely dies."

"No."

"And it smokes while it does this? White or gray smoke?"

"Yeah, actually. It does a little."

"That's your fuel filter, darlin'. There's nothing to fixing that." Effortlessly he lifted her off of him and sat up on the side of the bed, reaching for his jeans. "We can cure that in thirty seconds."

"Hey, no!" Her arms circled his shoulders from behind, her breasts giving a maddening embrace to his back. "I didn't ask you over here to work on my stupid car."

Charlie pulled away from her gently and stood up as he buttoned the fly of his Levis. "Susie, I don't know English or poetry or—whatever—history, but I can fix internal combustion engines." He was headed out of the bedroom toward the front door when he said, "Come hold the light for me."

By the time she had pulled on a loose robe and caught up with him, he had the hatch of the Mazda open and was unlatching his toolbox. Charlie handed her a flashlight and stuck a screwdriver in his back pocket.

"You got your keys?"

"Uh, no."

"Well, best fetch, 'em, darlin'. I'll have it fixed before you get back."

Her car was a small, yellow model of some kind of Ford, seven

183

or eight-years-old and in need of a thorough wash. When he opened the driver's door to find the hood latch, he saw the key ring, adorned with a large wooden "S," dangling from the ignition.

Charlie popped the hood and put the prop rod in place. In a moment he had the air breather off and was shining his flashlight on the fuel line near where it met the manifold. He could feel her gently press against his side.

"Uh."

"They're in the ignition," he said. "Here. Stand over on the passenger's side and point the flashlight right there."

Leaning all the way across from the driver's side, Charlie disconnected the fuel line without removing the filter from it. He looked up at her, resting on her elbows and shining the light down on the dusty engine. She was leaning forward and he could almost see all of her breasts, as delicious and distracting as the first moment he had seen them.

"This is the great part of being six-four," he said.

"What's that?"

"I can stand on the wrong side of an engine and still work on it."

And then neither of them said anything. They simply looked at one another in the pale, white light bouncing of the innards of the car. It came to him seconds later, as he bent down in silence over the little, malfunctioning four cylinder engine with the disconnected gas line in his hand, that they had had an instant of being completely present to one another. It was what he had heard called intimacy.

"Go, uh, pump the gas, will you?" he asked. "Don't start it. Just pump down on the pedal once or twice."

He watched her walk around the back and slide into the driver's seat. A strangled squirt of gas sprayed out in the Ray-O-Vac light.

"Shit, Susie. There's your trouble. Just stay there for a second." He ran the end of the screwdriver through the filter, reconnected it to the fuel line and tightened it. "Okay. Let's try it. Fire it up."

The engine roared to life with 1600 cubic inches of aluminum housed indignation. Charlie listened to it for a moment before standing up where she could see him and motioning downward with his hand.

"Okay. Shut it off." He handed her the light when she got out. "Hold the light for me again."

He was becoming very conscious of her silence as he reattached all the metal and rubber appendages to her engine. He could feel a sadness growing in her. And he did not know how to fix that. He had spent the greater part of the last year learning that he could only fix himself, and then only with the help of wise friends and a higher power.

"Your car is fixed. Kind of," he said. "When you get a chance, take it up to Tommy Thomas' service station. Tell him you need a fuel filter. . . . It also wouldn't hurt for you to get a new air filter. And your universal belt looks like it's about to give up the ghost."

"Anything else?"

He shrugged. "Well, you're running on four bald eagles. You're dripping battery acid on the a/c line. And you're throwing oil off a back plug. Apart from that, you just need to advance the timing. Although, I bet you're also due for a timing belt."

She was shaking her head. "You see. I told you I couldn't even afford to fix up my car."

"No, no, no," he said gently. "You don't have to do it all at once. You do it a little at a time, just what you can pay for as you go. See, people think their cars have to be perfect. That ain't so. Your car just has to be good enough to get you where you need to go today. Take my little rocket back there." He unhooked the hood, lowered and gently latched it. "It's not perfect. But it got me from Memphis to Melanna. And when my vacation is over, it'll probably get me back."

Even in the dim light, he could see her face drop. Susan turned and walked back toward his car. He followed her and put his tools in the box and shut the latch.

"Just what kind of car is this?"

"It's a Mazda RX7. They call them 'rotary rockets' because they have a Wankel engine in them. It's not piston driven."

She had a tired look in her eyes. "Why do you drive a car like this?"

". . . Nobody ever asked me that before. I guess because they're the only ones like it on the road. It's like you: different from everyone else."

He turned off the flashlight. She was standing close to him, near enough that he could smell the mingled scents of her perfume and the slight sweat that came from their arousal.

"You have a girl, Charlie?"

"Well, it's hard to explain. Sort of."

"'Sort of?' How do you 'sort of' have a girl?"

He smiled. "There's a girl I date. We are not engaged, going steady or in love. She's in the program and we are there for each other. It's not good to be alone."

He could hear her breathing, and then she asked, "Are you going to tell her about tonight?"

Charlie thought about it silently. "Well . . . it's like this: I'm not planning on rushing back and telling her. But, like I've been saying, I don't tell lies no more. If I tried to tell her a lie, she'd know it."

"Will she break it off with you over it?"

He scratched the back of his head. "There's nothing to break off. Knowing Bonnie, nothing will be different. She works a pretty good program."

"What does that mean?"

"She has a lot more sobriety than I do. Things don't upset her. If she felt different about me afterwards, she'd just end our relationship and move on."

She was very close to him, he realized. She was studying his face in the darkness. "Do you regret what we did tonight?"

"Regret? Shit. Regret? I regret we didn't do it fifteen years ago. But then, I try not to live in the past." He laughed. "I'm just glad we finally found this out about one another. Being with you has been—well, it's really been a spiritual experience."

"Spiritual?" she said. "That's not the way I'd describe it. . . . Charlie, want to do it again?"

"Very much."

"Will you carry me again, like you did?"

"Sure."

She was weightless in his arms, her face turned close to him as if she were breathing in his bare chest. As they were passing over the threshold into the cottage, she began to talk to him again.

"Tomorrow you're going to see Sloan Witt, aren't you?"

"Yeah. I expect so."

"Are you going to fight him?"

He shook his head. "I just want some information."

"But if you scare him or if he doesn't want to tell you, you'll fight. And if you do . . ."

He placed her gently on the bed. "If I do, what?"

"Grown men's fights don't end in bloody noses and torn shirts. He's already a killer."

He sighed. "Tomorrow is hours away. When it comes, I'll face it. Sloan Witt is not going to rob me of being with you tonight."

". . . Charlie?"

"Yes?"

"Can we do it slow and for a long time?"

There was an empty space near the front door where Charlie parked as he pulled up to the Pizza Palace. Almost immediately he saw Bonnie walk past the door. She went to a table by the window nearest him and began to wash it off. He sat watching her, thinking of the great joy she had brought to him.

He remember lying in her bed after the first time they made love, watching as she, unashamed, casually walked around the room straightening things and putting away clothes that she had ignored in the passionate minutes when they first arrived. Even in that rarified setting, she still bore an aura of serenity.

"You know," he had said, speaking not so much out of concern as of a desire to engage her in conversation, "my sponsor says you're not supposed to fall in love until you have two years of sobriety."

"You're not in love, Charlie," she had answered without turning toward him. "You're in bed."

He watched her disappear inside the restaurant and then reappear: bussing tables, speaking to customers, answering questions for youthful employees who rushed up to her. She was always unhurried. Always at peace. And when Charlie was with her, the serenity rubbed off on him.

She looked up and smiled when he came through the door. He went to a vacant booth and sat down. Within a few seconds she appeared beside him, setting a glass of tea before him.

"Hi. Surprised to see you. Want a pizza?"

"Naw. Just tea."

"I'll be back in a minute."

As he watched her walk away, Charlie felt a little guilty. Why, he wondered. Bonnie would not hold this trip against him. She had been in the program more than four years. She understood how

187

things worked and the unique rituals sometimes required to cement long-term sobriety. Why did he feel guilty? It was, he thought, residue from his old life, his old way of thinking.

"I'm back." She slid into the seat opposite him, setting down her own soda glass. "Whew."

"Busy night?"

"No. It's really sort of dead. But we do have a teenage soap opera busting out tonight. Two of my little server girls are causing me a problem. They're in love with the kid back there making pizza." She nodded toward the open kitchen area.

Charlie glanced over his shoulder at the boy: tall, pimple-faced, the faint fuzz of a mustache above his open mouth.

"Love is still blind, I see."

"And giddy," Bonnie said. "Neither one of the girls wanted to clean the ladies room. They told me they'd look bad to Jerod, the cook, if they did. So I told them that one of them could go home an hour early, but the other had to stay and clean the bathroom before we closed." She grinned at him. "Now one is cleaning the ladies room and the other is cleaning the men's room."

"I don't get it."

"Whoever stayed to clean the bathroom got to spend an extra hour around Jerod. So they both volunteered."

"Ah, the light dawns. Whatever they pay you for working teenagers, it isn't enough."

"They're good kids. Sometimes you have to manipulate them a little."

"Sometimes? Is there any other way to get them to do anything?" he asked. He gazed at her. "Bonnie. I have something important to talk to you about."

Her face was placid.

"I have to go to Texas. And I'm leaving in the morning." When she didn't respond, he continued. "I just called my boss and asked for two weeks of vacation. It may not take me but a couple days. Maybe longer. But I'll be coming back as quick as I can."

His eyes were like windows to her, and he knew it. She sat just looking at him, then nodded and said, "Okay."

"I'm working on my Ninth Step," he volunteered. "Making amends?"

"Yes. If I can. If it's at all possible." Propping his elbows on

188

the table, he rested his chin in his open palm. "Teenagers. We all were once, weren't we? Isn't it crazy how the things we do as kids can haunt us when we get grown?" He arched his eyebrows the way Pastor Werner had as he had listened to Charlie's Fifth Step. "The things we did as kids can keep us from sobering up or growing up.

"Here I am thirty-four and still torn up over shit I pulled fifteen years ago. I don't know if I can make the amends I need to or not, but if I can track a couple people down, I need to apologize. I need to explain a few things. . . . I talked it over with Desmond tonight and he understood."

"This is about a girl, isn't it?"

His jaw dropped. He nodded slowly. "Yes."

She smiled and said quietly, "You don't have to convince me or anybody, Charlie. Whatever you have to do for yourself, just go do it."

He studied the soft, spherical shape of her face, the sea-blue eyes and straw colored hair.

"I guess I've never told you," he said, "how much you mean to me. Seems like ours is the first really grownup relationship I've ever had. You are a different than anyone I've ever known. You absolutely do not play games. You don't expect me to be anybody but Charlie Cherry."

Without the slightest change of expression, she said, "I'm also loyal, trustworthy, true, obedient, neat, punctual—"

He burst out laughing. "I'm just trying to say thanks, okay? Thank for being you and thanks for being in my life."

She reached across the table and took his hands in hers. "Charlie, this is a selfish program. I'm only in it for me. If you stay sober and do the things you need to, it will help me with my program. Being with you has made me feel very womanly, Charlie. But I have to make a confession to you: wherever you go, whatever you do, I'm not going to drink over it. Go do what you have to and, if you can, come back to me."

His head rolled slightly to the side. "Can I tell you what I've got to do?"

She nodded.

"When I was eighteen," he said, "I secretly married a girl. Before we could leave town together, she was tricked by this—" he shook his head "—really weird bimbo into thinking that I was

fooling around on her. Which wasn't true. Believe me. When I tried to talk to her, her uncle beat me up bad. Her family sent her away. I had already signed up for the Navy and I had to go in. All these years and I've never tracked her down to tell her what happened. I need to set the record straight with her about how she was tricked. And I need to find out where I stand on this marriage thing."

He watched her closely, waiting for her response. He said, "Does it bother you to think about being with me? I mean, seeing how I might still be married?"

Bonnie sighed. "Look, Charlie, I'm not going to get into swapping horror stories with you. Mine are worse than yours, lover. And if I told you what I've done, you might not come back to me from Texas."

He straightened, surprised. "Oh no. No. I'll be back. No matter what I find out or what happens, I'll be back."

Chapter Six

Throughout the night her tiny, naked frame had been pressed against him. She slept so soundly. Charlie was awake from 5:30 on, but Susan slept until he roused her at 7 a.m.

Startled by the lateness, she quickly began to go through the personal, private rituals each human being acquires as preparation for another day. Charlie propped a second pillow beneath his head and watched her in silence, intrigued by her precise, feminine movements. They did not speak.

And when she had prepared herself, Susan stood in the doorway of the bedroom facing him. She was willing to go to school because denying her immediate desires was something she had learned to do, and had done over and over. She was, he knew, an adult. In her eyes, though, he could see fierce emotions raging. Silently Charlie wondered if this would become another atonement he would have to make, only possible when their passions had abated.

"Don't say anything," she said. "Especially, don't say 'goodbye.' . . . I hope you find her. I hope you don't kill Sloan Witt and that he doesn't try to kill you." She turned abruptly. He knew she was going to walk out of the house without hesitation.

"Susie," he said quietly. "I've been laying here watching you for hours."

She stopped, her back still turned to him. She was listening.

"You know, I thought my higher power was bringing me back to Melanna to make amends to Madelyn. But I've been wondering if, instead, it was so that you and I could discover how we felt about each other. And so we could have last night."

He saw her head droop slightly. Then, without turning or responding, she walked straight out the door. The car started up and he listened as it pulled away.

In the quiet that followed, he thought of his coming encounter with Sloan Witt.

He skidded to a stop in front of Madelyn's house, set the brake and opened the driver's door of the service truck. Before his second

191

foot hit the ground, Sloan Witt had burst out of the house and marched halfway across the yard.

The sight of him—the belligerent, scarcely controlled, undirected anger always present, but now entirely focused—caused Charlie to stop for a moment. He drew a quick breath and set his jaw and did not make eye contact with Witt. He made to walk past him as if he weren't there. Witt slithered to the side, directly in front of Charlie.

"Right there, cocksucker." His voice was low. Menacing. "You don't belong here. Get the hell outa here right now."

His mouth tasted as if full of brass. His nostrils were flared and his head turned slightly as he responded. "I ain't here to talk to you. I need to see Madelyn."

He snorted a laugh. "She don't want to see you, boy. Get outa here. You don't get no more warnings."

Charlie stood still, struggling to understand how to proceed. Madelyn's front door was a dozen feet in front of him, but seemed distant and inaccessible. He took a step back and stood up straight, a small demonstration of peaceful intent.

"I'm not looking for trouble. I have something very important to tell her."

And suddenly, without another word spoken, Witt lunged at him, swinging wildly with his doubled fist and striking Charlie just above his left ear. The blow stunned him and he staggered to the side, turning backwards in a complete circle. He tried to straighten himself and Witt hit him again, a solid lick on his chin. Charlie's arms went forward as he tried not to fall. He sat down hard. His eyes watering, he tried to gather his senses.

He leaned forward, propping himself off the ground with his extended arms, aware that Witt was moving toward him. Charlie charged forward and hit the older man with his shoulder. He began to flail his arms at him, missing wildly. Witt ducked low. He came up beneath Charlie's groin with a knee. Charlie helplessly heard the wind burst from his lungs as he fell forward. Witt grabbed him by his longish hair and the back of belt and slung him awkwardly in the direction of the truck.

They both paused to breath then. Charlie was on his hands and knees, facing the service truck. He could hear Witt take two steps and felt a boot connect with his behind, as if kicking a football.

192

Charlie Cherry's Ninth Step

Charlie rolled forward. He looked up—his face awash in blood, tears and snot—for the sanctuary of the pickup.

"Goddamn you boy!" Witt was screaming at him. "We don't want you here! We know what you done! Get out of here, sonabitch!"

He pulled himself into the truck. It took a moment for him to remember what to do: engage the clutch, turn the key, slowly pull away. It was the pain that kept him alert.

Charlie found the address in an old part of Garland, where the streets were narrow and the blocks short, the houses packed closely together and no deference given by the builders to different styles of architecture or design. All that set the home, that he supposed and hoped belonged to Sloan Witt, apart from the dozen other box-like houses on the street were the numbers tacked on the front door and a yard badly needing to be mowed.

He sat in the Mazda staring at the screen door and rehearsing what he would say to Witt. What would he do if Witt refused to talk to him about Madelyn? Or was that refusal something he truly wanted, something that would give him just the provocation he needed to restart their fight? Was he—after all the years and the brooding, the playing of the drama again and again in his memory—really more after revenge against Witt than amends with Madelyn?

An image flashed through his mind of Desmond, a huge grin on his face. He could hear his voice: "Keep it simple, man."

He stood on the chipped concrete steps and pushed the doorbell. From inside he heard the ringing of the bell. A moment later he heard a door open—an exterior door, he thought—and then quick, young steps walking through the house.

The girl who answered was twelve or thirteen. She had the disproportionate face of a young adolescent. One day she would be pretty, he thought. Charlie noted with resignation that she bore the characteristic features of all the women in Madelyn's family: light, very curly hair, a round face, upturned nose, and stocky legs.

"Yeah?"

"Yes. I'd like to speak to Sloan, please."

"He ain't here." She was, he believed, accustomed to lying for her father. "What do you want him for?"

Charlie shrugged. "I'm an old friend of his."

She frowned in doubt. "What's your name?

"Charlie. When will he be home?"

"Oh—he's working late tonight. Why don't you give me your phone number and I'll have him call you."

He started to back away, turning toward the street. "It's no biggie. I was just passing through. I'll drop him a letter sometime." He was walking toward his car.

"Well, okay." There was relief and a little regret in her voice.

When the girl closed the door, Charlie made a sharp turn and walked around the side of the house. The backyard was enclosed with a corroded chain link fence. Quietly he lifted the latch and opened the gate.

Stepping casually around the back corner of the garage, he saw a pallid, plump, balding, middle-aged imitation of Sloan Witt. Charlie felt himself lean forward in disbelief, then back in astonishment. Could it be that, sitting in the yellow lawn chair, staring vacantly across the backyard, a Pearl beer can drooping from his fingers, was the same person for whom he harbored years of dreams of sweet retribution?

Charlie felt ashamed. Time and the natural progression of his nature had devastated Witt beyond Charlie's meager intent.

He stood, hands in his pockets, watching Witt for a long minute. He could've stood there forever, he thought, without Witt ever becoming aware of him. Charlie shook his head and walked forward.

Quietly he said, "It's a little early for that beer, isn't it?"

Witt, unalarmed, turned toward him. "It's too damn late for anything else." He studied Charlie, looking up and down his frame. "Well, well. If it isn't Charlie Cherry. Here you are, the last of the vultures of my wasted youth—looking for your revenge too, I expect."

"How are you, Sloan?"

"Not bad. Not bad, Charlie. Yourself?"

"Oh, been taking it a day at a time."

The backdoor of the house burst open. The girl stood at the top of the wooden steps, her face aflame with indignant rage.

"I told you he wasn't here! Now get outa here before I call the cops!"

Charlie couldn't stop the grin from spreading across his face.

194

"Didn't your daddy teach you better than to tell lies?"

"I'm warning you, mister!"

"Calm down! Calm down." Sloan held the palm of his free hand up like a stop sign. "Charlie, this is my daughter Melissa."

"Hi, darlin'."

Her eyes were angry squints and her voice was spite itself as she said, "Daddy, I still think I should call the law."

"Call 'em," Charlie said. "'Fore they get here, I'll have what I want and be gone."

"Melissa." There was, for the first time, a hint of irritation—a pale throwback to Witt's old constant hostility—in his voice. "Go in the house, honey. Stay away from the phone. Mr. Cherry is a— an old friend of your Aunt Madelyn."

Madelyn! Melissa knew Madelyn, was apparently part of her life. So Witt must also know how to find her.

The girl's angry face, her expression unchanged, receded and the backdoor gradually closed, scarcely making a sound. Charlie knew she was already at some window, watching him.

"Got a lot of spirit, that girl of yours."

"A real heller." Sloan nodded, taking a sip of his beer. "Unfortunately she has her mother's temper." He looked up at Charlie. "That temper was her mother's undoing, as you may know. You heard what happened?"

"I heard you did a little time at Huntsville."

"No. I was at Tennessee Colony out in East Texas. People never get things right." He finished the beer and dropped the empty can beside his chair. "I worked late one night, went out and had a few drinks. The next morning I woke up in the county jail. They told me I had killed my wife. . . .

"The hearing was most interesting. That's where I found out what I really did. Apparently I found my way home just fine—drove all the way around Wichita Falls, mind you—and my dear departed met me at the door in a rage. They could hear it up and down the street. Before it was over, there were plenty of witnesses." He belched, something that seemed to require an unusual amount of effort. "She hit me with one of them little fireplace shovels, you know. I took it away from her and chased her all over the house and, when I caught her, I beat her to death."

Witt's face was emotionless. He was staring again across the

195

backyard, as if he were expecting to see something or someone suddenly appear. The calm, late spring air was silent.

He cleared his throat. "So why are you here, Charlie? You after a little payback for the fight we had?"

Charlie took a breath. "No. Actually I need some information from you. I'm trying to find Madelyn."

"Madelyn! For god's sake, son. I'd think you'd want to stay as far away from that as you could, after what happened and all these years."

"What I did? One little kiss doesn't end the world, Sloan."

Witt cocked his head, a look of perplexed amusement on his face. "One little kiss?" He chuckled. "A little more to it than that, don't you think? Why do you want to get involved anyway?"

Charlie had a vague feeling that he and Witt were talking about two different subjects.

"I'm just trying to make amends, to clear up a misunderstanding," he said. "You mind me asking if you know where she is?"

"Melissa!"

The backdoor opened instantly.

"Melissa, what's the name of that beaner your Aunt Madelyn is married to?"

"He's not a beaner, Daddy. He's Portuguese."

"Great. What's his name?"

"Jimmy Appadocca."

"How's that for a name? Appadocca." He glanced back to his daughter. "And don't they live over in Irving by the stadium?"

"Yes."

"Thanks, honey. Would you bring me another beer and one for Mr. Cherry too?"

"No," Charlie said quickly. "None for me. Thanks anyway."

The door closed again.

Witt was smiling at him. "That was it? Was that really all you wanted?"

"Yeah."

"I can't believe that you don't want to throw a punch or two at me."

He felt himself shrug and step closer, some odd need for community rising in him. "I'll be honest with you, Sloan. I suffered

196

a lot of years over what you did to me. But if we got into it now, it just might be a mismatch the other way. And then I'd find myself with another reason to be sorry."

"I wouldn't fight you, Charlie. I don't think I could've whipped you the first time if I'd fought you fair. And, by now, you know all the dirty tricks." He snorted a laugh. "You poked me pretty good, even at that."

"Poked you? I never landed a blow."

"The hell you say. You knocked the fool out of me."

"I did not."

"Bullshit, son. I've got a scar inside my bottom lip to this day where you busted me in the mouth."

The worn memories of the fight, so long unquestioned, began to play again. Had he in fact landed a blow?

"You hit me two or three times," Witt said casually. "Sounds like you don't remember your fights any better than I do mine."

"Hmm. Well. Guess I'd better be on my way."

Melissa opened the door and came to her father's side. He took the beer from her and opened it with a casual, fatigued repetition.

"Well, look, Sloan," he was pulling out his billfold, taking out his damp, creased business card much as Tommy Thomas had done for him the day before. "Maybe sometime you'll get tired of popping open those tabs. If you ever want to get sober and add a year or two to your life, give me a call." He handed him the card. "That's my number in Memphis."

He turned and walked away as Witt stared curiously at his card. Moments later, as he sat in the Mazda revving the engine and trying to remember the best route to Irving, it occurred to him that a strange transformation had taken place. He had come looking for Witt, he realized, to settle a score. Instead of inflicting the pain he had for so long assumed was due, he had offered instead to help take the pain away. And again through his mind flashed the image of Desmond laughing.

The home of Jimmy and Madelyn Appadocca was two houses from the corner of a major street. Across that street was a little city park with wooden playground equipment, a few large trees, a duck pond and parallel parking just off the road. Charlie positioned the RX7 in a parking space a little after noon. He had a box of chicken,

197

a large tea and a Dallas newspaper that looked like four Memphis papers piled together.

He had found Madelyn's house an hour earlier and parked in the driveway and immediately went up and rang the doorbell, less out of eagerness than as a way of fighting a growing case of nerves. Waiting for someone to answer, he came to the conclusion that both Madelyn and her husband must be working. Since he had come this far to see her and had nothing else to do, he decided, he would just wait.

It was cool enough with the northerly breeze that he could sit in the car with the windows down and the sunroof open and read the paper without being uncomfortable. Periodically he would glance out the window at home, waiting for a car to arrive, for some sign of activity. He was trying not to rehearse what he would say to her. Still, visions of her slamming the door in his face or throwing her arms around him competed in his imagination. And he had begun to ask himself if he should even confront her at all. Clearly she had divorced him. The marriage question was resolved. Was this a case where the amends would do more harm than good. Yet, there was Arletta and her treacherous kiss to be accounted.

"This going back and forth is stupid," he muttered. "The only stupider thing would be to come this far and go home without making amends."

Making amends, the ninth of the twelve steps in his program. So much of the time during this strange homecoming adventure, he had forgotten the purpose behind what he was doing. His intent in being here, he reminded himself, was to undo the "big thing" he had shared with Pastor Werner. Now he was perhaps only minutes from untangling the last knot that would free him from the mass of mistakes that had helped to perpetuate his drinking, that would free him to recover fully. What a crazy, yet undeniable truth in his life— at eighteen he had made decisions from which he was still trying to escape at thirty-four.

"No," Desmond would've said, "that's stinkin' thinkin'. The past has power over the present only if you let it." The past, as he heard so often in meetings, is nothing more than a proving ground for the decisions you make today. The past can be a cruel master or, if you choose, a wise teacher.

Charlie rolled the paper over in his hands. A story on the bottom of the front page told about the school children's final day of the year. He knew it was also the last day for the kids in Melanna. He wondered if, in Texas, the kids all started and stopped on the same day, the way they had for years. And if so, he wondered, why wasn't Witt's daughter Melissa in school. She hadn't been yesterday either, when he had called from McKinney.

Charlie smiled as he thought school ending for Susan. The sweetness of the time he had spent with her lingered in his senses, much as her small frame had lingered against him through the night.

After the second time they made love, she had teasingly said, "God, this is the most expensive sex in the world."

He had raised up on an elbow and looked at her. "What?"

"I was just thinking: I've been taking birth control pills for years—just in case, just hoping I would need them. At $15 a month for the past 100 years," she giggled, "man this is costing me."

"Well," he had replied slowly, snaking an arm around her, "we'd better make sure you get your money's worth."

For Charlie, at the new, very present place he found himself in his life, last night was nothing but exciting and beautiful. For Susan, though, he knew the regret had already begun—regret not for being with him, but because she perceived their time together to be only a fleeting respite from unfulfilled monotony.

He glanced out the window at Madelyn's still house. So much had happened to him on this trip of rediscovery. Even if he had never found Madelyn, he had at least found some parts of himself he had not realized were lost.

His old boss had almost revered him, and now felt a deep bond of brotherhood. His old enemy had said that the unforgettable fight between them had been much closer than he had realized. And the prettiest girl in his graduating class had confessed to him that she had always liked and wanted him. It was almost as if his memories of the most pivotal days of his youth were a faulty recording, an inaccurate record of misunderstood facts.

His body jerked. Sluggishly he straightened his lanky frame. The cool breeze and long wait had lured him to sleep. Now there was a nearby discordant noise that had startled and awakened him. What time was it—3:15? And what was that sound?

A car full of teenagers was sitting at the intersection of the road and the residential street just beside him, waiting to turn left. The car windows were down and music was playing at about three times louder than was humanly enjoyable—or even comprehensible. The boys in the car were shouting excitedly above the noise of the radio.

Charlie smiled. School had been out for only a few minutes and already they were wired for high decibel celebration. His mind was flooded with the affectionately remembered flavors of Leonard Skynard, the Rolling Stones and Loverboy playing loudly as he had circled the Royal Drive Inn in an endless loop—sixteen and completely stud. There were those things in life, he recognized, that were from generation to generation constant.

He watched the car turn, squealing its tires and speeding up rapidly. It was the sort of behavior to be expected. But he was unprepared when it halted suddenly in front of Madelyn's house.

As he wrestled with why teenagers would stop there, it occurred to him that he had been sitting for four hours watching the wrong house. He shook his head. Perhaps he had misread the map, or written down the address incorrectly. Now what should he do?

He could see the teenagers shifting around inside the car, heads bobbing, arms lashing out in mock assault.

Again he shook his head and frowned. Maybe it was better to find out this way that it was the wrong house than to have waited all day and have had the door answered by a puzzled total stranger.

As he sat staring at what he had believed was Madelyn's house, the passenger door of the teenagers' car opened. Charlie Cherry watched himself get out of the car.

The boy was an inch or two shorter than Charlie had been at fourteen, his hair a lighter shade of brown. But everything else was as he had been: the gaunt frame, the angular face thrust forward, the dip of his bony shoulders as he moved. Watching the boy was like watching a home movie of himself made nineteen years before.

He felt his hand open the door and he pulled himself, shaking, out of the car, not really standing up all the way, but supported by the low roof, the metal warm against his back. Charlie watched as the boy backed across the yard to the front door, playfully making obscene gestures to the others in the car. Then he disappeared into the house and the teenagers roared on down the street. And Charlie stood in shocked silence, trying to grasp the reality that he had just seen his own son, the child he never knew existed.

He slid back down, the car door wide open and his feet on the pavement, his head down. Was this what Witt meant? Was this part of the uproar at Madelyn's house the day of the kiss and the fight? Was it not only because of Arletta's trick, but because Madelyn was pregnant?

But how could she be pregnant? She had been taking birth control pills. No—she had only been pretending she was on the pill. She must've been afraid to go and get them. Afraid her mother would discover them. Afraid to tell Charlie she wasn't taking them. Just afraid. And the risk of having sex with him must've increased the fear she carried.

What did this mean for him, he wondered. What did this do to the whole idea of making amends?

"How do you make amends for this?" he asked himself aloud.

If he went to Madelyn now, would he be wandering into a legal abyss of child support payments and past bills? And what about his own legal rights? The boy was obviously, undeniably his. Should he see him? Didn't he have the right? Would it be a good thing, or something very destructive?

"Lordy. And I thought this trip was surprising up until now."

He raised his head and saw that a car, a blue Chevy, was pulling into Madelyn's driveway. The driver's door opened and out stepped Madelyn.

She was a bit taller than he had remembered, and her strawberry blond hair was longer, but still curly and full. She was thinner, he thought, or maybe it was the dress she was wearing, very business-like, very grownup. Charlie shook his head. Even across a major street, two front yards and fifteen years, he could tell that she carried a very different air about herself.

She was talking to someone, leaning down and looking across to the passenger's side of the back seat. In a few seconds a little girl, four or five-years-old, appeared at the driver's door. Madelyn took her hand and she jumped off the seat onto the driveway.

Charlie stood up again. He leaned back and watched Madelyn take things out of her car: some thick kind of briefcase, a backpack that must've been the girl's things. As they closed the car door and started toward the house, Madelyn glanced in his direction, looked away, then glanced back quickly. She stood still, staring at him. Leaning down, she said something to the girl, and they continued on into the house.

201

"Well, Charlie old buddy, it's now or never."

He got in and fired up the Mazda and made a tight circle off the parking space onto the residential street. The feelings of fear and hope mingled in his chest as he parked in front of the house. He got out of the car and walked to the front door slowly and, filling his lungs with air, he rang the bell.

Almost immediately she opened the door. Her round face was smooth and unlined. Gone was the chubbiness of adolescence and in its place was a fine, womanly prettiness.

"Charlie. It was you."

"Hello, Madelyn. I hope I haven't come at a bad time. I was wondering if I could speak with you for a moment."

"Of course." She stepped back and opened the door wide. "Come in."

So, she neither slammed the door in his face nor threw her arms around him.

The inside of the house was surprisingly spacious. There was a cathedral ceiling in the living room and everything that Charlie could see had a feeling of quality to it. A vision of Susan's tiny, dark TV room came to him. How very differently the lives of the two women had turned out.

He glanced over his shoulder at her. Madelyn was looking up at him patiently.

"I saw him, Madelyn. Just before you got here, he pulled up with a carload of kids. . . . I had no idea until that moment."

"Would you like to meet him?"

"Could I?"

She took a step toward a long hallway and called, "Wesley!"

A rough adolescent voice answered. "Yeah?"

"Would you come here please?"

"What'd I do?"

There were shuffling sounds from around a bend in the hall, then the boy, his shirttail out, barefoot, came walking toward him. He stopped a few feet away, transfixed by the sight of Charlie, the unmistakable resemblance between them.

"Wes, this is Mr. Cherry. Mr. Charles Wesley Cherry. He's an old friend of mine."

For an instant the boy stood silently. He exhaled suddenly, as if he had been holding his breath, and smiled. He held out his hand.

"Hi, Wes."

"Hi. Far out."

Charlie stood, his son's hand locked in his, their eyes upon each other. What should he say? What strange new feeling was turning inside of him?

The girl, the little one he had seen Madelyn walking with, appeared between them. Charlie stepped back, surprised. She must've been standing behind Wes. Her arm was snugly around the boy's leg.

"Oh yes!" Madelyn exclaimed. "This is little sister, Rebecca."

"Beck-y!" the girl corrected.

"Becky." Madelyn smiled. "You're right. I'm so sorry."

The girl was darker than her mother or brother. She must have taken after the Appadocca side of the family. But the pouty look on her face was pure Madelyn.

"How old are you?"

She forced her fingers toward him. "This many."

"You can say it, honey."

"Four-years-old."

Charlie smiled. He was never around children this age and had no idea what to say to Becky.

"Wes, dear, would you be willing to put on your shoes and take your sister across the street to the park for a few minutes? Mr. Cherry and I can have a chance to visit that way."

"Sure." He started back down the hall, then stopped and said to Charlie, "Say, you're still going to be here when I get back, aren't you?"

"I got all the time in the world." Charlie glanced at Madelyn. "I can stay as long as I'm not in the way."

"Okay, man. Maybe we can—you know."

"Yeah. I'd like that."

When he disappeared from view, Madelyn nodded toward an open doorway. "Let's go sit in the kitchen."

He followed her into a long, narrow, bright eggshell colored kitchen with a round butcher-block table.

"Sit down and I'll get us something to drink. What would you like?"

"Uh—what do you have?"

"Tea, water, milk, Kool Aid or scotch."

"Let's go with the tea."

She smiled. "Good. Lemon and sugar?"

"No, just over ice."

Charlie watched her silently as she filled two tumblers with ice and water and spooned in instant tea. Her back was toward him and he observed the feminine nuances of her motions. How very different it was now from the girlish way she had carried herself as a young woman. Was this truly the woman who had opened herself to him and allowed him her flower, who had borne his child in secret, and been the object his undiminished memories through so many years?

"Charlie?" She was speaking without looking at him. "You look the same. I mean, almost exactly. It's like you haven't changed."

He laughed. "Thanks, I think. Is that good or bad?"

"It's good. Where do you live and what do you do?"

"Memphis. Tennessee. I run a shop that works on diesel engines. . . . You've done well for yourself, you and Mr. Appadocca."

"Jim."

"Yeah. What kind of work do you do?"

"I'm a counselor."

His eyebrows arched. "A counselor?"

"An MSW. I do therapy in a community mental health center in Oak Cliff. I'm hoping, when Becky starts going to school all day, that I can go back and get my doctorate in clinical psychology."

". . . You, on the other hand, have changed completely, Madelyn."

She nodded. "Time changes us."

"Yes," he agreed. "And the hard lessons can help us grow."

"If we let them." She sat down across the table from him and stirred sugar into her tea. "So what caused you to want to find me, Charlie?"

He laughed. "I knew exactly why I came to see you and what I was going to say until about ten minutes ago. Talk about things changing. Uh—it's like this: my original reason for coming was a misunderstanding. The last day you lived in Melanna, something happened that I think you had the wrong idea about. I've wanted for the last fifteen years to explain what really happened. And I want to make amends for any hurt feelings I might have caused you."

"Make amends?" She tilted her head and wrinkled her nose. It was a girlish look of curiosity and the first familiar expression he had seen. "Charlie, are you in a Twelve Step program?"

"Yeah, actually. What do you know about the Twelve Steps?"

"Of all my clients, I'd say that easily a third of them are hooked up with some kind of Twelve Step program." She studied him silently. "Do you mind me asking which one you're in?"

He grinned. "Just plain old A.A."

"How long you been in it?"

"I've been sober for a little more than nine months."

"Well, I'm glad you're in the program and straight," Madelyn said. "Although I'm sorry you have a problem like that, and especially sorry if I had anything to do with it."

He pursed his lips. "I was trying to remember if you ever held a gun to my head and forced me to take a drink."

She smiled. "Charlie, what exactly do you feel like you need to make amends for?"

"It doesn't just leap out at you? It's about Arletta's little show."

"Arletta?"

"Sure," he said incredulously. "You have to remember. On your last day in Melanna, Arletta pulled into the service station and got me to stick my head into the driver's window of her car to look at a warning light on her dashboard. When I did, she grabbed me and gave me a great big kiss. An hour later, Gary calls and tells me that it's all over town that Arletta and I were making out. . . . That's why I came to see you. I had to explain it was a trick. Only, I never got the chance."

Madelyn stared at him. "Charlie, I never knew anything about that."

". . . You are shittin' me."

"No. That's the first I ever heard of it."

He leaned back in his chair. "Then why did Sloan beat the hell out of me?"

"Obviously," she said, leaning toward him, "because I was pregnant. . . . They wouldn't let me come to the door, but I watched you two out my bedroom window. That was the awfulest thing I ever saw in my life. I cried for days over what he did to you. They wouldn't let me call or write you.

"Sloan. Well, you know, he killed my aunt. He has an emotional

205

problem, as well as being a multiple substance abuser. But the reason he attacked you is because I was pregnant.

"Charlie, I lied to you about taking the pill. I never had them. When I figured out that I had missed a couple months, I went to the doctor and took a test. It was supposed to be confidential. The doctor's office called my house Friday with the results. Mom answered the phone. They asked for me without saying who they were.

"When they told me I was pregnant, I thought I would die. And when I hung up the phone," she shrugged, "well, you know how Mom was. 'Who was that on the phone?' She just kept at me. And I was so upset and feeling so guilty, I just gave in and told her. Of course she knew immediately it was yours."

"Why didn't you tell me? I mean, we were married."

"They wouldn't let me. I couldn't talk to anybody. All Mom could think of was getting me out of town before anyone found out. By ten that night they had arranged for me to go live with my Aunt Louise. That's why she and Sloan were there the next day."

"Well, like I say, we were married. Why didn't you just tell them that?"

She shook her head. "I was scared. I never told them. I guess, in my mind, I imagined that that would make things worse, somehow. That that would be the last straw. I don't what I thought they could do to me that was worse than what they were doing. . . . To this day, no one I my family ever knew that we were married. In fact, I've never told anyone."

Charlie stared at the floor. His breath came in deep, slow sighs. "Jesus H. Christ. For fifteen years I've been living with the guilt of thinking you believed I was cheating on you. And you never knew a thing about it."

The spaces under her eyes had turned a dark rose color and her chin crinkled. Tears began to well atop her cheeks, and he recognized a second familiar face.

"If either of us has any amends to make, Charlie, it's me. All these years I concealed the fact that we were married. I never even tried to . . . find you." She took the handkerchief he offered, knotted it and pushed at the corners of her eyes. "And, worse than that, you've had a beautiful son, who's become a beautiful young man and I never made an effort to track you down, to tell you."

He leaned forward, putting his elbows on his knees and looking down. "I don't feel like I've been sinned against, Madelyn. I don't feel like you've done anything I need to forgive you for."

"Maybe you will, when you think about it. Maybe you will."

"Probably not." He smiled. "The way you describe it, I understand perfectly how the Madelyn I knew would be afraid and make all those scared decisions." He shook his head. "What I don't understand is how you got to be so different. What made you change?"

She swallowed twice and took a sip of tea. "When my aunt was killed, my mother had a psychotic break. She had always been borderline, but that pushed her over the edge. She has never recovered. About eighteen months after that, my father died of cancer. It was not like he was ever that much help, but at least he was there. After he died, I was totally responsible for my mother, and my little boy. . . . I knew I either had to figure out how to be healthy or I would go crazy too. That's when I first got interested in counseling. I was in therapy myself for three solid years.

"I still take care of Mom. She can't come live with me though. I know I couldn't handle that." Madelyn pushed his handkerchief back toward him gently. "But I go see her every week. I take her grandkids. And, I guess, I'm emotionally sober."

Charlie nodded in agreement. "Yes. I'd say so. . . . Madelyn, did you ever have our marriage annulled? Did you ever get a divorce?"

She gave him a quick, sheepish grin. "No. I never did. I guess that makes me a criminal. I'm not going to tell anybody. Are you?"

"Uh, no. I never told anybody about us being married either, until a few weeks ago when I was working my Fifth Step."

"What are you going to tell people now?"

"They won't ask," he said. "If they should, I'll just say you've remarried. Which is true. You just left out the middle step." He took a big breath. "What about Wes?"

"What do you mean?"

"Would it be possible for me to get to know him?"

"I think it would be wonderful. He knows a lot about you: what you were like, that he has your name."

"How'd you pull that off?"

"They knew your first name was 'Charlie,'" she said. "But they didn't know that 'Wesley' was your middle name."

Charlie took a long, cool drink of tea. "What can I do for him?"

"What would you like to do?"

"Well. . . . I make pretty good money. Not as good as your husband, but pretty good. I'd like to start a fund for him, you know. College or trade school. Whatever."

"His stepfather is a systems analyst. Wes wants to go to A&M and be one too."

"I don't know what the hell that it, but I'm willing to help pay for it." They laughed together. "What will your husband think?"

She gave him a slow, relaxed smile. "Jim is a very secure person. In a lot of ways he reminded me of you. He can share your son with you."

He nodded. "Can Wes come to Memphis some time?"

"Sure."

Charlie rested his chin on his knuckles. For nearly a full minute neither of them spoke. A sweet feeling of relief began to spread through his chest and he smiled.

Madelyn looked at him curiously. "What?"

He sighed. "Well, I guess I'm through with my Ninth Step."

Susan answered the door, barefoot and wearing the clothes she had worn to school that morning, her shirttail out.

"Charlie!"

"Hi."

"Uh—did you—did you find her?"

"Yep." He nodded. "I did."

"Are you—did she—"

He shook his head. "She's remarried."

"Oh." She tried not to show the relief that spread across her face. "What about Sloan? What about, you know, your amends?"

"Well," he said slowly, "I can tell you all about all that. But that's not really the reason I came back."

Susan slouched against the doorframe. There was a hint of anger in her voice. "Just looking for a cheap place to spend the night?"

"Not really." He looked over his shoulder at the Mazda. "You have a week-and-a-half off beginning now, don't you?"

"Yes," she replied cautiously.

"Well, I got my doings done and I've still got the better part of two weeks myself. I have a few hundred bucks just burning a hole in my pocket, and I was wondering if you'd like to go down to San Antone and walk the river with me."

For a moment she hovered in the doorway. She stepped toward him and leaned forward, looping her arms around his neck and pressing her lips to his.

She breathed at length and said, "Do you want to leave in the morning?"

"Well look. We kind of rushed into things last night. Surely we can slow down and do thing a little more romantically."

Her expression was curious. "More romantic than last night? Like how?"

"Well, let's go pack your stuff, and I'll take you for a moonlight ride with the top open on my rocket. We'll cruise on down to this barbeque house I found in Dallas. Best pecan pie I've had in fifteen years."

She was smiling, her arms a swing and her face moving gently a few inches beneath his. "Then what?"

"Well, then we'll drive on down the road 'til we find just the perfect spot to spend the night."

"Salado."

He shrugged. "Wherever you want, darlin'."

They kissed, a deep, sweet kiss. He straightened.

"Come on now. I'll help you."

She turned and went inside. He watched her graceful steps. "Pack light. I imagine I'll be picking you out a few things. How do you suppose you'd look in one of those white senorita dresses?"

"A senorita with freckles?"

"I love freckles. . . . Susan?"

"Yes?"

"How do you feel about stepchildren?"

www.ingramcontent.com/pod-product-compliance
Lightning Source LLC
Chambersburg PA
CBHW070747180626
46818CB00007B/3026